Wild Girls

Pam Keevil

Happy reading!

Pam Keevil

November 2022

Wild Girls

First published in 2022 by Black Pear Press
www.blackpear.net

Copyright © Pam Keevil 2022

All rights reserved.

ISBN 978-1-913418-62-5

Cover design by Black Pear Press

Black Pear Press

Dedication

To anyone who enjoys living in a village.

Contents

Chapter one Mona

As the plane finally broke through the clouds, a faint cheer echoed through the cabin. It didn't last long. It was replaced by a groan. The ground below was sodden. Rain streamed down the window. That was right for Britain wasn't it? Or should that be England? Mona smiled. 'Little old England. Hello there,' she muttered under her breath before turning it into a cough. No point in appearing crazy. Although she was, wasn't she? Anyone else would have pitched up to her ex, demanded a fair share of the business, house and furniture and high tailed it to the hills. Except she couldn't. Not yet. Something was stopping her. Fear? Probably. How on earth had she let herself become sucked into his web of spite again? At least in England she'd be free to figure out what she was going to do. She sighed. Something would turn up.

'First time in England?' her neighbour said. It was good it was a nighttime flight. There hadn't been any excuse to exchange more than a name before the cabin crew dimmed the lights, turned up the heating and they sped across the pond in a cocoon of dry air and other people's smells, fearful that any small tremor and the damned thing would plummet out of the sky. Her neighbour had been a deep sleeper. Once the eye shades were on, she was out. And she hadn't moved. Either she had a bladder the size of an elephant or she wore special protective pants. Mona hoped it was the former.

Mona acknowledged the question and the interest with a smile. 'No. I've been on holiday a couple of times to London. This is something different.'

'Oh?' the Botox wouldn't allow any expression. The voice gave it all away. *Tell me, I'm bursting to know.*

'Yes. I'm staying for a couple of months, getting to know the countryside, that sort of thing,' Mona said. Should she get Botox? Or a tattoo? What do you do to mark leaving an old life behind? Perhaps she could go blonde? It would make a change from grey with a few streaks of red.

'Rather you than me,' the woman patted her hand. 'They just don't do decent coffee and as for iced water.' She let her words dribble away. 'Oh, but the history. You must see Stratford, Bath, York and there's Windsor and Stonehenge,' she counted off the places on coral tipped fingernails. Her hands were marked with brown spots and suggested she was at least seventy. 'I'm eighty-three,' she said. Mona smiled her approval and awe. 'This time I'm off to Edinburgh. Just have to see those men in kilts.' She flapped a hand smothered in gold rings in front of her face. 'Phew. Getting hot already.'

There was no time for any more discussion. The pilot's announcement that they were preparing for landing sent everyone into a flurry of activity and before Mona could blink, she was outside in the damp, early morning air as black taxis and coaches vied for the limited space at the terminal arrivals area. She checked her itinerary; a coach to Reading station, a train to Stroud and a taxi to the cottage. She yawned. Her coach wasn't till eleven. She needed coffee and prayed her neighbour had been wrong.

Starbucks. She knew that name. 'A latte with almond milk, a double shot and a cinnamon twirl to drink in,' she said and handed over a brown plastic note.

'At the end,' a clipped voice said. Marika was the name. She didn't sound English. Or not as Mona imagined English people sounded, sort of a cross between the Queen and the family in Downton Abbey. Still, Americans didn't sound alike. It was probably the same here. She collected her drink. Mrs Botox had been wrong about the coffee. It looked good and smelt perfect. She sat down surrounded by her two cases and hand luggage. Like the wagons in the Wild West? She took a sip and swirled the liquid round in her mouth. Perfect. She dipped the corner of the cinnamon twirl in the coffee. Yes. Tasted just as good. If this was England, they'd get on fine. She messaged.

Landed safely.

What else could she put? Miss you all? She did. That wasn't the point. She'd come here to get away, to take stock of what she wanted to do with the rest of her life. She counted on her fingers. If you believed in the old three score and ten of the Bible, she had fifteen left. Not much. She added a few more words to the text.

Will message again later. Miss you.

A lump formed in her throat. It stuck there. Accusing. What the hell had she done? She took another sip of the coffee and stopped; the cup poised. Who was that? It was him, wasn't it? He'd followed her. Her hand shook. The coffee spilt. She stared at familiar hunched shoulders; greying hair curled onto the collar of a check coat. He never wore a coat, did he? The head turned, an arm shot into the air as a black cab lumbered to a halt. It wasn't him. She closed her eyes in relief and took several deep breaths.

'You all right?' Marika was stacking used mugs and cups on a trolley. She swiped at the spilt coffee with a cloth.

Mona opened her eyes. 'What? Oh yes. Sorry. Just a bit jet lagged.'

'I make nice clean table for you. Enjoy,' Marika said and wheeled the trolley away.

Mona sniffed and blew her nose on the paper serviette. It wasn't him. She was safe here. She'd make the best of it. All she needed was a bit of peace and quiet for a short time. Please? She was about to lift her eyes to heaven when she stopped. All that churching on a Sunday from the age of three months to fifteen years had seared its message into her soul. If she had one. 'You're the boss,' she told herself. 'You're in control now.' It was scary. She got out her phone, logged onto free WiFi and checked the news. *April temperatures smashed. Britain on course for a summer sizzler.* Mona looked out at the rain still pouring down. 'Yeah right.'

Four hours later, tired, dirty, hungry, and ready to burst into tears at the slightest word of cruelty or kindness, she opened the door of Lavender Cottage. The email had said the key was under the blue plant pot It was. What about security? Were the Brits so laid back? Mona glanced along the narrow road, hardly wide enough for a car to pass. It was deserted. A curtain twitched in the window of the cottage opposite. Probably anyone acting weirdly would be locked up or burnt at the stake.

Mona dragged her cases into the lounge, closed the door and sank against it. The place looked smaller than in the photos. The front door opened straight into the main room. A black stove huddled in the chimney breast next to a pile of logs. In front was a red and blue rug, partly covering the wooden floor. The pale walls were decorated with someone's photos of a misty field, a snow-covered pine tree and a woodland in spring with lime green leaves above millions of blue plants. A white sofa smothered with mismatching coloured cushions and throws was like her grandmother's house in Kentucky. She sniffed. Was that Lavender? Or something else? She sniffed again. Fresh bread? Where the hell was that coming from?

She moved across to the stable door. From the floorplan, the kitchen was on the other side. She lifted the latch and the door swung inwards. A square room with a red tiled floor and a window with a curtain covering the lower half, grey painted units and a deep, white ceramic sink greeted her. On a table, set in the centre of the room was a scrubbed wooden table. A wicker basket sat in the middle. Mona lifted the starched white cover. Underneath was a freshy baked loaf and a note.

4

Dear Mona,

I've taken the liberty of buying you a starter pack. In the cupboard you'll find tea, coffee and a few tins of essentials (beans, tomatoes) enough for a few days. In the fridges are milk, butter, local cheese and a present from the girls. I've cleaned from top to bottom and there are towels and plenty of bed linen in the airing cupboard. Hope to see you around in the village.

Sheila (Rose Cottage opposite the church)

The girls? Which girls? Were they neighbours? Mona went across to the small, white fridge with what looked like a rabbit hutch on top. Was that a fridge freezer? She'd never get her food in there. She opened the lower door. A bottle of milk, some packets and a red and white ceramic bowl of eggs perched on the lower shelf. Each egg had some spidery black writing. She picked one up.

Love from Hettie

She replaced it and picked up another.

Love from Clarice

And another.

Love from Brenda

What sort of person names their hens? And can remember which chook laid which egg? One of the eggs had a small brown feather attached. She picked it out.

Another from Hettie

In that moment, any doubts about being there flew away like the feather she blew into the air. It fluttered to the floor. She bent and picked it up and searched for a place to put it. No. She'd keep it in her purse. Or was that a wallet? The feather was a talisman. Everything would be all right. She'd spend a wonderful summer here and go back refreshed and ready to kick some ass and that would include her ex and anyone else who got in her way.

Could she? The doubts returned. He'd told her so often she was stupid she had believed him. All the times he'd changed stories, hidden things, made her feel she was losing her mind and when she challenged him, he'd back down and for a few days, all would be wonderful. Then it would start again until she had run away from him, left her job, and arrived here.

'Forget it,' she spoke aloud. Her words echoed through the silent room. All she needed was a decent bed, some good food and she'd be back to her old self. An omelette with some of that bread and cheese would be perfect.

'Thanks Hettie,' she said as she opened the cupboard doors. Where the hell was the omelette pan?

Chapter two Sheila

Twenty-five past nine already? It can't be. At least the parking fairy is on my side. Hooray. As I swing the car into the last remaining space, there is a scraping sound on the passenger side. I get out and inspect the damage. How was I to know there was a low stone wall stuck out above the edge of the tarmac? Probably explains why no one else has parked here. I run my fingers along the white mark. This is more than a scrape. I trace a long deep scratch. I stay crouched down and punch at the damage. Damn thing. I slump back in the driver's seat and cover my face with my hands. I shouldn't cry. It's just a car. Just a dent. My life is heaps better than many peoples. Except today it doesn't feel that way. Not at all. I'm a drudge. Everyone's servant. Good old Sheila. The reliable mum, wife, grandma, co-worker. Sheila will save the day. I can't stop the dry sobs of self-pity. That's what it is, isn't it? Even my main purpose in life as a breeder is departing with each bloodless month. I grip the steering wheel. I'm being stupid and selfish, and I hate myself.

And I'd so much planned for today. A whole day for me? Fat chance. It had started so well. I'd woken before the alarm, the water in the tank was still hot and I'd slung on a faded tracksuit and a pair of Mark's old football socks. OK I wouldn't win any beauty contests. I'd tidy myself up later; my chin needed attention, or I'd look like Gandalf and my hair was matted and greasy to the touch. I'd skipped downstairs and that was as good as it got.

In the kitchen an empty pizza carton with the remains of ham and pineapple congealing on the white marble worksurface, a can of lager and a mug with cold coffee next to a puddle of spilt milk greeted me. Mark was treating the place like a student house and his student days finished years ago. He must have been out again with his old mates. Talk about boomerang kids. Breakfast for Brian then I'd tidy up.

Too late. Footsteps clattered down the wooden stairs. 'I'll grab a coffee before the meeting. Need to double check these figures. Can't make a mistake with the merger and that promotion up for grabs.' With a curt nod, Brian grabbed his jacket, laptop bag and car keys.

'Will you be late tonight?'

'Dunno.' The door slammed. The silver Audi A4 scrunched on the gravel, and all was quiet again.

If only Brian had said, 'What are you doing today? How do you fancy a meal or even a drink tonight? You look nice.' Even goodbye and a peck on the cheek would be welcome. I picked up a paper towel and wiped away the beer and coffee slops. I reckon I talked to myself as much as Shirley Valentine. At least she had a wall.

Yes, the promotion was a big one. Was it really worth it? Brian had insisted everything would settle down once the new appointments had been made. If he wasn't one of them, God knows how he'd take it.

I threw the sopping towels in the bin. And looking nice? Do I? No. Fifty-five going on five hundred feels more like it. Funny how I can manage to walk round the house and avoid all the mirrors. If I can't see the lines and the grey hair, perhaps others might do the same. I picked up the pizza and its packaging and dumped them both in the waste bin. Sod the recycling for once. I poured the milk down the drain and stuck the mug in the dishwasher. Another quick wipe with the cloth removed a bit more of the stale smell. I opened the patio doors and let the breeze from the valley flow through, disturbing the cream muslin curtains. It smelt better already.

The clouds were building up in the west. It'd rain soon.

I was certain Mark had an interview today. Should I check on him? Or was it tomorrow? I'd decided coffee first. Everything else could wait. I switched on the kettle and waited as it boiled. I suppose if I was one of those super fit, organised glam grans, I'd be doing a three-minute meditation? Or perhaps a few exercises to strengthen the pelvic floor? The coffee jar was empty. I checked the cupboard. No more ground. Damn. Instant would have to do. I shook a little of the granules into a mug. Did people really follow all those do's and don'ts to help the menopausal woman? Who cares? Today was my day. For me. No one else.

I'd sat down at the kitchen table and scanned the list; collect dry cleaning, shop, bank, get card for Aunt Mary's birthday. So much for a day off. I wouldn't have time for a pee if I got all this done.

The phone rang. My heart pounded. Why does any mother always suspect bad news? 'Claire, what's up?' I switched to speaker mode.

A breathless voice exploded in the quiet room. 'It's the twin's assembly this morning and I can't get time off. Could you go along and give them a bit of grandmotherly support?'

Everyone's all right. Temporary relief was replaced by something else. I thought it was all arranged. Claire is usually so organised. 'Weren't you taking half a day as a holiday?'

'No. Well, yes, it was except there's a virus going around the office and the Big Man has promised time and a half if we can go in and get the shipment out today.' She paused. 'It'll mean more cash and we need all we can if we're to take the kids to Florida this summer.'

All I can think of is our rain sodden family holidays camping in Wales We felt we'd come up in the world when we could afford a caravan. I opened my mouth to say something and stopped. Claire had explained it all to me as if I was a half-wit. *Children today expect more. No one stays in England. They'd be the only ones in their class who hadn't gone.* And the killer. *Most grandparents treat their grandchildren to a big holiday now and again.* Not if they've relied on one income, have put both kids through university without letting them run up a huge debt and dipped their hands into their savings to help with the deposit on their first house. Now I knew what that something else was. Resentment. Have I really turned into such a mean, spiteful old woman? I couldn't refuse or I'd feel crap all day. I fold up the list. 'What time?'

'No rush. Half nine and they last about twenty minutes. It shouldn't take up much of your day. You are a life saver. Got to go. The twins will be so excited. Make sure you take plenty of photos.' There is a pause. 'I don't know how I'd manage without you, Mum. Thanks.' The call had ended.

I'd glanced at the clock. Eight fifteen? There were still the hens to feed, and I'd promised Lydia I'd clean the cottage for the new rental. Trust Lydia to muddle her doctor's appointments. Again. I ran a hand through my greasy hair. I can't go out like this. I wasn't turning up at the school with all the elegant mummies looking like a mad old bag lady.

'Hens first.' Outside the air was fresh and cool. I'd sucked it in as if it'd give me life and energy for the day ahead. I collected fresh water and a scoop of pellets. I trudged down the path, past the tiny tendrils of peas, struggling to grow after the cold, spring weather and snipped off the heads of some purple sprouting broccoli. The flowers were forming, yellow pinpricks against deep-sea green. How had that happened so soon? I needed to pick and freeze them.

Well, the hens will eat them if I don't get around to it. They enjoy a bit of fresh veg, don't they? No one else does. If Brian doesn't grass over the veggie patch, I'd get someone to do it. All this grow your own. A bag of peas from Iceland is a bag of peas, isn't it? The sound of clucking increased as I got closer. They recognise the smell of food. I bent down and unlatched the wire gate. I replaced the water and scattered the food pellets on the ground with the broccoli.

'Breakfast' I called and opened their door. One by one the girls descended, clucking gently at my feet. I held out a stalk of broccoli to Hettie who pecked at it, contentedly. 'If only the rest of the world was as easy to please as you.' I straightened up and stood for a few moments to breathe in the aroma of sawdust, bran, decaying cabbage stalks and what was certainly hen smell. It was comforting. Below me, the valley was criss-crossed with fields, stone walls and pathways. The towering grey clouds above the green would make a wonderful photo. If I got rid of the veggie plots, I'd have more time. Not today though. I turned back to the hens scratching around at my feet. 'Let's find out how generous you've been.' I reached into the hen house to collect today's eggs.

I should have collected the eggs and not wasted time on my stupid daydreams. It meant I was in a rush. I jumped into the shower but there was no time to dry my hair properly. A quick brush and I'd rely on the car's heater to do the rest. I'd poked my eye with the mascara wand. Both eyes watered and my makeup smudged. I'd cleaned if off. There was no time to reapply. No one was going to look at me, were they? Damned tights snagged. And it was my last pair. I pulled on a pair of black trousers. They're tight around the waistband. Surely, I haven't put on more weight? I tried the brown ones. Same thing. The grey stretch trousers would have to do even though they're due for a wash. There is a stain at the front where I'd splashed grease as I was frying onions for a casserole. A long black sweater covered it up. Except the sweater should have been worn with black tights and riding style boots. Shabby chic? I reckon I was born that way.

So here I am, late, scruffy, rushed, stressed…and what else? I'm just a middle-aged woman, of no interest to anyone and of no use except as a skivvy. God, bloody self-pity again. I sit up and wipe my eyes and nose on a crumpled tissue. I'll get out of the car, paste on a smile and be everything everyone else wants me to be.

Except it's not enough. Is it too much to want some time and space to be me? To be Sheila. Although who is Sheila? I don't know. I just know she isn't this.

Chapter three Sheila

'Come on, Sheila, you've got stuff to do,' I say as I hoist myself out of the car. Everything else can wait. My grandchildren need me. I hope they do. I push open the entrance to the school, sign in and collect a lanyard with VISITOR printed on it and scuttle along the corridor. I'm ashamed of my appearance. I'm sure the school secretary disapproves. Since when did school secretaries dress in suits? Or is she a business manager? At least the children don't seem bothered. A long-haired girl with a metal badge that says she's achieved the lofty heights of house captain stands by the entrance to the hall. 'There's some seats at the back.'

That's the trouble with school events. Anywhere else and front row seats are avoided. Here, seats at the front are grabbed by eager families leaving late comers to negotiate the stares of those already seated and squeeze along narrow rows into the last available spaces. I mutter a thousand sorries as I jostle against knees and folded arms, step over huge leather bags and avoid knocking toddlers off laps to flop onto the far seat at the end of the back row.

'I think we're all here, are we?' A young woman with pale blonde hair swinging round a heart shaped face stands up. Must be the class teacher. Doesn't look old enough. 'Please note that all photography is banned until the end and only photos of your own children are allowed. No photos of any children should appear on social media unless with the written permission of the carers.'

She looks over towards Mr Dhand who nods. 'Sorry, Safeguarding and all that,' he says and holds out his hands in mock surrender.

I settle down and scan the rows of children. Where are the twins? The usual strong readers are seated on chairs on the small, raised area that serves as a stage. They all have sheets of paper in their hands with their words. The twins are not amongst them. The rest of the children are seated on the floor, and everyone is wearing some kind of animal mask. Is Nick the lion with spiky hair? Is Emily a frog? No. Her hair is too short for plaits. I relax. I'll spot them soon. Must be doing a story about Noah's Ark.

A red-haired child stands up. 'Welcome to our assembly,' he says. 'Today we are going to tell the story of Noah's Ark.'

I watch, listen and join in clapping to the songs and booing the bad rain clouds. How does a Biblical story fit with the need for conservation before all species are wiped out? At least I manage to spot Nick and Emily as they take part in the final dance before the animals enter an imaginary spaceship and are whisked away to a distant planet where life will be perfect and everyone lives in harmony. Nick is an elephant and Emily is a panda. Interesting how the animals represented are all of the cuddly, cute variety. What about slugs? Snakes? Fish?

The children crowd onto the stage and the whole school joins in a rousing song all about a big blue planet swinging through the universe. What happened to *All Things Bright and Beautiful*? I clap loudly as the children remove their masks and bow. Nick's face screws up as he searches for his mum or dad. I wave. He smiles and flutters his fingers at me. It is a sad smile.

I squirm on the plastic chairs. It creaks. Not long to go now. Mr Dhand thanks everyone. There is more applause and a general shifting of bottoms on small chairs. Time is getting on and people need to be back at work or elsewhere. 'You can all go and say thank you to the adult who has come to support you,' he says to the class as the other children file out.

'Where's Mummy?' Nick says as Emily clambers onto my knee. She smells of strawberry soap and her soft hair

14

tickles my face. She snuggles closer. Always likes a cuddle does our Emily.

'Working,' Emily says. 'She told us she might not get here. Don't you remember anything, Nick?'

Nick's eyes fill with tears. I reach forward and draw him closer. 'Mummy is very sorry. She asked me to come and take a photo of you.'

'Oh.' Nick is not reassured.

Emily clambers off my knees and replaces her mask. She poses, one hand on a hip, the other stretches out like a dancer. 'Come on, Nick. Like this.'

Nick pulls his mask over his face and shuffles towards her, arms tightly folded. Is he sulking or still upset? 'Smile,' I say and press the button several times. One of them must be a decent shot. 'There. One last hug and it's back to class.'

Emily does as she is told and skips off to join a group of girls laughing and chattering like budgies. Nick remains where he is. 'She promised,' he says and his lower lip wobbles.

Poor lamb. I hold out one hand. He walks closer and glances round. 'Hug, no sloppy stuff,' he says as I pull him close and breathe in the small boy smell of soap, toothpaste, and slightly sweaty socks.

'I know, lovey. Sometime life just gets in the way. I mean work does for mummies and daddies and grandads too.' It does, if Brian's crazy schedule is the norm.

'Are you Nick's grandmother?' The class teacher hovers over.

'Yes.'

'Run along, Nick,' she says. 'Mr Dhand is taking you back to class for English. We're writing a story today.'

Nick pulls a face, but does as he is told. 'Bye, Granny,' he says as Mr Dhand shepherds them all out of the hall.

'I was hoping to have a word with Nick's mum,' the young woman says. 'I'm Miss Bell.'

'I remember the twins talking about your art lessons. They both love drawing. Is anything wrong?'

Miss Bell shakes her head. 'No, just wanted a word. You know how it is? Nothing to worry about, I'm sure.'

This sets me off. Instinct springs into action. 'Is he being bullied?'

'I do need to speak to his mum or dad.'

In other words, not me. 'There's nothing wrong at home,' I say. Defensive? Yes. 'I will ask my daughter to get in touch.' I want to know if there is anything bothering him at school. She won't tell me. I'll text Claire as soon as I'm out of here.

'Good. She can contact me on email via the school any time,' Miss Bell says and breezes off. 'Thank you for coming.'

I follow the other families out of the hall and return the lanyard. How come the other women are all so elegant? Do they make a special effort? Is *glam at the school gate* another Instagram fashion style I'd voided?

Back in the car I text.

> *Got a few photos. No video. Not allowed. Nick a bit withdrawn. Emily full of beans. Miss Bell says can you contact her. Won't tell me why. Says nothing to worry about. All OK with you?*

The reply pings back within seconds.

> *You could have sneaked a few photos and a video. Everyone does. Nick is going through a whiny phase. He wants to sleep with Ted and Action Man. Ted alone is not enough. Miss Bell is an interfering old cow. Told the class last week they shouldn't eat junk food or have more than one hour a day screen time. She should try keeping two kids quiet over the long summer holiday. Must go. Team meeting. Love you xxx*

16

Thanks? Nice of you to help out? Nothing. I drive away hurt and worried about Nick. How can she be so dismissive of his fears? I remind myself I am grandmother, not mother. It's hard.

I take a short cut through town. I've still got to clean Lavender Cottage, shop, cook and God knows what else. And there is the small matter of the scrape and dent. Brian will be furious. Except what is a dent in a car when something might be wrong with Nick? Perhaps if we have the children over for a night, Brian can take him for a kick around. Young children often open up more to a grandparent than a parent. I slow the car. Ahead of me is a queue of traffic and in the far distance a red light and several white vans take up half the road. I'll be here for another twenty minutes, at least. Sod it.

It is six o'clock before I get a proper break. Brian will be late. Mark had gone out by the time I got back and left a message to say he didn't know when he'd be home. It's only Thursday but I deserve a glass of wine. I wonder if the American woman has arrived. I open the back door and peer towards Lavender Cottage. An upstairs window is open. I want to go across and introduce myself. It's too soon. Let her settle in first.

I pour a glass of Shiraz and look out over the valley; the cottages clinging to the hillsides, a wisp of smoke from an early evening bonfire curls up to the sky. I should be worn out and proud of everything I've achieved today. I'm worn out and fed up. I really am becoming a miserable old bitch. I must shake myself out of this. Except there must be other women like me. Women who want a bit of time for themselves. A bit of time to do things with people they choose. Not just family. Likeminded people and perhaps a chance to experiment a bit. Try something new. Something outrageous.

That's it.

I go to the computer in Brian's office and start to type. I'll put the poster up in the local shop and stick it on the village Facebook page. Something might happen.

Are you tired of sitting in front of the TV?
Do you want to meet like-minded women, who want to try new things and have a bit of fun before old age comes calling?

I add my phone number, email address and an image of a bird soaring in the air.

We need a name. A wild bird is free to roam anywhere, isn't it? Wild Birds sounds more like a 60s band. Wild Girls? Yes. I add the name to the top of the poster.

Chapter four Mona

What the hell was that? Mona jerked awake and sat up. It was an old man coughing underneath her open bedroom window. No. Can't be. She froze. There it was again. Do you call the police? And say what? There's someone having an asthma attack in the back yard? What was anyone doing in her back yard anyway? 'This is England, not Chicago,' she said as she slipped out of bed, her feet sinking into the soft carpet. As her eyes became accustomed to the dark, she searched for something to throw or use to threaten. Surely any potential burglar would run off if they saw an angry figure waving a stick? She crept closer to the window. The moon was bright. So were the stars. They almost made up for the lack of streetlights.

She flung open the window, cleared her voice and spoke deeply. Would they be convinced she was a six-foot quarterback for the San Francisco Forty Niners? 'Who is it?'

Only a small bark drifted up from the garden below. She peered out. In the silver light, silhouetted against a rose bush was a small deer. It looked up at her before opening its jaw and snapping off a green shoot. It repeated the action.

'Well, I'll be darned' Mona said to herself. She leaned out. 'Shoo. Go and eat some of the forest, not my garden.'

The animal trotted off obligingly. It stopped at the end of the path, looked back at the window, barked once and sprang over the hedge.

'Spooked by Bambi, eh?' Mona smiled. What a great story that would be to tell back home.

She climbed into bed and snuggled below the duvet. She closed her eyes. She turned over, punched the pillows, sat up and rearranged them before turning the other way. It was no use. She was wide awake. Jet lag had kicked in. Her stomach growled a complaint. She was hungry too. The green light of the alarm clock her landlord had provided showed five ten. What was that in West Coast time? Nine pm? No wonder she was hungry. What did she fancy? Would it be fish chowder? A Mexican taco before hitting the cinema or a drink before the theatre with the promise of a late supper? Her mouth watered at the thought.

Sleep would be impossible. She pulled a sweatshirt over her pyjamas and trotted downstairs. Coffee and toast would have to do. She placed two slices of bread in the toaster and waited for the kettle to boil. She searched the kitchen cupboards. No honey? No preserves? That would be her first task tomorrow. No today. She found a scrap of paper from her travel documents and a pen. Some decent peanut butter would be good too. And ground coffee. Tea? English people always drank tea, didn't they? No. She'd stick to coffee.

The warm, nursery smell of browning bread filled the kitchen. There was a ping. Buttered toast would do for the moment. She poured coffee into a small blue and white mug, spread butter thickly on the hot toast and watched as it melted into a golden pool. She sat in the armchair she'd dragged in front of the lounge window, curling her feet beneath her for warmth. Wasn't April supposed to be Spring? Perhaps T. S. Eliot was right when he wrote. *April is the cruellest month.* Probably why she'd always preferred Robert Browning. What was the verse? She checked her phone. At least there was decent WiFi here. She read aloud:

> *Oh, to be in England*
> *Now that April's there,*
> *And whoever wakes in England*
> *Sees, some morning, unaware,*
> *That the lowest boughs and the brushwood sheaf*
> *Round the elm-tree bole are in tiny leaf,*

While the chaffinch sings on the orchard bough
In England - now!

There was something comforting in those words. She shivered. It still didn't make the damn room any warmer though. She fetched the duvet and snuggled down again. A shard of light along the hills in the East pierced the grey sky. Her first dawn in her new country was on its way. She had to stay awake for that.

'What the hell are you doing here?' Ethan's face glared at her.

'Get out. Get out,' she screamed. No sound came from her throat. 'I said get out,' she picked up a brick and threw it.

Ethan caught it and squeezed it between his hands. It crumbled into dust and fell to the floor. His thin lips twisted into a smile. 'You really thought you could get away from me, didn't you? Stupid bitch. That's all you are and always have been. Stupid bitch.' It turned into a chant from a thousand unseen voices. Bitch. Bitch. Bitch.

He came closer. Mona backed away. She was flat against the wall of their apartment. Behind him the lights of the city shone through the picture window. The red, winking tail lights of aircraft crossed the night sky as people arrived and departed. 'You'll never leave me. Don't have the guts, do you? I'll make sure you don't get a cent. Crazy that's what you are, and everyone will know.'

Mona lifted her arms and beat at him. Except her fists made no imprint on his chest. With every punch he grew bigger until he towered over her. She fell to the floor and cowered, waiting for the first blow. She screamed again.

Mona jolted awake and opened her eyes. What the fuck? She looked around. Where was he? Where was she? Her hands shook. Breathe. Breathe, she repeated as the fear subsided and her pulse rate returned to normal. Sunlight beamed through the window. A little bird with a red breast was singing from the apple tree at the edge of the garden path. Its chest was puffed up and she could see its beak opening and closing as notes poured forth.

She'd been told she might have flashbacks and night terrors for years. It was early days. It would be fine. She'd sort herself out. Get help if she had to. Twenty odd years with a man like Ethan was a life sentence. She was out on parole. She'd recover, given time. Her shopping list fluttered to the floor. 'Time to get a move on. Shower and shopping.'

There was a village shop, wasn't there? She'd check that place out first. She consulted the manual left by the letting's agency. If not, a bus would take her into town. That would be a good start.

An hour later after squeezing herself into the small cubicle and washing under the trickle that pretended to be a shower and restored by more toast and coffee, she dressed in what she thought would suit a country village; jeans, a navy and white sweater and her favourite necklace made from red circles of glass. With red lace up boots, she was ready. She checked the hand drawn map in the folder. If she went out of her cottage, followed the main road for a few hundred yards before turning left, she'd see a sign for the shop.

A few minutes later, Mona pushed open a green door into a structure that was more shed than shop. A bell tinkled a warning. There was no need. A group of mums with babies were seated at the far end in front of a table, with mugs of coffee and a plate of cakes. A man in his seventies was reading a newspaper and a woman in the corner was knitting while the woman next to her was tapping away on her laptop. The few shelves were packed with essentials, but it was more like a café or community centre than a shop.

'Hi,' Mona said, acutely aware of her accent.

A small, thin woman bustled forward. Her hair was cut in a silver bob, and she wore a pale pink sweater with black trousers, spattered with white marks. A string of pearls hung from her neck. 'You must be the new lady at Lavender Cottage,' she said. 'I'd shake hands except I'm a bit messy' she held up flour dusted fingers.

'Fancy you remembering that.' A lady came forward. 'Don't mind us. Lydia has a mind like a sieve, except for recipes,' she added with a wink. 'Try a slice of her cherry and almond tart. I'm Jen and I run this place.'

Lydia flushed slightly. 'Just because I mislay things from time to time. They're called *senior moments,*' she said. 'What did you say you wanted?' Lydia wiped her hands down her trousers. More white marks appeared.

'What about your bread, Lydia?'

'Ooh yes. Sorry. Must check.' She scurried into the kitchen area and opened the oven door.

'There's a few things I need.' Mona got out her list and handed it over.

Jen scanned the items. 'Yep. We can do all that. You sit down while I put everything in a box. Lydia, get the lady a cup of tea. Or would you prefer coffee? I noticed the accent.'

'No. Tea would be fine,' Mona said. 'When in Rome and all that.'

She glanced around. There was a bookshelf of second-hand books and more shelves with locally made cards and pottery. A noticeboard was covered with posters. One in particular stood out.

An Invitation to the Wild Girls club
Are you tired of sitting in front of the TV?
Do you want to meet like-minded women, who want to try new
things and have a bit of fun before old age comes calling?

Mona took out her phone and typed in the number. Jen spotted her. 'Sounds fun, doesn't it?'

'Is this a local group?'

23

'Sheila from Rose Cottage came in this morning and asked us if we could put it up. It's attracted a lot of interest.'

'Rose Cottage? Is that by the church?'

'Yes,' Jen said. 'Do you know her?'

'Someone from Rose Cottage cleaned mine and left me a pack of groceries, bread, milk, stuff like that. Does she keep hens too?'

'That's right. We'll soon have you up to speed with the locals.' Jen sat down. 'Tell us a bit about yourself. You don't have to hurry off, do you?'

'No,' Mona said. 'I've got all the time in the world.'

As she said the words, she realised it was true. For the next few months, she could do what she wanted and when. It felt so good.

Chapter five Sheila

Three text messages, a voice mail and one call from Jen. At least there'll be five women and it is early days. People round here never respond till the last minute. Is it FOMO? More like lastminute.com. Still, five is a good start. Must have touched a nerve. Mona? Where have I heard that name recently? I shrug. It'll come to me sooner or later. I shred spring cabbage and add the pale green ribbons to the saucepan of leeks, already sweating in butter, a splash of water and they'll need to steam for five minutes. I can heat them through if and when anyone decides to come home.

What now? I wipe the surfaces and the top of the hob clean and place the chicken and bacon casserole next to the cabbage and leeks. Should I eat? I like my food freshly cooked. God knows when Mark will be back, if at all, and Brian said he'd be late. That probably means eight o'clock at the least. What happened to all the long evenings we'd dreamt of when the children had left home? I lean on the countertop and stare out at the evening sky casting long shadows and bathing some houses in a rosy golden glow. We'd take a walk, call in at the local pub or just sit with a glass of wine and talk about the day's events; Brexit, who'd make a good Prime Minister, climate change?

We'd reckoned it would be good to have a proper discussion and not about possible GCSE subjects, the advantages of a local university, if the children were spending too much time on video games (Mark) or another disastrous boyfriend (Claire of course). Except all Brian wanted was to moan about the boss, his chances of getting the promotion and the new members of the board. Perhaps when we were both retired? Damn it. I can't wait that long. I pick up a bottle of wine. What was it I'd read somewhere about drinking alone? Was it the first stage of dependency? Would one glass matter?

No. It's too early. I'd eat and at seven, pay a visit to the new lady in Lavender Cottage. My excuse? Had I left the place neat and tidy? Did she need any information? After all, I don't want to let Lydia down. If there is a problem, it'd be better to sort it out before it gets too bad. I'll take a bottle of wine. To be neighbourly of course.

At ten past seven I'm on the doorstep of Lavender Cottage and ready to retreat. Is this really a good idea? A light is on in the kitchen and in the front room. The cottage was always a bit dark and gloomy so someone must be home. Here goes. I lift the doorknocker in the shape of a woodpecker and rap the beak against the wood.

'Coming,' a voice calls from inside the cottage. The door opens. The grey-haired woman who looks out is frowning, not helped by the ruby streaks. I knew this wasn't a good idea. 'Yes?'

I hold up the bottle of wine. 'A welcome present from all at Rose Cottage. I'm Sheila.'

The woman claps a hand over her mouth. 'The girls? Hettie? You're the egg lady?'

'I've been called plenty of things in my time, never that.'

'Come in, come in. I'm sorry. You must think I'm so rude. I didn't thank you for the eggs or the message and the groceries. What do I owe you?' She steps back and holds the door open.

'Nothing,' I say. 'I wanted to make you feel at home.'

'You did that.' The voice has a warm slow drawl.

'To welcome you, I wonder if you'd like to join me in a glass to toast your new home…er…Miss?' I sound too formal, too British.

'Mona. Call me Mona. She holds up one hand. 'After Desdemona. My mother had a Shakespeare fetish.'

'Could have been worse. She might have called you Bottom. Or Bagot, not to mention Old Gobbo.' I follow her into the front room.

For a moment there is silence before we begin to laugh like a couple of kids in the infant class after someone has said a rude word behind the play house. 'Bottom I know. A Midsummer Night's Dream, are the others really Shakespeare characters?'

'Yes. I assure you they are. Minor ones maybe. Characters yes.'

Mona smiles to reveal perfectly even white teeth. 'Now I'm living the dream. To be talking about Shakespeare with a real English person. That deserves to be toasted. Let's go into the kitchen. It's warmer in there.' She heads towards the interior of the cottage.

I shiver. Cottages like these are often dark and don't benefit from the sunshine. This feels damp. It might be April, that doesn't mean a blast of central heating or a lit stove won't be needed. 'Have you tried the heating?'

Mona flaps a hand in the direction of the boiler on the wall. 'It rattles and burbles from time to time. There's no heat though.'

I check the radiator. It's warm. 'What about a fire? That makes a place feel toasty?'

'I wouldn't know how to start. A gas barbeque I can manage. Anything else. No.' She pulls the cork like an expert and pours two glasses.

'I'll come over tomorrow with an Allen key.' I run one hand down the radiator again. The pipe at the bottom is hot. 'I'll bleed it.'

Mona hands over a glass. 'What's that?'

'Air gets in the pipes and it stops the hot water circulating. I think.' Wasn't that what Brian said? 'If not, my husband can come over at the weekend and have a look.'

'You are very kind. I'll pay of course.'

'Nonsense. It's what neighbours are for. Cheers.' I hold up my glass. I'm happy to offer help and feel appreciated.

'Cheers. Take a seat.' Mona sits at the far end of the

table. I sit opposite. There is silence.

What can I say? I don't want to appear nosy. Why did an American pitch up here and take a lease for six months on an old cottage? Is she an artist? 'Do you have family round here?'

'Me? No.' Mona looks at me over the rim of her glass. 'You want to know why I've come here?'

I feel my face flush pink. 'Sorry. The Brits might be reserved. It doesn't mean we aren't incorrigibly inquisitive.'

Mona holds up her glass and swirls the liquid around. 'I wanted to get away for a break. I stuck all my favourite places from novels into a hat and out came the Slad Valley. *Cider with Rosie*? Laurie Lee?' She doesn't wait for an answer. 'This was as close as I could get at short notice.'

'Wow. That could have been a bit dangerous. Imagine if it had been *The Kite Runner*. You'd have ended up in Afghanistan.'

Mona smiles. 'I was careful. I had Laugharne in Wales for Dylan Thomas, Edinburgh and *The Prime of Miss Jean Brodie*, even Whitby for *Dracula*.'

'Not Transylvania?' I'm enjoying this conversation.

'No. I have some standards and a mediocre budget,' Mona adds.

'I always reckon this place is a bit like The Shire in *The Lord of the Rings*. Tolkein had visited the Forest of Dean so he might have been inspired. I like to think so anyway.'

'That figures. As long as there aren't any Orcs around. I got spooked last night by a small deer. I didn't know they made such a noise.'

'Oh, the country is far from a quiet place. You'll see.'

There is silence again. 'Have you lived here long?' Mona says.

'No. Yes.' I count on my fingers. 'I can't believe it's been over twenty years. We couldn't afford much when the children were small. Rose Cottage was cheap because it was practically falling down round our ears. We did the work; the children went to the local school and we've been here ever since.' Is it nerves making me talk so fast?

'Is this home?'

The question hangs in the air. It needs an answer. Until today, I'd never thought of dying in the village. There's still more to do and to explore. It's too final somehow. 'Who knows?' Perhaps if Brian gets the promotion, we might find a bigger place. If he doesn't, we could go for a complete change. I'm ready for it.

Mona raises her glass. 'I think we ought to toast a summer of exploration. Who knows what we might find?'

It is gone ten when I get back to Rose Cottage. Brian's car is on the drive. He hasn't been in long. The car bonnet is still warm as I brush past. 'Have you eaten?' I call as I open the front door.

Brian is slumped on the sofa. A plate, piled high with chicken, mashed potatoes and the leek and cabbage mix is balanced on a cushion on his knees. A tin of beer dribbles foam onto the coffee table and he is staring at the ten o'clock news. 'I'm eating now, aren't I?'

'I only asked.' If he is in one of those moods, I'll leave him to it.

'It might be nice if my wife was in when I get home,' he speaks like a sulky child.

'I went to see the new lady in Lavender Cottage. I didn't know when you were due back.' Why am I making an excuse?

'I told you.'

'You said you'd be late. That was all.' When had the carefree young man with the long curly dark hair turned into such a misery? The lines around his mouth turn down. When had he stopped smiling? Or when had I failed to notice it? 'I'm going to check on the chickens.' I escape before he can say anything more.

Chapter six Mona

She was back as a teenager. A short, plump, insecure little thing with a tendency to break out in spots when under stress (except she'd never heard it referred to like that—it was just being a teenager). Ethan was three years older, a basketball player with a car, a huge collection of music cassettes which he lent out to everyone, and a weekend job, so he was always flush with cash. He'd asked her out and she'd fallen in love. Even today she could recall those first few months when she'd thought she was the luckiest person in the world. When did it start to go wrong? At first, she'd explained the putdowns and the ridicule, the silences and the sneers because he was off to college, leaving her to complete her studies at High School. He told her over and over how much he hated the small town where everyone knew each other's business and were keen to judge before they were judged.

Only once had she questioned him on why he was ignoring her or why he expected her to wait for him to call. 'What's up? What's wrong? What have I done?' She'd say as the tears formed in her eyes and her throat constricted.

'If you don't know, you must be stupid.'

She should have told him to fuck off. There and then. She didn't. She watched as his face contorted into a mask of suppressed anger. He was taller than her. Stronger. She'd flinched under his gaze. Was he going to hurt her? No, he was too clever. He knew just when to smooth talk her with attention. Instead, he'd ruffled her hair and told her she was mistaken. She'd imagined it. Of course, he hadn't been out with anyone else. He'd told her to call on Monday evening, not Tuesday. She'd made a mistake. Had she? She certain he'd said Tuesday, but he was so convincing, she'd believed him. So, it went on. She'd escaped when she was twenty-five, to be sucked back ten years later.

This time there'd be no going back. Why did the same dream keep on recurring? It always ended the same way, her running down the street and him following as she tried to open locked doors and find safety in a house. His voice sounded in her ear and his breath was on her neck. 'I'll find you,' he said. 'You'll never get away.'

She'd wake up in bed, sweat dripping from her forehead and her heart thumping. She'd be sitting upright, the covers clutched in her shaking hands. Why had she thought he'd changed?

Mona yawned and sat up in bed. The jet lag was kicking in again. Moonlight shone through the open window. The only sound was a faint tap tapping of the branches of an old lilac tree, disturbed by a faint breeze. It must have been the Facebook message with a photo of her and Ethan at a friend's wedding this time last year. She'd hated every minute. Ethan had left her sitting alone while everyone else enjoyed themselves. She'd hidden in the cloakrooms for a while which is when she'd had a very drunken conversation with her own sister. 'Leave the bastard, Mona.' It had taken her a year. She'd done it. She was safe. No one knew where she was. Except seeing that photo brought it all back. 'Think of something else, girl,' she said out loud and punched the pillow.

Sheila was an interesting character. And this *Wild Girls* thing sounded a hoot. The text message she'd received last night from someone called Sheila about a meeting in the café tomorrow night would tell her more. Sheila? Could it be the same one? Or was Sheila a popular name in England? No. It had to be the same person in such a small village. She'd soon find out. She'd close her eyes for a few minutes. Sleep would be unlikely.

When Mona woke again, the sun was shining in through the bedroom window. She checked the alarm clock. It was eleven. How on earth had she slept so long? Today she had stuff to do. She needed food and money. That meant a trip to the town. She'd walk down and get a taxi back if needed. She could explore. She'd find a bank in the centre and set her phone to show her the way. It would be fun.

It was nearly mid-day when Mona stepped out of Lavender Cottage. Her phone told her to walk down the hill, past the school and follow the road. It looked easy enough. She set off. The sun beat down. Wasn't England supposed to be wet and foggy? Or was that just in old movies? The weather forecast on the BBC had said it was going to be unusually warm for this time of year. Is this what they meant? She passed the school. Lessons were going on and voices filtered through the open windows. Music lessons? They were singing *All things Bright and Beautiful*. Nice. Mona hummed along. Her phone bleeped. Turn right.

She stopped and looked for a gate. There was a small gap in the stone wall. A green sign said *Public Footpath*. It pointed upwards. Must mean straight on. She checked her phone. Yes. This was a short cut. It would save five minutes. Good job too. Sweat was pooling on her upper lip. Her throat was dry, and she hadn't got any water with her. She'd remember next time. She squeezed through the gap and crossed the grass down the hill, avoiding the cow pats. They were dry. Nothing to worry about there. Fresh cow pats meant cows nearby.

Mona lifted her head and started to sing. Here she was, free, safe, on the verge of a new adventure in life and when she went back, she'd tackle her ex and get her share of the house. She might even move somewhere. New England? Connecticut? Alaska? What was it her grandmother used to say? 'Cross that bridge when you come to it.' That's what she'd do.

The sound of padding behind her made her turn. She stopped. The cows stopped. She took a step backwards, the cows moved forwards.

'Be brave,' she said. She turned her back on them and continued down the slope. 'Head up. Shoulders back, they're only being inquisitive.' What if they charged at her? She was in the middle of the field. There was nowhere to hide. Heavy breathing meant they were getting closer. Should she speed up? What if they did the same? A brown head butted her under the arm. Was this the start of the stampede? Would she end up squashed? What would the headlines say back home? Woman trampled in freak accident. Would she be repatriated? What if this was it?

She turned. 'Fuck off!' she yelled and waved her hands at the first cow. It stopped. 'I said fuck off. Go on. Shoo. Vamoose.'

The lead cow backed away. It ambled off to the side. The rest followed and stood in a group, watching her every move. Mona quickened her step. Could she get to the stone wall and clamber over before they realised? She hurried on, expecting at any minute to be mown down. She reached the drystone wall. Where the hell was the gate? She looked along the line of thorny bushes. There was a strange wooden thing at the far end of the wall. It looked like a series of steps. That must be the way over. That was funny. The grass was beaten down here as if it was a well-trodden path. Weird. She reached the steps and clambered over.

'The footpath is along the side of the field. Not across the middle,' a deep voice said. She looked to her left. A man in green cord trousers, a green and white check shirt and heavy boots stood, arms folded. His hair had once been sandy brown. It was sprinkled with grey. His face was red and lined as if he was used to outdoor work. At his feet was a black and white dog.

Mona readjusted her jeans and shirt after climbing over the steps. 'The sign for the footpath pointed down here and so did my sat nav.' She waved her phone at him.

33

'Those cows are in calf. You shouldn't frighten them.'

'What about me? They came at me, you know. All I did was take evasive action. If the footpath sign was wrong, get the people who fix footpath signs to fix it. Or stick up your own sign.' Mona looked up at him.

'I'll let you off this once but—'

'But what? What are you going to do? I have a right to roam. I read all about it. Get your signs fixed. If you'll excuse me,' she stepped away. Her foot sank straight into a very large and fresh cow pat. 'Shit,' she said.

'Yes,' the man said. 'I think it is.'

Chapter seven Sheila

'Brian, breakfast,' I call up the stairs for the third time.

There is a muffled bellow from the shower. 'Must be on his way.' I spoon two poached eggs on slices of buttered toast, place the plate on the counter as the latch on the staircase door lifts.

'I see he's not back yet,' he says and sits down on the stool.

'Mark said he might be away for the night.' I cross my fingers he won't ask where.

'Where?'

'Oh, a mate. Said something about going back to university.'

Brian snorts and shovels toast and egg into his mouth. 'He needs to get a bloody job. Fast. Start at the bottom, like I did.' He waves a fork in the air. 'No. He's too educated to be a clerk or what do they call it today...project management? Crap. We all did some very boring jobs so we could move onto the next one.' He looks around. 'Any chance of a coffee?'

I take a blue china mug and pour the coffee. I pass it over, carefully making sure it doesn't slop. How many times have I done this? Made breakfast? Poured coffee? Washed up before rushing the children to school and ending up in a boring job myself so I could be at home or take time off. I tell myself it was my choice. 'Will you be late tonight, again?'

'Probably. I'll text you.'

'I'll be out at the shop. Remember? I told you about the women's group.'

He sits back on the stool and pushes his plate away. 'Another? Aren't there enough places for you lot to gossip already?'

I ignore the taunt. 'It's new. A chance to do something

35

different. That's all.'

He stands up. 'I forgot to say Claire called while you were feeding the chickens.'

My stomach goes into free fall again. I grip the countertop. 'Is she all right? Are the children OK?'

'She wants to bring the twins over to stay on Saturday night. She and the lad want an evening to themselves. I said it'd be fine by you. I'm golfing on Saturday afternoon and on Sunday morning. I'm sure we can rustle up a pizza for tea?' He stands up.

'You should have asked me, first,' I say.

'Why? You wouldn't have refused, would you? Or is that women's group going to take up more of your time?'

'That's not the point.'

He shrugs. 'What was the point? I knew you wouldn't mind. Must be off. See you later tonight.' He picks up his laptop bag, jacket, keys and phone and bends forward. I tilt my head and receive the proffered kiss on the cheek. 'See you,' and he is gone.

I pick up the plate and scrape the crusts into the recycling caddy. Why doesn't anyone realise I might want some space for myself? For the two of us? My mother never expected granny to help out. We met for tea once a week and there was the very occasional stop over, perhaps once a year. Claire thinks this house is an extension of her own.

Guilt punches me in the stomach. Would I have refused? Probably not. I just want to be asked. Not taken for granted. Assumed I'll fit in with everyone else. I wipe non-existent breadcrumbs from the countertop. I'm a mean old woman. I should be delighted to have the grandchildren. Isn't that what all the adverts show? The perfect family with doting granny and grandpa?

I love them, of course I do. The suspicion that yet again everyone expects me to drop my plans and be at their beck and call niggles like a dull ache. Tears prickle my eyes.

Damn hormones. I must be menopausal again.

The back door flies open and slams in the breeze. 'Hi, Ma. Any food?' Mark slumps into the old nursery chair. 'What's up?' He must have noticed my wet eyes.

'Nothing. Just being a silly old woman.'

He stands up, comes over and places an arm round my shoulder. 'You are not a silly old woman. Never have been and never will be.'

I lean against his jacket. There is a strange smell, pungent, grassy and sweaty. Oh God, is he taking drugs? No. He's too sensible, isn't he? I push the thought away. 'Hungry?'

'You bet.' He perches on the countertop. I can't be bothered to say anything. 'Remember John. He's just landed a great job… barman in Brighton for the summer. He reckons he needs help. I've told him I'll let him know by the end of the week.'

I turn away and focus on cracking eggs into a bowl so he can't see my face. All that money on a degree and he wants to pull pints? 'Isn't there anything closer to home?'

'Not yet. After all those years studying, I want some fun. There's plenty of time to get started on a career.'

Except every year, there are more and more young people all trying for the same posts. And some will have masters, doctorates, or intern work, won't they? I heat up some butter in a pan and wait for it to melt. 'Your father was asking about your plans this morning.'

'You can tell him the more I think about it, the better it'll be for me to get away. I suppose it's my gap year.' He sniggers. 'Gap decade more like. Any juice?'

'In the fridge.' The door opens. 'Get a glass, please,' I say as he lifts the plastic container to his lips.

'OK. OK. Chill,' Mark says and collects a glass from the dish washer.

'You could empty that,' I say and pour eggs into the hot

fat. They splutter. From the sound of crashing, Mark is doing as I've asked. I place two slices of bread in the toaster. 'Are you really serious about bar work?'

'Don't knock it, Ma. The entertainment industry is awash with great careers. Event management, bar management. Did you know there are huge chains, desperate for keen managers? And it doesn't stop there. Hotels, theme parks. The list is endless.'

'And the best way to start is a bar in Brighton?'

'It'll give me experience,' Mark says. 'I'll take these upstairs.' He butters the toast, adds two more slices of bread to the pile and holds out the plate. I spoon the eggs on top. 'Great. Got a facetime with Syd from uni. He's in Thailand. I might join him with the money from the summer.'

His feet thump on the wooden stairs as he climbs to his attic bedroom. What was worse? No job or a bar job? He could get a bar job, here, couldn't he? If he'd been more like Claire, he'd be on his second promotion. Admittedly she'd left to take care of the twins when she discovered she was pregnant. A mistake? When I was her age, we didn't dare make a mistake.

I pour myself a coffee and sit down on the patio. The day is already warm. I must give the hens some extra water and the peas and beans will need another soaking if this weather continues. There it is again. Why am I the one to fuss about the hens? Why do I worry about the garden? Why is it all down to me? Damn. Mona's radiators. I'd meant to ask Brian. Too late now. I'll mention it tonight. If the twins are coming on Saturday, I'll have to get the beds in the spare room made up and shop for food. Claire preferred ready meals. And all the hours I'd spent so they had home cooked food. What for?

That's enough. I drain my mug. I'm being a miserable old grouch. The weekend will be fine. Next week I'll have a bit more time to myself. Tonight is the first meeting of the new group, if anyone turns up. So far there are seven. That's enough. Two would be enough. One would be plenty as long as it was someone with a bit of grit. That's what I need. A bit of grit to tell everyone to back off, even for a while.

At seven o'clock I'm standing outside the shop and café. 'There you are,' Lydia says. 'Got to open up and switch the alarm off.' She unlocks the door. The alarm bleeps. She waves a small black fob in front of the alarm box. It stops. 'Good thing this. Can't do with all these pin numbers and logins.'

Once inside I look at the odd assortment of small tables and chairs at each and a three-seater sofa. 'Any ideas?'

Lydia bustles over. 'Let's move the tables back and put the chairs in a circle with the sofa. Gives it a cosy feel. How many do you think you need?'

'I've got seven down at the moment.'

'Better make it ten,' Lydia says and stops. 'What was I going to do?'

'Make a circle of chairs.'

'Yes. I remember.' Lydia and I move the tables to the side of the room. She holds ono the back of a chair. 'Do we need all of these?'

'You reckoned ten.'

'Oh, that's right.' Lydia places the chairs in a row. 'Can you put the kettle on for coffee?' she says. 'We can use the biscuits from this afternoon. I didn't have time to make a cake.'

I am about to remind her about putting the chairs in a circle. Instead, I fill two kettles with water and switch them on. I collect cups and saucers and arrange biscuits on a plate. Lydia is placing the chairs in two rows. 'Didn't we say a circle?'

Lydia stops and stares at the chairs. 'Oh, yes.' She moves

one chair and stands back as if she is lost. That's when I spot Lydia's shoes. They're odd. And not just two black ones in different styles, or a navy and black one. She'd done that on a couple of occasions. Haven't we all? No. This time one is brown and the other is navy. Strange.

'Oh, look at me,' Lydia says. 'What a silly thing to do,' she points down at her feet. 'I must replace the light bulb in the utility. I grabbed the first shoes I could find. She giggles. 'Now what was I doing? Oh yes. Chairs.' She picks one up. 'How many do we need?'

'You reckoned we needed ten in a circle.'

'Did I? Ten it is then.' She places the chair back in the row.

This is not like Lydia. What is going on? The noise at the door stops any further thought. It's the sound of voices. The first meeting is about to get underway.

Chapter eight Mona

The man continued to stare at Mona. She burst out laughing. 'I guess you are right on that score,' she said.

'You're not from round here, are you?'

'Nope. How did y'all guess?' She added a Southern drawl. Make what you can of that, mister.

He wasn't fazed. 'In future, follow the footpaths. We have rules in this country.'

She deliberately continued with the drawl. 'At least we make sure folks know about them and they're correct. A sign that says Beware Rattlesnakes don't mean in the next county.' She wiped her foot on the grass. 'Don't have no objection 'bout me making a dent in your lawn, do you?'

He turned. 'Use the footpaths,' he said and walked away.

Mona continued to wipe her messy foot on the grass. It was no good. Cow shit sticks in any country. She had two choices; go back and waste the afternoon or carry on and find a cheap pair of sandals in the first shop. A run in with the local landowner was not going to put her off. She'd have to ask Sheila who he was and if there were any rules about leaving dangerous animals in an open place where people walked. She continued down the hill. She needed a cold drink.

Two hours later the taxi dropped Mona off outside Lavender Cottage. Her smelly trainers were in a plastic bag and she had a pair of pink sandals with toe poles on her feet. Not bad for ten dollars. No. She must think in pounds. What was that? About eight. She heaved two shopping bags out of the taxi and paid. The taxi reversed and shot down the road, ignoring the flashing lights and signs that warned the maximum speed was twenty miles an hour. The signs were particularly interesting; a child's drawing of a clown and the words, 'Don't be a clown, Slow down'. The English were so polite. Except for the man she'd met today.

She walked up the path and opened the front door. Leaflets fluttered to the floor from the letter box. She picked them up and flicked through; fast food, double glazing, a cut price deal at a nearby mall. Nothing of interest. There was an envelope. All it had on it was one word. Mona. She opened it up. It was a card. On the front was a picture of a house and a cat with the word *welcome* in large white letters against a blue sky. She looked inside. There was no verse. Someone had scrawled a message.

Hope you have settled in. Any problems, call us.
Frobisher and Kingswood Lettings Agencies

It was a nice touch. She closed the door and kicked off the sandals. The toe poles were already making red marks on her soft skin. She'd have to get the trainers cleaned. Should she use the washing machine? That was for later.

She placed the card on the shelf next to the stove and stepped back to admire it. Like the release of a small coil of tangled wire, something eased inside her. Was the tension beginning to go? At least she didn't expect her ex to turn up at any moment. He had no idea where she was. He'd threatened her before if she ever left him, he'd find out where she lived and camp outside her door if he needed. She'd laughed it off at the time. As his behaviour became increasingly erratic over the last few months, she no longer had any doubts. He'd stoop to anything to humiliate and hurt her.

'No more,' she said out loud. She had to stop these silly thoughts. 'You're safe.'

She busied herself for the next ten minutes unpacking her groceries. How the hell was she going to keep all this stuff in the fridge? She'd have to leave the peanut butter and blueberry jam in one of the cupboards. At least they had a salad crisper. How did people survive without a full-size freezer? Ten minutes later she sat down at the kitchen table with a cup of lemon and ginger herb tea. What a surprise to find as many different teas as anyone might ever need. Didn't the English only drink the ordinary sort? She opened her tablet and scanned the recent emails. She'd told close friends and a few members of the family who could be trusted not to tell Ethan anything that she was travelling around but wouldn't post photos until she got back. Only one person knew where she really was, and her sister Janey Lee wouldn't say anything. Ever.

She read, clicked, deleted, and typed. She had three more to do. Her hand froze. Ethan. She pulled her hands away as if the keyboard was on fire. Why had he written? What did he want? Should she close it down? Delete it without reading it? No, that was weak. One finger stretched out. Like ET. It touched the screen. The email opened and a page of dense text unfurled.

Dear Mona,

I know you won't want to read this email. Please don't delete it. Not just yet. I only want to know if you're safe. I was very concerned when I heard you'd gone travelling. I know we said we'd have a trial separation (Where the hell had he got that idea from?). *I expected to see you round at our old haunts. The news you'd gone abroad for six months came like a bitter blow. Has our relationship meant so little you felt you couldn't tell me?* (What relationship?)

I understand I can be a pain in the butt (You said it). *Just let me know from time to time if you're safe and please don't block me.*

I've spent a lot of time thinking since you wanted a break. There are plenty of things I'd do differently (That's what you always say). *Whatever happens, let's remain friends and I'll be here for you when you get back.*

Please just reassure a very worried man that you're not in some flea ridden hostel with malaria or dying in a ditch (That would suit you, wouldn't it?)

The weather here is fine and dry. The mist hasn't been down for days and Josie and Ben's party was great. Marcie was dressed in purple lurex. At her age? And she's got a new man. He's called Silvio and he's from Brazil. Must be all of twenty-two. Everyone said they missed you. (She missed them too)

Remember, a simple email every so often just to reassure me is all I want.

Miss you and our life we had together.
Ethan

She reread the email. What the hell was going on here? Ethan sounded genuinely concerned for her safety too, not for their status as a couple. Poor old Marcie will never learn, will she? This lad will fleece her. Thank God she'd got her first husband's millions to fall back on. Although after the marriage to Luka, she'd taken a big hit in the divorce courts. If Mon was at home, she'd take Marcie to lunch and talk some sense into her.

No. She gritted her teeth. She was getting sucked back in. She did miss her friends though and it would be good to keep up with the gossip. One email wouldn't matter, would it?

Hi Ethan,
Quite safe thank you. Good to hear about the party. Poor old Marcie. Will she ever learn?
Mona

That was OK, wasn't it? Not too friendly? Not too brusque? Her finger hovered over the *send* button. If she

44

didn't reply, he might think she was being deliberately difficult and that might cause problems when she got back. No. 'Manners are cheap' her grandmother would say. That's what she was being; good mannered. She pressed the button. Too late now.

Mona jumped up and closed the tablet. Food. She was hungry. There was the meeting tonight. What should she wear? Who would be there? Would Sheila know anything about that awful man she'd encountered? It was strange how any worries about Ethan disappeared when she was busy, or her mind was occupied. It was good of him to be so concerned though. She wasn't fool enough to think he'd changed. He hadn't so far. This was simply concern. After all, they had been through a lot together, they shared mutual friends and had known each other since they were in High School. That deserved manners and since she was in England, even more so. She'd never encountered so many please and thank you's as she had in one shopping trip. Apart from that man. The Brits certainly knew how to be polite.

At seven twenty-nine Mona closed the door of Lavender Cottage. It was still light and warm enough not to need a jacket. Although she hoped her jeans and a sweater would be enough. What would people back home say if they knew it didn't rain all the time? She followed the path she had trodden earlier that week. No. It wasn't earlier that week, it was only a few days ago, wasn't it? Weird? She'd been here a couple of days and already she was feeling she knew a bit of the place. As she approached the shop and café, another small link in the twisted chain unfurled. She stepped forward, placed her hand on the door handle. 'Here goes.'

Chapter nine Sheila

'Hi, am I in the right place?' The door closes. I squeeze my way between the tables and chairs and hug Mona like the proverbial long-lost sister. 'I'm so pleased to have you here. We need a bit of inspiration, I think.' I nod my head in the direction of the clusters of women in groups and the words university, grandchildren, my son's new job floated above the general noise. 'This is not going to turn into a grannies' gossip corner. Nor is it about whose got the newest gadget in a kitchen they won't use in case it gets a scratch.' I hold up my hands. 'Sorry. Too bitchy, too soon.'

'I agree. When I start banging on about an exciting find in Walmart, shoot me,' Mona says and grins.

I think I've got an ally here. 'Let me introduce you.' I clap my hands and the chatter fades away. 'Ladies and whatever else you happen to answer to, this is Mona. She's from the States and over here for the summer.'

There is a general murmuring of welcome, nice to see you.

'It's great to be here too. Hope I'll get to talk to you someday soon, if not here.'

I'm forgetting my manners. 'Coffee? Tea? Lydia, can we get Mona a coffee?'

'Not sure if it's up to New York standards,' Lydia says and pours hot water into a pale green china cup. 'I reckon it was the best I'd ever tasted when I was over there in the 80s.'

'Too darn right,' Mona says and sits down. 'Whatever you've got will be fine, I'm sure.'

'Once we're all settled with a drink and something to nibble, perhaps we can start to discuss what we want from this new club?' I speak quickly as if they'll disappear soon. Either that or we won't get around to anything and everyone will spend the evening bickering about details.

Mona raises her hand. 'If you don't mind, I'd like a space to talk and get to know people, while doing interesting things. How about getting onto the real stuff and we can exchange pleasantries later?' She rolls her eyes in mock horror.

I could kiss her. 'Anything else?'

'I think we all know each other, don't we?' A large woman with long silver-grey hair in dreadlocks and a patchwork skirt waves her hands around to the accompaniment of her jangling oversized jewellery.

'Do we, Virginia?' Another woman with a sharp pointed face crosses one leg over the other. A white sandal dangles from a foot with black nails and several large toe rings. I recognise her as Nancy from the eco new build. 'We might say hello or even share a pew in church. Does that constitute knowing someone?'

'What do we mean by doing interesting things? Lydia raises her hand and speaks hesitantly. 'If it's anything to do with horses, count me out. Or sky diving.'

'What does everyone think?' Here's my chance. I jump up and pull a flip chart stand closer to the group. 'You shout out ideas and I'll write them down.'

'I'll top anyone up with tea and coffee,' says Lydia. She goes into the kitchen area and comes out with a tea pot.

For a few seconds there is silence. It feels like a few hours.

'I like gardens and stately homes,' Lydia says.

It unleashes a torrent of other ideas; theatre trips, spa afternoons, walks, days by the sea.

'Hardly wild?' Nancy says.

Virginia raises her hand 'Circus skills? Wild swimming? Nude life class? Not us, the model.'

'Some great ideas here. Any more?' If we carry on, they must come up with a few that will appeal.

'I hate to be a party pooper,' Nancy says.

Mona frowns and looks at me for clarification. 'That means someone who puts a dampener on things. Nothing to do with dog poop or any other type,' I say.

'I had visions of us trawling the streets with pooper scoopers,' Mona says and laughs. 'Like a doggie vigilante squad.'

Nancy is not deflected. 'Cost. Not all of us are on big money,' she says. 'What if we want to encourage the young mums? They'd have to pay for a sitter too.'

'As far as I was concerned, when my three were young, the only thing I wanted was a quiet evening in with a good film or a night out with my partner. I hardly expect them to be interested in being with a group of older women,' Virginia says. I cross my fingers. These two had form over that sneak, James Frobisher, if the village gossip is to be believed. The last thing I need is the inaugural meeting to be remembered for a stand-up row between two of its potential members.

'They'll be old too, one day,' someone else chimes in.

'That's it.' I've found the answer. 'We can make this an event for women of a certain age. How to grow old disgracefully but gracefully?' I smile at the assembled faces. Come on, you lot, give it a go I want to say. I don't.

'I like the idea,' Mona says. Is she emphasising her American drawl? 'This would go down a storm in California. All those widows and divorcees love a good party and a chance to let it all hang out.'

For a moment no one speaks. A few heads nod in agreement and the first quiet murmurs of approval increase, like the swell of the ocean on a stormy day.

'Are we in agreement?' I'm waiting for the usual excuses. Nothing happens.

'This is all about us and growing older but not with false teeth, floppy oversized sweatshirts and sensible flat shoes. This is growing older with heels, fancy tights, painted nails and attitude,' Jen says with her usual enthusiasm.

'Ground rules,' Nancy says. 'We need some rules.'

'OK, Nancy, you take over.' I hold out the marker pen.

'Well, if no one minds?' Nancy looks round. No one else offers. She stands up and takes the pen, turns to a clean sheet of paper and writes at the top, *Wild Girls*. She underlines the words with a curved line. Below, she prints one word. RULES.

This is better. I'd hoped it wouldn't be left to me. I like things to have their own momentum. After another half an hour and topped up with Lydia's excellent tea, coffee and cakes, the list of rules stretches to ten. Not everyone was expected to attend each meeting. Meetings would be rotated round people's houses and the hostess provided the refreshments. Interspersed with the monthly meetings, there will be activities and these might cost. At the meetings, there should be discussions on topical interest and if they could involve local people who were experts and willing to share their expertise, that would be an advantage. There was to be no talk of children, grandchildren, new kitchens, holidays, cars or Christmas (at least not until December). The meetings would take place on the second Tuesday, Wednesday or Thursday of each month to give people a chance to fit them in with other commitments.

'I'll type this up and if you let me have your emails, I'll get this to you by the end of the week.' Nancy tears off the sheet of paper and rolls it up.

'Great. Thanks.' I take a deep breath. 'What does anyone fancy doing for our first session?'

'Can I suggest something?' Mona raises her hand. 'I'd love to visit Laurie Lee's village and have lunch in his pub. It's not something I like to do on my own. Not until I know the area,' she adds.

'That's easy and cheap,' Virginia says. 'I'm happy to arrange that.'

'At our first evening meeting we might want to ask everyone to bring a book they've enjoyed, like an exchange. That usually gets everyone talking and will help us get to know each other,' I say.

It is decided. On Saturday 12th May, Virginia will arrange a walk from ten till one with lunch. On the second Tuesday we will meet at Jen's and bring a book that has made a big impact on us. We'll decide on later events at that meeting.

It is ten to ten when I finally stand up. 'Ladies, I declare the Wild Girls Club open for business.' There is applause and people ease stiff bottoms. At least their own homes will be more comfortable. I make a mental note to ask Brian to check the summer patio chairs are clean. The radiator! Damn. I'd forgotten to ask Brian and I'd promised Mona. Brian wouldn't mind.

Lydia is packing away the spare cakes and telling Mona her recipe for Raspberry Buns. 'My gran used to make them,' she says. 'I never weigh the ingredients. I measure the flour and the fat in tablespoons.' She smiles at anyone who is listening. 'Did I tell you my recipe for these buns?' she said.

'Yes. A thousand times,' I say and turn to Mona. 'Saturday morning, ten o'clock and I'll send Brian over with his plumbing kit. If he can't get the heat working, it's probably the boiler and you might want to contact the lettings agency.'

'Thank you so much,' Mona says. 'It won't give me any decent water and the bathroom is so cold in the mornings.'

'Brian will do his best,' I say. I'll tell him tonight. He can spare a few minutes from the golf club, can't he?

'I suppose you know plenty of people around here?' Mona says to me as we wait outside in the clear evening air. Lydia is still inside. The alarm console peeps as she sets the alarm.

'I knew a lot more when the children were small. All those birthday parties, play dates and school events.' I pause. She isn't talking about mums and toddlers. 'Why? Have you met anyone interesting?'

'There was a guy this afternoon. Said he owned the fields down there.' She wafts a hand in the direction of the football pitch and the stream.

'Big bloke, grey-haired, gruff voice and as miserable as sin?'

'Perfect description,' Mona says. 'He told me to keep to the footpaths and I pointed out his signs were misleading.'

'That is James Frobisher. He bought Valley Farm and gradually he's buying up any bit of land and any property he can get his hands on. No one's got a good word to say about him.' I want to tell her to steer clear. There is no chance. I'm interrupted by a long, piercing wail.

Lydia runs out, the key fob in her hand. 'I can't remember what to do,' she says and bursts into tears.

Chapter ten Mona

Saturday morning and what the hell was there to do in this place? Mona paced the small kitchen. Should she go down into town? Why? She'd never liked aimless browsing and the freezer was stuffed with enough food. Had she been naïve? Imagining she'd wander round a small village and there'd be plenty of people to stop and talk to? Everyone was either out somewhere or in their gardens, hidden behind high hedges, stone walls and wooden fences. She needed a car. That was it. Then she could explore further. She sat down at the kitchen table and switched on her laptop. Buy or lease? She searched and was about to click on one interesting site that promised a small run around for a lease cost of less than three hundred dollars a month when a knock on the door made her jump. She paused. The knocking was more insistent this time.

'I'm coming,' she called to the unknown visitor. It was probably a poor parcel delivery guy trying to find a Lavender Cottage. She'd already come across that. The Jenkins of Lavender Cottage somewhere else in the village had a prodigious online shopping habit. She opened the door. 'If it's for the Jenkins, they don't live here.' She stopped. The man standing at the front door was not a delivery guy. He held up a tool box. 'Sheila's sent me to sort out your heating,' he said and emphasised the word *sent*.

'Come in,' Mona opened the door wider. 'You must be Brian?'

The man entered. He was taller than Mona had imagined and his bulk filled the small entrance. 'First things first,' he said and placed his tool box on the floor. 'I'll check the radiators. Can you show me where they are?' He slipped off his trainers to reveal smooth, bare feet with neatly trimmed nails.

'There's two in the main room and one in the kitchen,'

Mona said. Shit. He'd need to go into her bedroom. Had she made the bed? Yes. Or at least pulled the duvet cover straight. She still missed proper blankets and a good old-fashioned quilt. Besides he wouldn't take any notice. He was in a rush or was he usually so brusque and to the point?

'Right. Let's get these bled.'

'What are you doing?' Mona asked as Brian squatted on the floor. He fiddled with a valve on the side of the radiator. There was a hiss and brownish water spurted out.

'Got a paper towel?' he said as he cupped his hands under the water.

'Here,' Mona said as she rushed to the kitchen, tore off a few sheets and scurried back.

Brian dabbed at the spillage and his hands. 'Thought so. Air lock. I'll check them all and you should be right as rain.'

'Right as rain,' Mona said out loud as Brian straightened up. 'What a cute expression.'

'My gran used to say that to me. She had plenty more too,' Brian said as he looked around for the next radiator.

'Under the window,' Mona said and went to move the sofa away.

'Here let me,' Brian said as his hand closed over hers. Mona moved away and he manoeuvred the sofa towards the middle of the room. 'Never at a loss for words, my gran,' Brian said. 'Raining cats and dogs, it's black over our Will's mum's, bent as a nine-bob note.' He repeated the action with the second radiator. This one hissed and gurgled like a geyser in Yosemite. Mona felt a wave of regret. She could be cycling there today if she was home.

'I'll get some more paper towels,' she said. Wasn't that the best action? Keep busy? Keep thinking of the next thing to do? She went into the kitchen. Brian followed her. 'That one was easy. More like that please.' He took the proffered paper towels and fiddled with the kitchen radiator. There was a rush of air and water spurted out over Brain, the floor

53

and the wall. 'Sorry' Brian said.

'Here let me,' Mona wiped at the water. It was orange brown in colour. There was a streak down the front of his lilac polo shirt.

'Bugger,' Brian said as he grabbed the paper towel and scrubbed. 'I'll have to go home and change and I wanted to get off to the golf club. I'm late enough as it is.'

'Give me your shirt. I reckon it'll come clean with a little cold water.' She held out her hand.

Brian hesitated. 'I'm not sure.'

'If you're embarrassed about stripping off, pretend you're on the beach. You don't wear a shirt if you're sunbathing, do you?'

'No. I suppose not.' He lifted his arms and pulled the material over his head. The few hairs on his chest had a greyish tinge and apart from a small bulge of soft flesh over the top of his chinos, he still had the remains of a once toned body. He caught Mona watching him and smirked.

She turned away and went to the sink. The splashing of running water drowned her embarrassed muttering. 'Water and a bit of soap.'

'What did you say?' Brian was right behind her and she could smell pine body wash. He dropped the shirt on the draining board.

'Soap and water is the best. I'll get on with it. You can find the radiators?'

'If I get lost, I'll shout,' he said and ambled off.

Ten minutes later Mona was drying the clean, wet patch on his shirt with the iron when he came down. 'The stain's gone. It's still a bit wet though.'

He peered at the shirt. 'That's brilliant,' he said. 'As good as new. All the radiators are done. I'll fire up the boiler and test they are working properly,' he said and walked over to the white box on the wall. There was a whoosh as the thing lit and a rattle as water flowed through pipes. Mona

54

continued to iron the shirt. Wasn't there something dangerous about wearing damp clothes? Brian continued to press a digital display. Random green numbers flashed up.

'Is there anything wrong?'

'With the boiler? No. It was set too low. See this here,' he pointed to a number eighteen. 'This was showing seven which meant the heating would never come on unless it was really cold. I've adjusted it. You should be OK now, unless we get any freak weather.'

'Like what?'

'We have had snow in June and 2012 was a real washout. Fingers crossed we'll get a good one this year. Right, I'll check the radiators.' He bounded off, whistling.

Mona picked up the shirt and pressed it against her skin. It felt dry. The smell was nice too. She stopped. Must be Sheila's washing liquid. She'd ask her what it was.

'All done. You should be fine.' Brian held out his hand. 'Thanks for the shirt.' His fingers lingered over hers as he took the shirt. She snatched them away. He slipped it over his head and peered at the front. 'Brilliant job. Thanks.'

'Can I get you a coffee or tea as a way of saying thanks?' Mona said, unsure of what she should do.

'I would say yes, except I've got to be at the golf club by eleven.' He checked his watch. 'I should still make it.'

'It's very kind of you to do this for me,' Mona said as he collected up his tool bag. 'I really appreciate how neighbourly everyone has been.'

'That's Sheila for you,' he said. Was there a trace of bitterness in his voice? 'She knew I had to get out early. I nearly didn't come. I'm glad I did now,' he said and smiled. 'It's nice to meet someone new and interesting.'

Mona moved towards the front door. 'Thank you once again,' she said.

'If you do get any more hassle, let Sheila know and I can pop round after work. I'll take you up on that cup of coffee.

Or a glass of wine?' he said.

Mona opened the door. 'I'm sure it'll be fine and if this weather holds, I hope I won't be needing it.'

'You can never second guess an English summer. That's why the English have so many clothes,' he said. 'We need something for all eventualities.'

He was hovering on the doorstep. Didn't he have a golf match to go to? 'I hope you won't be late,' she said and held onto the door and edged it forward slightly. Can't he take a hint?

'Talking of clothes, your secret is safe with me.'

'What secret?' Mona frowned and clapped a hand over her mouth.

'Yep. Black and red lacy ensembles are not often seen on the washing lines round here. I'd dry them inside if I was you.'

Mona had piled her dirty washing on the floor of the bathroom. There didn't seem to be a linen basket. Her bra and knickers must have been on the top. 'Thanks for the tip,' she said.

'My pleasure.' Brian winked before he set off down the lavender-edged path, brushing one hand over the new heads of flowers as he passed. Mona closed the door behind him. Was he flirting? Did he do that with all Sheila's friends? Was it part of being friendly? No. The English were a reserved lot. Not like Ethan. That was it. He was behaving just the way Ethan did when he was introduced to a new female. Instinctively she knew why. If ever there was a man looking for a quick away game, it was Brian. And not golf.

'Well, it's not going to be with me, buddy,' she said. Should she say something to Sheila? What? 'Your husband behaved like a teenage jerk and talked about my panties?' No. She'd make sure she kept a distance from Brian in the future. She went into the kitchen and resumed searching for a new car. She needed to find where she could buy a linen basket too.

Chapter eleven Sheila

With Brian out of the way, I dial Lydia's number. It was a good job I knew where the alarm number was written and how to use the fob. The villagers don't take kindly to any unexpected noises. Poor Lydia had been upset by the whole episode and kept repeating weird things. As if she was telling herself off for being stupid. I hope nothing is wrong.

'Hallo, Sheila. What can I do for you today?' The voice is cheerful enough.

'Just wondering if you're alright?'

'Yes. Why shouldn't I be?' Was there a slight tetchiness?

'After the shock of the alarm…I never thought my ears would recover.' Was that upbeat enough?

'What alarm?'

'The shop? When we had our meeting?'

'Oh. Yes. No. I mean did it?' Was she being deliberately vague to cover her embarrassment?

'We were outside with the American lady, Mona.' Had she forgotten?

'Oh …yes…of course. Well everything is sorted now isn't it?'

There's that vagueness again. Or am I imagining it? 'That's fine.'

'I must go. Got lots to do this weekend.' Lydia hangs up.

For a moment I stare at the phone. This is odd. Lydia is usually up for a chat at any time. It's hard to get away. Or it was. Perhaps she is busy. Or tired? Or was that stuff about the alarm a senior moment, as people liked to call these small lapses of memory? Even Terry Wogan used to talk about them. I replace the phone in my bag. If Lydia says she's fine, she must be.

I go back into the kitchen. Where do I start? There is a clatter as Brian drops his toolbox by the garage door. I poke my head through the open window. 'Did you get Mona's

58

heating fixed?'

'Yes. The boiler timer needed a bit of adjustment, and I bled all the radiators. Nice lady,' he says as he slams the garage door shut. 'I'll be back at about six.' He climbs into the car and drives off.

'Thank you,' I call. He waves at the mirror and is gone.

My hands grip the top of the sink. I know he works long hours during the week but when we could have spent some time together, he goes off golfing. I am left to look after the grandchildren. I could do with a hand this weekend. Isn't that what the adverts always showed? Doting couples playing with their grandchildren? The girls all scrubbed faces and gleaming hair? The boys laughing as Granddad swings them round? I press a hand to my temples and scrunch up my eyes. I really am becoming a miserable old hag. What was it? As women you are either lover, mother or crone?

'Yeah and I'm fast becoming a crone,' I say out loud and clamp a hand over my mouth. I'm talking to myself again. Shirley Valentine would be proud of me.

'Pull yourself together. Today will be wonderful. We'll bake some cakes, go to the park to play on the swings and have an ice-cream.' I nod at the cupboard. It's not the same as a wall. I imagine two sleepy children tucked up in bed by seven after a story and hot milk. It will be like the old days again.

It isn't. Claire arrives in a rush with a list of instructions about the twins' schedule. Saturday and Sunday morning are planned with meticulous detail, even down to the time they must spend practising their spellings ready for Monday's test. She has brought two sets of clean clothes, a huge bag of toys and their own duvets which she said they couldn't sleep without. Nick is clutching his tablet and Emily's eyes are glued to her phone. At eight?

'Nick's been complaining of stomachache. He'll be fine.

He just wants attention,' Claire whispers behind her hand as she dumps their bags in the hall. 'Have a lovely time, you two?' She hugs them both. They look mutinous.

'Come on, let's bake some cakes for tea,' I say as enthusiastically as I can. 'We like baking, don't we?' Neither child replies. It used to work with Claire and Mark. Am I losing my motherly touch?

I must be. The cakes burn. The twins sulk on the trip to the park. Nick wants to know why they couldn't have really exciting rides, like Alton Towers and Emily complains she is missing a party that everyone in her class is going to, and she'll be left out on Monday when everyone is talking about it at school. Every minute is hard work. Where is all the joy I'd felt when I knew I was to become a grandmother?

At least they enjoy the pizzas. Brian arrives back at six and, after tea, a bath, and a short story, the twins are tucked up in the spare room by eight thirty. A late night won't matter for once, will it? Except it isn't late. Emily reminds me they don't usually go to bed till ten on Saturday. I refuse to budge. Eight thirty is late enough. I don't like them sharing the same room. Not at their age. I wonder if Brian could turn the dining room into a makeshift bedroom next time. We can talk about it tonight over a glass of wine.

By ten o'clock, all is quiet. I sit down on the sofa by his side. Brian's eyes are already closed. 'Brian, can I ask you something?'

'What?' he says without opening his eyes.

'Can we put a spare bed or a sofa bed in the dining room next time the twins come?'

'Mm?'

'I said—'

'Granny, Nick's been sick and it's all over the walls.' A wail comes from the upstairs bedroom. Emily appears at the top of the stairs. Her face is white. 'I don't feel well either.'

I run up the stairs two at a time and push Emily into the bathroom. The smell of fresh vomit is already floating my way. Nick has indeed been sick. I'd forgotten all about projectile vomiting. 'OK, Nick. You're fine. Let's get you cleaned up,' I say and strip off his pyjamas.

The rest of the night is spent bathing Nick's forehead, reassuring Emily he is fine, it's just a bit of a bug. I call Claire and leave a message. Her phone has been switched off. Must mean she trusts me whatever. It is slightly reassuring.

At eight o'clock Nick wakes. He's spent the night on the sofa wedged between me and Emily who'd refused to go back into the bedroom. She said it made her feel sick. The sheets are on the line with Nick's pyjamas. Brian was out for the count. It is like the old days. I am in control. I am important as mother while the man of the house, the provider, sleeps peacefully. The idea is ridiculous. It shouldn't have been like this. It rankles. We should have shared more. Or is that only modern parents?

I ease my body away from the two smaller ones. 'Come on, wash time and we'll get some breakfast. Toast for you,' I say and ruffle Nick's curly hair.

By the time Claire arrives back, both children are rushing around the garden like maniacs. 'Hallo darlings?' she says. 'Did you have a nice time?'

'Nick was sick,' Emily says. 'I wasn't.'

'It must have been the bug doing the rounds of the class,' Claire says. 'Nick always cops it. Can you bring his clean jammies over when they're dry?'

'Thank you,' I mutter as they drive off. There it is again. Shouldn't I be waving them away with cries of 'Love you lots'. All I feel is relief and sadness. I am a miserable old crone after all. I wander into the small study where Brian is hunched over the computer. 'How do you fancy a walk and a pint?'

He continues to stare at the screen. 'Sorry. Need to get this presentation changed. I told you I'd have to work today. That's why I thought you'd enjoy having the twins here.'

'That was yesterday. You made the arrangements, remember?'

'Sorry.'

He hasn't even looked at me. That was it. Sorry. No explanation.

What next? As if I didn't know. Sunday will be spent doing the same things; chores all morning, cook the Sunday lunch and what then? Who needs a roast mid-day anyway? Or is it tradition? Yes. That's it. I'm stuck, following the same rituals that had seemed fine in the 50s, 60s or even 70s and 80s. Not now. This is the 21st century. It's time for a change.

I could always talk to Karen and ask about changing jobs. Could I take on a bit more responsibility? I'm intelligent and I could learn. It might mean more money. It would be good to have some extra cash. My cash. Not in the joint bank account.

After lunch I leave Brian snoring on the sofa. I go upstairs and open my wardrobe. What could I wear tomorrow to show Sheila means business? I pull out the navy suit I bought for Marks' graduation. I hold it against me. Shirley Valentine never wore clothes like this. If I remember she dressed in a belted raincoat. 'What do you think, Shirley?' I say as I hold it against me.

I know she'd approve.

Chapter twelve Mona

The days settled into a pattern. A walk. Breakfast. Shopping. Tidying the house and experimenting with the garden. Another walk. Saying hello to a few people. Emails. Facebook (not telling anyone where she was). Television and bed. It was calming. The shaking, the fear, the trembling as she opened her laptop or checked her phone for messages was fading. Ethan must have decided he didn't need to contact her anymore. Had he found someone new to terrorise? He wasn't a monster early on. Clever man. He was the perfect boyfriend and partner, later husband.

Mona looked out at the gentian blue sky. It was a perfect day with a few fluffy clouds and a slight mist over the valley. She looked at the pile of washing. That could wait. The car would be delivered later. A walk and a cup of coffee in the shop was needed. She reached for her make up bag, something she hadn't done in ages. 'No point in looking like a down and out, is there?' she said aloud and reached for a pinkish-beige lipstick. She smoothed the colour over her bottom lip. Lipstick. That was when it had all started. 'Don't wear lipstick, you look like a painted doll' he'd told her, and she'd gone along with him. Not at first, of course. He'd been insistent. She'd given in.

She smoothed a layer of colour over her top lip and rolled both together. She ran the tip of her tongue over the silky surface. Once he'd won that battle, others followed. 'Black suits and white shirts are the only weekday clothes for a professional woman.'

Mona went to her wardrobe. She'd ventured into the Factory Shop and the local stores and bought a few new things in bright colours. Today she'd wear the red shorts, as it was still warm, with a floaty, floral top. It felt decadent.

She'd even had her hair coloured a deep copper red. It was one expense she had insisted on until Ethan tried to take away her charge cards. She still felt guilty. Waiting expectantly for a hand on her shoulder and a threatened whisper. 'You don't need that, do you?'

She'd ignored it at first until he became more and more morose and picked an argument either with her or the shop assistant. How many times had she hurried out of places in case there was a scene? It had been easier to give in and each time she had, he had grown stronger in his control.

Mona collected her purse and phone. It would be good to meet up with someone in the shop. Ethan had hated her to keep in touch with friends and even family. 'They don't really care. No one does, except me.'

Gradually she'd lost contact except for those who were strong enough to accept she couldn't see them often and ignored Ethan's rudeness when they met. When she was back, she'd change that. People would understand, wouldn't they?

She closed the front door and walked down the path, past the lavender bushes. Later they'd be smothered in bees. Today there were only pale grey green shoots. What was that heady, rich scent? She sniffed the small purple-mauve flowers in spear like clusters on the small tree in the next-door garden. It was lilac. She took another breath. It filled her lungs, like a life-giving force. She'd enjoy her walk today.

Mona climbed the small track away from the village and headed towards the woodlands. The acid bright green of the beech leaves had not reached the canopy, so the spidery branches spread out against the sky. That would make a good photo. She clicked and moved closer under the trees to get a better view. If it was good enough, she might even post it on Facebook and perhaps Instagram. No one would recognise the place. After all, brown trees, green plants and white clouds were common to most of the countryside, weren't they?

Mona clambered up a small bank, head down, watching where she placed her feet. When she straightened up, she had to grab onto a nearby sapling. 'Well, I'll be darned.'

In front of her, spread like Texas Blue Bonnets were a raft of curved bell-shaped flowers. Early morning sunlight filtered through the acid green leaves of the trees under which they sheltered. She bent down and sniffed. Sharp and flowery like a basket of apples. She crouched on the dry leaf mould and lined up the head of a plant in the centre of her screen and clicked. A bit wobbly. Another couple of shots and there it was. A perfect mix of greyish brown tree trunks and mauveish blue flowers.

Mona stood up and stretched her back. Years ago, she'd have run home and got her paints or sketching materials. Come to think of it, there was a time she never went anywhere without a small pad and a couple of pencils. What had happened? She moved away, reluctant to leave the view behind. Jeez, she'd live here if she could. She scanned the patch of flowers. Was that a path? A slight space where there should have been flowers called to her. She picked her feet through the delicate blooms, muttering, 'Sorry little plant,' as she moved closer. A well-trodden path stretched through the flowers, like Moses parting the sea. She'd follow it for a while.

Ethan again. He'd stopped her painting. What was it he'd called them? 'Mona's little daubs.' He'd laughed at her idea to paint water colours of fruit and vegetables, cupcakes, flowers even, frame them and give them as presents to friends. There'd been plenty of compliments when people noticed the small pictures she'd put up in their galley kitchen. Except Ethan hadn't wanted them. They didn't fit with a sleek chrome and white room with clear walls and surfaces. It didn't matter that she'd preferred the homely, handmade look, like her grandparents' country kitchen. Ethan always got his way.

She'd stopped painting soon after and taken all her equipment and the small collection of canvases she'd created and disposed of them in a friendly neighbour's dumpster. She could hear her neighbour's voice. 'Why Mona, you can't get rid of these?' Sherelle had pointed to a collection of three small rectangular canvases with images of cookies. Mona had been particularly pleased with the one with pink frosting.

'I don't have any use for them,' she'd said.

Sherelle had grabbed them. 'They'll look so good in the family room.' That is where they had ended up.

Why didn't she have another go? She could go into town today in her new car and get some paper and watercolours. Unless Ethan had been right, and she wasn't any good. Did it matter? She could use them as a record of her time in England, couldn't she? That was it. She might do a special one for Sheila as a thanks for her kindness so far. All she needed was the materials.

Mona turned. 'See you later little guys,' she said and headed back home. What was it Laurie Lee had once written? That he knew every blade of grass in the area? She smiled to herself. She was in good company.

Mona was waiting in the front porch. The hire car was due at two. It would be good to get her own transport. She hadn't realised how close the UK was getting to the States where no one walked anywhere unless they lived in the middle of the city. The buses were fine if you wanted to get out and about during the day. So far, she hadn't ventured out much in the evening. This might help.

A small white car drew up on the space hewn from the front garden. A man got out. He looked a kid. He grinned when he saw her and waved. She opened the front door. 'Here she is,' he called out. 'Your transport for the next six months.'

She? It was a car, wasn't it? 'I hope you've got plenty of

time,' Mona said. 'I'm not sure how close a UK car is to the States models?'

'You'll be fine with this baby,' he said and held out a hand. The white shirt contrasted with his brown skin. 'Ahmed,' he said.

'Pleased to meet you.' Mona peered inside the car's spotless interior. 'This is kinda cute.'

'Not your usual Chevvy?' Ahmed sounded pleased he'd spotted her accent. 'Hired a Chevrolet Malibu in Florida last year. The kids loved it.'

'Did you do Disney and the theme parks?'

'Yep. Spent all day there. I'd like to go again. Where are you from?'

'San Francisco.'

Ahmed's eyes bulged. 'Wow. That is one place I'd like to see. Alcatraz and all that?' His eyes misted over for a few seconds before he snapped back. 'Let me show you round this baby before we complete the paperwork.'

He opened the door for Mona, and she slid into the seat. 'Seems pretty straightforward,' she said moving the automatic drive.

'Good job you didn't hire a manual. You'd a need a shedload of lessons.'

'I know. It was worrying me.'

'No need to worry about this car. She drives like a dream. Are you confident in roundabouts? Stop signs? Highway code?'

'I've looked it all up on the net. Should I get some lessons?'

Ahmed shrugged. 'Might be wise if you intend driving a lot.'

'Oh no. It's just for local journeys.'

'You should be fine. Let me go through the lights, heaters and the onboard Sat Nav.'

Thirty minutes later her head was spinning. She'd better

go slowly for the next few days. Ten minutes after that, Ahmed handed over the agreements, spare keys and a card with a phone number. 'In case you get stuck or there's anything I haven't explained properly,' he said.

'Thank you,' Mona said and meant it. Here was her freedom. She hadn't needed a car in the city and when she married Ethan, it was always his car. She took another look round the interior. This was perfect.

Once all the paperwork had been completed, Ahmed had bounded down the road like a young deer. His wife was collecting him at the end of the road, and they were taking the kids for a pizza. Mona waved him off. If only she had a smidgen of his energy.

Time to try the little car out. Mona collected her purse, locked the front door and climbed in. This was it. Her bid for freedom was taking on a new lease. She'd pop into town and buy some cartridge paper, pencils, and water colours. She edged the car slowly out of the driveway, turned right and headed downhill. The twenty mile an hour speed limit was an excuse to go as slowly as she needed. She was passing the pub when she spotted a small figure by the side of the road. Was that Lydia? What was she doing here? Waiting for a bus?

Mona slowed and opened the window. 'Lydia?' The face that greeted her was expressionless for a moment before it broke into a smile.

'I'm off to church,' she said. 'Everyone should go on a Sunday.'

'It's Saturday,' Mona said.

'Is it? Are you sure?'

'Yes. Today is Saturday. It's three o'clock in the afternoon and I'm heading to town. Do you want a lift?'

The face clouded. 'No. I'd better get back. Saturday? Not Sunday?'

'No,' Mona said. 'Not Sunday.

'Are you sure?'

'Yep.' Mona got out her phone and showed Lydia the screen with the date and time.

'I can't see properly. Don't like these things.' Lydia stepped back from the car. 'Do I know you?'

'I met you a week back at the shop. We both know Sheila.'

'Sheila?' There was that weird vagueness again.

'Yes Sheila. Are you sure you don't want a lift?'

'No. I'm quite all right. Thank you.' Lydia turned and walked away up the hill.

Mona waited until she had turned the corner at the top. Should she mention what had happened to anyone? Next time she saw Sheila would do. After all, the English were known for their eccentricities, weren't they?

Chapter thirteen Sheila

Funny how Sunday still feels the same as it did all those years ago when the house was filled with the smell of roast meat, the kitchen windows steamed up from bubbling vegetables and Mum would send me into the garden for a sprig of parsley or mint. After lunch and the mountains of washing up, the afternoons stretched interminably. Mum and Dad would fall asleep in front of a film. My older brother would take his latest LP to whichever of his mates was allowed friends to visit and I'd be free to curl up with a book and lose myself in Hardy's melancholy, Lawrence's repressed sexual energy or the exotic thrill of Steinbeck and Hemingway. That peace would take me through the long afternoons until I was called down for cheese and cucumber sandwiches and chocolate cake.

After washing up, there was only time to get ready for school, check my homework, wash and dry my hair and, if there was enough hot water, I'd have a bath with a few precious drops of Pretty Peach or Aquamanda bath foam with its cloying orange smell. I thought I was so sophisticated. Claire had grown up with the extensive delights of Body Shop. Some things had changed.

Except not the somnolent stillness of Sunday. It is still there. The shops might be open till 4.30pm. There might be Sunday League football, cricket, packed pubs and restaurants for Sunday lunch or brunch but at five o'clock, a hush descends, as it does on Christmas Eve. As if the world is holding its breath. Or more likely taking a giant breath in readiness for the breakneck speed of the working week. I put down my book. Brian is working in the study. Genesis and Deep Purple filter through the door. At least the house isn't shaking as it used to when we were first married. I flick through the remaining chapters. I'm bored with murders of young women. What is it about young men, and old ones too, and their fascination with rock, played loudly? I check my watch. Mark hasn't returned. Where did he say he was going? I'd bet my last penny he won't be fit for job hunting on Monday. What was it he'd said once? 'A decent weekend means you need the week to recover?' Yes. If you have a rich trust fund so you don't have to work. The rest of us have to be ready. Although perhaps I'm the one in the wrong. No. I don't believe that. If you take someone's money for doing a job, you need to be sober and energetic enough to do it properly. How many mistakes in people's bills, overlooked emails and cock ups are the result of people too knackered to take care? At least doctors and pilots have more sense. What about care workers administering drugs? Or bus and coach drivers?

I close the book and stuff it under the coffee table. I can't be bothered. I am becoming my mother and grandmother all rolled into one. I'd never have had miserable thoughts like this a few years ago. Is that what people mean when they say as you age, you lose your oxytocin goggles? I slump into the armchair and switch on the TV. I flick through reruns of comedies, a few ancient films, and endless American series. Why did the programmers think that what happened in some Boston suburb, a New York attic or a Californian mansion is remotely of interest to someone in a Leeds terrace, a high rise in Tottenham or a cottage in the Dales? I switch off.

What is Mona doing today? A rich American, over here for six months, no expenses spared, no worries about cash flow. She's probably online, catching up with vast numbers of family and friends all about her exploits. She'll have eaten a healthy meal. Vegan most likely and would now be relaxing with a glass of chilled Californian chardonnay. Or was Chardonnay old fashioned?

I check the clock. Nearly five. Sod it. 'Brian, I'm off to see Mona. There's plenty of bread and cheese for a sandwich and the rest of the roast chicken from lunch.' Should I explain? Say I need to discuss the club? Had I mentioned it to Brian? Hell. I don't need to explain anything. If Mona isn't at home, I'll take a brisk walk and get back before he's realised I've gone.

I collect a coat from the rack under the stairs, find my keys but leave my phone on the table. For once I'm going to be free from all contact. I step outside, walk along the uneven path, and past the lawn which is showing patches of brown. Weird for this time of year. Should I water it? I count on my fingers. It's been a couple of days since there has been any rain and in this warmth the grass is struggling. I loosen my shirt. It's muggy. Typical. A few weeks ago, we'd been cowering under the onslaught of the beast from the East. A blackbird calls from the apple tree in the cottage garden of number forty-five. He's one of the few remaining old-style gardeners. I peer over the drystone wall. His beans are already a foot tall. The peas are following fast behind and the tops of early potatoes poke above the black soil. In the greenhouses, small shoots of summer salads luxuriate in the warm, moist air. The blackcurrants, gooseberries and raspberries are in bud and his strawberries have been tidied and wait for their beds of straw. How does he do it?

Here it is. Lavender Cottage. Outside is a small white hybrid. Has Mona got guests? No. The cottage is quiet. No people milled around in the front rooms. If I did intrude onto a small gathering, I'd make my excuses and leave after a respectable and very short time. I ring the bell.

'Coming,' a voice calls from the back. Mona's smiling face appears as the door is flung open. 'Jeez. This is a nice surprise.'

What's my excuse? 'Any more problems with the heating?' That's it.

'No. Seems fine to me.' Mona tidies a strand of hair behind her ear and leaves a blue smudge on her cheek.

'I won't keep you if you're busy decorating,' I say and back away down the front path.

'Crap,' Mona says and holds the door open, 'come in. I was about to stop for a drink. Join me. There's something I want to talk to you about, anyway.'

I mutter some thanks and step inside. I follow Mona into the kitchen. The table is spread with paints, pencils and paper. One sketch is in the process of being painted. I recognise the scene. 'You've been to the bluebell wood.'

'Yep. Sorry about the mess. Chardonnay suit you? Californian of course.'

I'm about to say that's exactly what I thought Mona would drink. I stop. It might appear too intrusive. 'Sounds lovely,' is better. I lean over the painting. 'This is beautiful,' I say, and I mean it. The pale colours with a distressed white frame would be perfect for the guest bedroom, although not if it's going to be covered in vomit. It would be nice to have a proper guest bedroom and some guests that weren't family.

'Do you really think so?' Mon stands back, her head tilted on one side. 'That's what I'd hoped. I'm planning on taking some back to the States for presents.'

'Lucky recipients,' I say and accept a glass of buttery yellow liquid.

'That's the idea. Or at least the start. I've thought about setting up in business doing little paintings for kitchens for years…you know bowls of ice-cream, popcorn, cupcakes. Olives and tomatoes for people without a sweet tooth.'

'You're obviously talented, I'm surprised you haven't done this before,' I say. Mona's face changes. The smile disappears. The forehead creases and the eyes dart from side to side. Have I upset her?

'There are some people in this world who think I am the least talented artist ever born and no one except a blind or partially sighted, uncultured Red Neck would have my work on their walls.'

I don't know what to say. This other person or person's snide remarks have cut deep. Any effusive denials will be met with scepticism. I can't say nothing though. 'Taste is very personal in art,' I say. 'I'd get a load and have a stall at a local flea market. If you have such things in the States especially before Christmas. They'll either sell or they won't. I reckon they would.'

Mona looks from me to the paintings and back again. A small smile starts at the corners of her mouth and spreads. 'That's the nicest thing you could have said. I'll give it a go.'

I smile back. There is something left unsaid. It will come out sooner or later. I change the subject. 'You said you wanted to talk to me about something?'

'Yes.' Mona settles back in her chair and curls her bare feet up beneath her. Her toenails are painted purple and on her big toe is a narrow, silver ring.

'Go ahead and I'll see what I can do. If I don't know, I might point you in the direction of someone who does.'

'I got my little car yesterday.'

I hold up one hand. 'I can drive them, check the tyres and fill them up, anything else is beyond me.'

'It's not that. It's Lydia. I was driving down the hill and spotted her waiting at the bus stop. I pulled up and asked her if she wanted a lift. She told me she was going to church because it was Sunday.'

'Sunday? Are you sure it was her? We do have a lot of rather strange people in the area. Not to mention our fair share of druggies.' I feel a sickness in my stomach.

'No. Short lady, silver hair in a bob. Couldn't remember the code for the alarm?'

'Yes. That's Lydia.' The feeling intensifies.

'I thought so,' Mona said. 'She was acting real strange.'

Chapter fourteen Mona

Mona explained she'd stopped the car. When she'd waved, Lydia didn't recognise her. That wasn't a surprise. They'd met twice—not enough time to be on name terms. Enough perhaps to be on 'Ooh I remember your face' sort of thing. There was nothing.

'If I didn't know better. I'd have said she was on drugs. She seemed sort of spaced out. Not here. If you know what I mean?'

Sheila nodded. 'I had the same experience once when Mark, my son, was at school. He'd been to a party and when he stumbled in through the back door, I knew he wasn't drunk.'

'Could she be on medication? Some stuff makes you a bit cranky until you get accustomed to it?'

Sheila paused. 'Lydia hates doctors and medicine unless there's no alternatives. Come to think of it, I've never known her to have anything worse than a cold.'

'What about children? Husband? Is she alone?' As Mona said the words, she dreaded the answer. Is that what might happen to her? A lonely old woman who loses track of time?

'There's a son in Dubai and another in Scotland. One visits when he can, and Lydia goes up to Scotland at Christmas and in the summer holidays to see the other one and his family. She's been to Dubai a couple of times. Her husband died years ago. Car accident.'

'Poor Lydia. She must have been quite young.'

'Late forties. She said she'd never marry again. Dedicated her life to her job, the children and the church.'

'She was pretty insistent she had to get to church,' Mona said. 'I showed her the date on my phone, and she became tearful. I wanted to drive her home. She insisted she'd walk.' Mona looked away. Had she been wrong? Should she have followed? Gone with her?

'That's Lydia. Stubborn and as independent as hell. I'll pop up and see her this week.'

'What do you think is wrong?' Mona said.

'It's probably nothing. Stress. Overdoing it. I know I still think I've got the energy of a teenager.' Sheila paused. 'Except I haven't.'

'If she goes to church would the pastor know anything?'

'By pastor, you must mean vicar?' Sheila didn't wait for a reply. 'That's the trouble, we have a combined benefice.'

'What's that?'

'Where the churches in the area share vicars and readers. They would know her but not very well, unless she attends regularly.'

Mona nodded. 'I see.' She held out her hand for Sheila's glass. 'I don't know about you, I'm ready for another?'

Sheila hesitated before handing over the glass. 'Why not? Brian can make himself a sandwich.'

'Good girl. After all, we are supposed to be *wild*, aren't we?' Mona refilled their glasses.

'Yes. Whatever that means.'

Mona sat down on the sofa and curled her legs beneath her. 'For me it's about shouting out, *Heh world, I'm still here.* I'm not ready yet to slink away into the darkness.'

'Except I'm not sure what I want to do.' Sheila twisted the stem of the glass between her fingers. 'No. I'm lying. I do know and I'm ashamed to tell anyone.'

Mona held up one hand. 'You don't have to say anything else. Except if you want to take a lover, be discreet and make sure he is too.'

Sheila threw back her head and laughed. 'Me? No thanks.' She was silent.

Mona knew to wait. People spoke when and if they needed to. Sometimes all you had to do was be patient. Years in therapy had told her that.

76

'I still feel I've got a lot to give and not just as mum and gran. Most of the time it's wonderful. I want more.'

'Change of career? New outlet? Writing? Painting?' Mona said.

'Something like that. I want to feel alive again. Sometimes when I look in the mirror, I see a husk of a person. I'm exhausted with being mum and gran. I want to be Sheila. Except I don't know who she is anymore.'

As she listened, Mona felt her throat tighten She blinked hard. She wanted to shout *I know what you mean. I feel the same.* She wanted to be Mona, not Ethan's or anyone else's version of her. 'I understand,' she said in a whisper and pulled a tissue out of her pocket. She dabbed her eyes. 'Ignore me.'

'Sorry. It should be me listening to you too.'

'No. I understand. I really do. For years I've been Ethan's partner. I want to discover who I am. That's why I'm here,' Mona said and blew her nose.

'Tell me about Ethan if you want to,' Sheila said.

For the first time in years, Mona wanted to tell someone. About his control. His put downs. Hell, his personality disorder because that's what it was. 'I met Ethan when I was at high school. He was popular, a great sport and clever. I admired him. Everyone did. We dated for a couple of years.'

'What happened?'

'I grew up and realised he wanted me to remain like I was in high school, in awe of him and perpetually in his shadow.' She smiled as the ridiculous images of Ethan's put downs filtered back. 'There was this one occasion and we were at a party. Ethan hands me a drink and goes off to talk to a group of his friends. I wander over, try to join in and he turns his back on me. Fine. I go and find a group of kids my age. That wasn't right. How dare I talk to men or women? What the hell did he want me to do?'

'You broke up, though?'

'I went to college on the other side of the country. It was before email, mobile phones, the internet. It was tougher to keep in touch.'

'Easier to lose contact too?' Sheila said.

'Exactly. We lost contact.'

'Did you meet anyone else?'

'They didn't last. At the back of my mind was a feeling I'd failed. I should have worked harder to make us work, if you see what I mean? What about you?'

Sheila grimaced. 'I tried to be the perfect wife and mother. I was what the adverts showed. I had the spotlessly clean home and the perfect home cooked food. I helped out at school, took a part time job on minimal pay to provide extras. Always the image of the perfect family came first.' She went quiet. 'I'm not even sure if it was what was best for the children, for Brian or for me.'

'What do you mean?'

'Wouldn't they have been as happy with a mum and dad and a walk in the park? Did they need all those computer games when we could have played cards with buttons? Like I did. It's not what they are doing it's the attention they receive. I don't know.' She clapped a hand over her mouth. 'There I go again, dragging the conversation back to me and my stuff. Tell me more about Ethan.'

Mona hesitated. What the hell. Sheila was a good listener. 'We met up again at a high school reunion ten years ago. He was divorced with two grown up kids. We talked, phoned and spent a long weekend in Chicago where he was working. Within six months we were married and he moved to San Francisco.'

'Had he changed?' Sheila raised one eyebrow.

Mona shifted in her seat. How could she say she'd been taken in? She'd fallen for the oldest trick in the book. She took a deep breath. 'It was fabulous for the first few months. Things started to change after that and we were back to where we'd been. This time I couldn't run away again, could I? I had to stick it out. To prove I could make a go of a relationship, our relationship, because when stuff between us was good, it was brilliant.'

'Like looking for a lost diamond ring in dog shit?'

Mona burst out laughing. 'Only a Brit would say that. It's true. I kept searching for that darned diamond and it turned up whenever I was getting ready for a confrontation or planning to ask for a break. Bang. Ethan was Mr Perfect. If I dared to challenge him, he made out it was all in my imagination.'

There was silence. Each woman was lost in their own realities or whatever passed as reality. 'I think sometimes in our life, we owe it to ourselves to become ourselves,' Sheila said.

'Whatever that means.'

'To "whatever that means" That's the toast,' Sheila said and held up her glass. 'Wild Girls need to know themselves and be happy with that or happy to make the changes.'

'I'll drink to that.'

As Mona got ready for bed later that evening she looked down at her naked feet. Purple nails and a toe ring were a small step to reclaiming herself. She could post a photo on Facebook. It would make her friends laugh and annoy Ethan no end if he saw it.

'Jeez, Mona girl. Is that all it takes? Could have saved a fortune and gone to Jenny's Nail Bar on East 23rd.'

Except she knew it wasn't. It was the beginning, like the paintings downstairs on the kitchen table. They weren't brilliant. It didn't matter. They were the beginning of her trying to define what and who Mona was after years of Ethan's…what was it? What do you call treating someone's achievements with contempt? Not even wanting to hear about them. Pointing out faults. Comparing her to more attractive women whenever he could. Mental abuse? Yes. That's what it was.

As she climbed into bed, she felt as if another link in the chain that Ethan had created to tie her down had fallen away. She hoped Sheila could feel the same.

Chapter fifteen Sheila

'Where have you been?' I'd hardly got through the front door when Brian's voice cuts through the guitar riff from some old rock band.

I close the door quietly. 'I've been to see Mona.'

There is a snort. 'I suppose you've got some more jobs lined up for me?'

'I wouldn't dream of it.'

'Glad to hear it. I missed the start of the match and had to partner Wilkins. He's deaf as a post and takes ages to set up each shot. We were holding everyone up.'

I want to tell him he's lucky if that's all he's got to worry about. I don't. If he wants to sound like a sulky teenager, he can. I'm not going to be drawn in. 'I think it's a sad day when we can't show a bit of neighbourliness. She was very appreciative.'

There is another snort. No words follow.

I feel guilty. Old habits are hard to shift. 'Have you eaten?'

'I made myself a sandwich.'

How does he manage to sound so hard done by? 'Good. Is Mark back yet?'

'No. Unless he sneaked in when I was working.'

'I doubt it. Mark likes to make his presence known.' I say and sit down opposite Brian on the two-seater sofa. This can't go on. Perhaps I need to take more interest in his work. Although lately he's been too wound up for any decent discussion. I can try. 'Did you get your reports finished?' I say.

Brian passes a hand over his face as if wiping away an unpleasant memory. 'Yes. Not that it'll do me much good.'

Come on, I want to shout. Stop being such a misery. I don't of course. Something tells me to hold back any judgements. 'Why is that?' I say and hope it sounds encouraging. My words act like petrol on a small smouldering bonfire. Brian jumps up and his words pour forth.

'Because I'm too old. Past it. An old crock. The place is swarming with youngsters, out of college with their ideas about podcasts, vlogs, blogs, online support. There's no respect for those of us who were with the company when it began.'

He is pacing the room, one hand on his head, raking through his hair. 'If I'd spoken to old Jenkins as if he was an idiot, I'd have been carpeted. Now? It's all, *'Yeah great idea. Takes us into the 21st century. Online phone support is such a waste of resources.'* It doesn't matter that Mrs Smith doesn't have online access. She likes paying by cheque or cash and if there's a problem, she wants to talk to someone.'

Usually when he's on a rant, I say nothing. This time is different. I want to help. 'What choices have you got?'

The rant stops. Brian swivels round to face me. 'Choices?'

'Yes. If the place is as bad as that, what else is there out there?' I want him to realise I understand his frustration.

He glares. 'That's not the point. I've been with that sodding company since 1993, through all the financial troubles. I've worked my way up and what for? To be told all posts at my level and above are open for grabs? My reputation counts for nothing?' He's waiting for an answer.

'I'm sorry I didn't realise,' I mutter. I know it's not the right thing to say.

'No. You didn't.' Brian flops back down on the sofa and picks up his tablet. He taps at it.

I move next to him and place one hand on his knee. 'I'm really sorry. If you'd talked to me earlier—'

He pulls away from my touch. 'So, it's my fault is it?'

'I didn't say that. It's—'

Brian stands up again. He looks down at me. 'I've

worked my arse off for this family and what thanks have I ever got? A son who's a waste of space, a daughter who's so caught up in her own life she doesn't think we might have something to do at the weekend. No. Mum and Dad will look after the children.'

'We did our best,' I say, amazed at how calm I feel. 'We did what we thought would give them a good start in life. I'm sure they don't mean to be so…' I hesitate. The word I want is unpleasant on the tongue. Selfish. That's what I want to say.

'I wish I thought the same,' Brian says. He picks up his tablet and laptop bag. 'I'll be in my office.'

'Do you want a cup of tea?' I call after him.

'No.' The door closes. More rock music blares out.

I can't sit here. It's time to get the house ready for the coming week. I collect a duster and wipe over the top of the wooden mantelpiece. It is a piece of driftwood we'd found and stuck in the back of the car on a camping holiday. The children had squeezed in beside it and we'd bounced uncomfortably home. We'd been so proud, and the children had loved hanging their stockings on the small hooks, specially placed by the side of the grate. Oh, the excitement of Christmas morning. Little squeals as they ran downstairs and tore open the small gifts, bought and wrapped since September. Big presents came later and there was never any argument. What had happened? Had we made a mistake? Had I made a mistake? I'd done all I could to make sure the children were happy. Was I too protective? Did they just need love and a hefty dose of reality which says, life is not all roses, deal with it, we'll help you but we can't make it all perfect?

I flick the duster over the other polished surfaces and get out the soft brush and pan so that the hoover doesn't disturb Brian. Not that he'd hear, anyway. I go into the kitchen. A loaf has been left on the draining board. The remains of the roast chicken wait for a cover. A buttery knife is parked on the chopping board. Crumbs and grease are scattered over the counter surface and the jar of pickles is left unscrewed. Couldn't he even make a sandwich and not leave a mess?

I am in the office by nine the following morning. I'd dressed in a plain black skirt, a white blouse and had added a necklace of coloured beads, bought from a craft stall years ago. It is too warm for a jacket. Thank goodness. I didn't want to look like a penguin, all black suits and white fronts. A garbled message from Mark about going to Brighton for a few days was hardly reassurance he was safe. It would have to do. By the time Brian came to bed I was nearly asleep. Did he have to work that hard or was it deliberate, to avoid me? We'd hardly exchanged two words this morning. I was pleased when he'd left and I could get ready.

Karen is already in her office when I knock on the door. 'Hey, good weekend?' she says without looking away from her screen.

'So so,' I say. Here goes. I cross my fingers behind my back. 'I'd like to have a word with you.'

'Sure.' Karen clicks on some keys, swivels her chair to face me. 'Fire away.'

Karen's face is still unlined. No dark shadows lurk under her eyes and her brows are naturally shaped and full. Her grey and white sleeveless shift dress shows slender, taut arms. Lucky lady. 'It's about my post here.' I blurt out the words. 'It's part time. I was wondering if there was any way I could increase my hours or get a post with a bit more responsibility.' There it's done. I've said it. I wait for the excuses and am ready to apologise and leave.

Karen punches the air. 'Hallelujah! There was me worrying all weekend about where I'd find someone to take on these.' She picks up a series of manilla files.

'What are they?'

'Similar to what you're doing at the moment, reviewing housing stock, checking allocations and tenancy agreements.' She pauses. 'With a new slant.'

I'm caught off guard. 'What's that?'

Karen folds her hands on the polished desktop. 'This is a new initiative. We want to allocate a case load to an individual housing officer and they will be the point of contact and, more importantly, a mentor. It will involve a regular fortnightly visit, check everything is OK. If there are issues, direct them to support and even be a link to Social Services.'

I need to sit down. 'Are you sure?'

'Sit down, Sheila, before you fall down,' Karen says and I collapse onto the chair next to her desk.

'It sounds brilliant,' I manage to stammer out.

'There'll be some training and you'll have to get enhanced clearance for dealing with possible vulnerable people.'

I can't believe my luck. 'I'd love it,' I say quickly in case she changes her mind or says it was all a mistake.

'You haven't asked me about the pay?'

'I'm assuming as it's a few extra hours, it will mean more anyway,' I say.

Karen shakes her head. 'That's why I like working with older people.' I flinch. She doesn't notice. 'You put the work before the wonga, if you get what I mean?'

'I suppose we do,' I say, remembering all the heated arguments we'd enjoyed at university. about finding ethical work and not joining the consumer rat race.

'Take a look at these today and we'll have a catch up later. I don't want you to take on something and regret it.' She pushes the files towards me.

'I won't.' I flick through the top one. Medical reports, police reports and more. I collect the files and hug them to me. 'I'm ready for a challenge.'

'It'll be that,' Karen says as her phone rings. 'The first problem of the week. Wish me luck,' and she turns away.

I leave the office and sit down in my own cubicle. Already the rest of the team are seated at consoles. I wave and smile, reply to a few well-meaning questions about my weekend and enquire about theirs. I can't wait to go through the files properly. I check the emails. Nothing that can't wait. I open the first manilla file and spread the paperwork out on the desk. Social workers' reports, police reports of abusive neighbours, credit checks, results of previous applications. A Syrian family in need of support and what do they get? Racism. Anger that they're taking up some pot of cash. Tittle tattle about the children to the authorities. It would be good to be of service to people who needed help.

Others follow. An elderly couple who had lost their money and their house. A young man out of rehab. Mark? Was he involved in drugs? No. Not after his early experiments. Except how would I know? I push the thought aside.

I flip another page. Someone for whom care in the community is failing. Another person who needs a transfer to a bungalow because of problems with mobility. An ex-offender. It is the vulnerable and needy of society spread out before me, except from my little village bubble, I could have believed it was a different planet. I make a new file on my computer, issues and actions. I'd do my best.

Chapter sixteen Mona

'Damn thing!' Mona rattled the door of the washing machine. It was jammed. Inside were the trainers smothered in cow dung. She flicked the switch on and off. Nothing. She twizzled the dial, pressed the surface of the console. Still no movement and no sound except a faint whirring as is a bee was stuck inside and trying to escape. Water continued to trickle into the drum. If she didn't do something, it'd start to spill out, wouldn't it? Who could she call? Sheila? No. It was Wednesday and Sheila would be at work. Besides, she didn't want to provide an excuse for Brian to come over. There was something creepy about him.

There was a file with important information. Of course, why hadn't she thought of that before? There might be something about a helpful electrician. Or did she need a plumber? She rummaged in the bookcase for the file. It was wedged between a battered copy of *Bleak House* and *The AA Guide to Birds of Britain*, dated 1989. She flicked through the loose-leaf pages. Garage? Doctor? Dentist? Nothing about a plumber. The agent's number was emblazoned on the front page.

In case of emergency or for more information call…

She picked up her phone and dialled. This was an emergency wasn't it? There might be a flood? What would that do to these old cottages? Could it damage the foundations? Images of the house falling down, of her having to pay extortionate amounts to repair it and losing her hefty deposit unnerved her. She'd lost so much confidence since she'd married Ethan, she was frightened of her own daydreams.

'Frobisher and Kingswood Estate and Lettings Agents,

how can we help?' The words were run together as if it had been well used by the bored sounding voice at the other end.

'I'm Mona Carter and I've taken on a six-month tenancy of Lavender Cottage. This number was given to me in case of an emergency and I think I've got one.'

'I'll pass you onto our lettings department. Hold the line please.'

Mona listened as the strains of Vivaldi's Four Seasons, spring played. It had been a long time since she'd heard that. She hummed along. 'Lettings. Richard James here.'

'Sorry,' Mona said. 'I wasn't expecting...or I was and got carried away with the music.'

'Yes. I like a bit of the Baroque myself. How can I help you?'

Mona explained the situation.

'No problem. I have the owner of Lavender Cottage here. He was enquiring how you were getting on. He says he can come around with a replacement washing machine. He was meaning to do it later this year anyway.'

'Wow. That is service.'

'The owner is very keen to make sure his lettings are up to date. He recognises there are a few improvements that need to be made.' The voice was muffled for a moment as if someone was talking and didn't want to be heard. 'How about late afternoon? Around five o'clock?'

'Yes. That would be great. I can't thank you enough.'

'Is there anything else?'

Should she mention the boiler? Brian had got it going for the moment although if the fine weather continued, she'd need air conditioning. Perhaps when she met the owner? That was time enough. 'No.'

'Good. Enjoy the rest of your day.' The phone line went dead.

Damn. She hadn't asked the name of the owner or what

he looked like. What if she answered the door and it was a maniac with a gun? What if she let him in and he was fake? 'Calm yourself,' she said. The person, whoever it was, would be laden down with tools and have a darn great washing machine in the back of his pickup, wouldn't he? Wasn't that evidence enough? She really needed to get more of a grip. Her imagination was going crazy.

She looked around at the cottage. Her paintings and sketches took up most of the table and counter space and there was a layer of dust on the bookcase. The floor was gritty under her feet. If Brian had spotted her dirty linen on Saturday, what else was there she'd left out? She'd better clean up and fast.

By four fifty-five the cottage was reasonably tidy. All stray underwear had been banished to a cupboard. Her paintings were in a neat folder with one that she was currently working on propped up on the kitchen table. It all looked very homely, rustic and she had to admit, rather Bohemian and artistic.

Someone was hammering on the door. Mona checked her watch. 'Spot on time.'

Through the front window she could see a van parked next to her car. The frosting on the door panel meant she couldn't see what the person looked like. Was it a man? Why not a female? Plenty of women could wield a spanner, why not a plumbing thing? What tools did plumbers use? She'd soon find out. She opened the door and looked up into a familiar face.

The man from the cow field held out his hand. 'James Frobisher. You're expecting me I think?'

'You own Lavender Cottage?'

'Plus a few others. I've got the washing machine. I'll just take a check on the old one.' He didn't wait to be invited in. He strode over the threshold, through the kitchen and into the small utility room.

Mona followed. He hadn't recognised her, had he?

He rattled the machine. It gurgled and there was a whooshing sound as water flowed away. He looked through the viewing panel. 'Are they trainers in there?' he said. From the tone of his voice, he was not amused.

'Yes. Perfectly common practice,' Mona said. 'It's the best way to keep them shoe box clean.'

He sniffed. 'I hope you scraped the mud and grit off first? Washing machines can't cope with stones.'

'There were no stones. In fact it was simply—'

'Cow muck?' James Frobisher straightened up. His bulk filled the small room. Mona backed away.

'Er yes.'

'You are the cow pat lady?' He folded his arms and a smile hovered over his lips. 'Sorry for being so brusque.' He held out one hand.

Mona took hold. It was rough and calloused but warm to the touch. 'Not quite the welcome I'd expected from Merrie Old England,' she said.

He smiled ruefully. 'Yes. Let's say there are a few people around here who don't like what I'm doing and want to stop me and if that includes upsetting my animals, they'll oblige.'

'People would do that?' Mona said. This was certainly not her idea of England and the English.

'Let's get this shifted and I can tell you later over a coffee. I haven't stopped all day,' James said.

'Coffee coming up,' Mona said and made a point of preparing a couple of sandwiches.

She ignored the swearing, the grunting and the odd clatter as something was dropped onto the stone floor. Half an hour later James wheeled the old machine out to his van, handed her a very clean pair of trainers and wiped his hands down his trousers. 'All done.'

'Thanks. Coffee and I've made a few sandwiches.'

His eyes widened. 'You did that for me? After my less

than polite welcome?'

'You don't know what I've put in them,' she said and smiled.

'If I drop down dead tomorrow, my movements have been tracked, you know.'

'I'll have a good attorney lined up,' Mona said. 'This way.' She led him onto the small patio where she'd placed a pot of coffee, two mugs and a plate of cheese and tomato sandwiches. 'Black? White?' She indicated the coffee pot.

'Not instant?'

Mona shook her head. 'One thing we do know about is coffee. This is as good as it gets here.'

'I'll believe you,' he said and took a sandwich. He ate it in three bites. 'Good,' he said. 'Black for me,' he added.

Mona waited until he'd had another sandwich and had refilled his coffee mug before she dared ask the question that intrigued her. 'What's all this about your plans and upsetting people. I thought that was the prerogative of our Mr Trump.'

'Ah ha. The next instalment of Frobisher versus the bigots,' James said and sat back on the small metal chair. It creaked under his weight.

'That's a bit harsh, isn't it?'

James shook his head. 'I want to create some units that local people can use as offices or for small manufacturing businesses. Did you know we've got soap makers, candle makers and craftspeople begging for space? That doesn't include all the people who spend their working life staring at a screen in a city centre office block. Why not stare at a screen here?'

'Encourage people to work from home?'

'Exactly.'

'Sounds like a great idea. What is their gripe?'

'Tradition and Nimbyism.' James picked up a third sandwich. Mona hoped he didn't want more. She only had two slices of bread left.

'Nimbyism?'

James pulled a face. 'Sorry. Short for *Not in my back yard.* N- I -M -B -Y get it?'

'We have a similar thing back home. Everyone wants to protect their own bit of paradise.'

'This is a way of protecting it.' James leaned forward; his eyes flashed. 'By creating decent job opportunities, people can live and work here. Saves on the commuting. Saves petrol. Good for the planet. Mums or dads could work at home and look after the kids. Saves cash.'

'I'm convinced. So why aren't people interested? Or are you planning an IKEA-size warehouse on the football pitch?'

'No. It upsets people's ideas that homes are for living, workplaces are away from the home and we travel between them.' There was no mistaking the contempt in James' voice.

'That's what people are used to. It's history, isn't it?' Mona said.

'Not here. See those three-story houses over there.' James waggled a hand in the direction of the far side of the valley. Mona nodded. 'Weavers used to live and work there until the factories opened and everyone was forced onto the twelve-hour-a-day treadmill.'

'In their own homes?'

'Yep. They each had a loom, were paid by the amount of material they created and could work when they wanted to.'

'Sounds perfect.' Mona said.

'All we're doing is returning to the best of the past and giving people the power to organise their own working life.'

'Good luck. I'm sure the people round here will understand, once it's made clear to them,' Mona said.

'It's not luck they need. It's a kick up the back side and I

92

expect I'll be the one who has to oblige.' James took a final bite of the sandwich. He chewed in silence for a while. 'Good sandwiches,' he said. 'Any chance of another?'

Chapter seventeen Sheila

I spread the documents from the thickest file on my desk and pull a plain piece of paper from the printer. I draw three columns and write three headings at the top: individual's name; issues; possible outcomes. I open the first report from Social Services and read. I'm so engrossed I'm still working when Karen pokes her head over the top of the cubicle partition. 'Overtime?' she says. 'It's gone two o'clock.'

'Really?' I double check. She's right. 'Sorry, I've lost track of time. I won't be expecting payment,' I add in case she thinks I'm eager to bump up my pay ASAP. 'I'm up to date with my caseload so thought I'd go through these.'

'You still have a life. Get some lunch and you can come back. If not, I'll ban you from the building.' Karen's fierceness is legendary. It hides the kindest heart.

At that precise moment, my stomach growls in protest at having been ignored. I smile up at her and tap my belly. 'Point taken. I'll nip out for a coffee and sandwich and if you don't mind, I'll complete these notes before the end of the afternoon?'

'Be my guest,' Karen says and checks her watch. 'I'm off to a meeting with a possible new developer. He has an idea to create a mix of small workplaces, private houses and sheltered units for vulnerable clients. Might be of interest. See you tomorrow.' She breezes out, her long blonde hair flowing behind her.

For a moment I wonder what I would choose if I'd had my time again. Could I have been as successful as Karen? Karen has a nanny for the children and a partner who works at home. For a moment I feel envious. It passes. It was how life is for her and for other young women. Do they have it easier? Who knows? Every generation has its own advantages and challenges. I stand up, pile the papers in my desk drawer, lock it and pick up my bag. I need a break.

I head towards a small café off the crossroads. I pass the market stalls. Out of habit I check what's on offer. Did we need anything? I have no idea. My mind is buzzing. The last thing I want to do is fuss over tonight's supper. There's plenty of frozen stuff if we run short. I push open the door. Steam hisses from the coffee machine and the smell of fresh bread and cakes welcomes me. 'Usual?' Carlos, the owner says.

'Yes.' I stop. 'No.' If I'm earning a bit more, an occasional change from the Americano to go and a sandwich from the supermarket is allowed, isn't it? 'Standard Americano, no milk, bagel with Emmental and ham and a slice of chocolate tiffin. To eat in,' I say and hand over a twenty pound note. It is a celebration, after all.

'Coming over. Take a seat.'

I find an empty space at a small round table in the window. Most of the lunchtime patrons have left. A few people are scurrying to and fro across the pedestrianised roadways, clutching paper bags with sandwiches or boxes of salad and a cup of coffee or can of drink. A few smokers and vapers chat around the fountain. I stretch out my feet and smile. This isn't the Sheila who spends her lunchbreak shopping for food, who grabs the cheapest items she can find and eats them at her desk. I feel liberated. Professional. A real working woman. Except what can I make for supper tonight? Guilt sits on my shoulder and whispers in my ear, 'Some wife and mother you are. All that stuff about looking after people, keeping healthy, doing it for the family.'

I shake the voice off. They can cope for one day with pizza, frozen chips and peas, can't they? It is probably Mark's ideal meal anyway and Brian will be back so late anything I cook will have dried to a crisp.

Carlos places my order on the table. 'Buon appetito,' he

says.

Thank you,' I say. I'm going to enjoy this. I take a sip of coffee. Mark? Has he contacted me? I check my phone. As usual there are no messages. I text.

Are you home tonight? Should I cook for you? Hope you had a good weekend. Take care and love you.

I take a bite of the bagel. My phone chirps. He's replied already.

No food Ta. Have popped home to get a change of clothes. Brighton job is defo. Will be away for a few days. Tell you more later.

A job? In Brighton? All my conflicting mothering instincts flood back as pride jostles with the need to protect my cubs. It's a long way from home. Where will he live? Would it be safe? But a job? Good for him. He's done it all himself. He'd already lived in Manchester for three years and survived, hadn't he? He'd mentioned bar work. Surely, he can get something better. He'd got qualifications in Media Studies. Why couldn't he be in films? TV journalism? Or a local paper? I chew slowly on the bagel, the hot mustard tingles on my tongue against the salty ham and sweet, nutty cheese. My son, the film maker? The TV pundit? Cocktail maker of the year doesn't sound so good although I suppose all great people have to start somewhere, don't they? He could end up sommelier to the Queen.

I finish lunch and walk back past the market. For a moment I'm tempted. A salad made from organic lettuce and tomatoes would be far better than frozen peas, wouldn't it? I join the queue. I'm almost at the head when I turn and walk away. Karen has entrusted me with an important task. I want to do it well. If it means I'm a bit late getting home, no one will know.

Once back in the office I unlock my drawer and pull out the papers. My fingers are tingling. My stomach's going topsy turvy. I'm looking forward to getting back to work. For months, years even, I'd clock watched, going through the motions, doing my best. To tell the truth, I was bored with box ticking, checking what other people had decided. This is different. I'm about to make decisions that will help or hinder other people's lives. It might be the deciding factor that changes someone's luck.

It is gone five before I realise the cleaner is hoovering round the desks. Everyone else has gone. I push my chair under the desk and go outside to the bus stop to join the swarm of commuters crossing the road to the station or heading towards the bus garage. I follow the latter and wait at the back of the queue for the half hourly bus to take me home. It doesn't matter if there isn't a seat. I quite enjoy swaying as the bus lurches round corners. I show my pass and squeeze into a seat on the top deck. I like it up here. I smile as I remember travelling home by bus as a child from school. Upstairs was where the teenagers sat, the Alpha crowd. Even when I'd reached their age and could join in, I always felt more Gamma than Alpha. Is that why I'd never dated around? Brian had turned up in the sixth form and that was that. I'd waited while he went off to university and had endured many a difficult phone call as he glossed over the parties he'd been to, the names of the women he was friends with and the times he'd promised to be home when an unexpected event kept him away. He had come home eventually and we'd married within a year. It had been a simple affair. Not like the one for Claire which began with an engagement party and ended up costing over twenty thousand.

The bus trundles through the city, out through the suburbs and into the countryside. Gradually people get off, each to their own homes, lives, their happiness and sadness.

The bus turns left and crests the brow of the hill. I love this point when the valleys spread out before me, and I can glimpse my own home tucked against the side of the hill. It's reassuring. The bus slows as it passes down the hill and through the village. I stand up and brace myself against the stairs. I signal to the driver I want to get off at the next stop. The school is closed up. The pub door is open.

I spot something. Who is that parked outside Mona's house? Next to a small white car is a large pickup truck. There are no words on the side. Couldn't be a tradesman. Has the boiler gone wrong again? No. Tradesmen today have fancy vans with pictures of catchy names emblazoned on them. The bus squeezes past. The driver glares in the direction of the vehicle and tuts several times. I peer through the window as Mona's door opens. Out comes James Frobisher. What is Mona doing with him? Or more likely, what the hell does he want with her?

Chapter eighteen Mona

'Tell me more about this plan of yours?' Mona said and indicated the coffee pot.

'Yes please,' James said and held out his cup.

He seemed reluctant to speak. 'Well?' Mona said.

He sucked in the breath between his teeth before continuing. 'Do working people commute long distances in the States?'

'Yes,' Mona said remembering the tailbacks on the freeway.

James leaned forward. Coffee slopped into the saucer. 'What if you had the option to work from home?'

'I'd love it. Except it's not possible for most people. They need access to specialised machinery, like food production, engineering, manufacturing the big stuff. What then?'

'We're no longer a manufacturing country. Ask most people what they do, and they stare at a screen all day long.'

"Not everyone, surely?' Mona said. She reached out her hand to take James' cup and saucer.

His eyes fixed on her. 'There's scope for small units and anyone who could work at a screen should be able to do so from home, don't you agree?'

'What if people like going to work?' Mona said. 'It is a way of meeting people and getting out of the house. There are a lot of lonely people out there.'

'If you could work where you lived, you'd get to know people locally, wouldn't you?' James sat back. The cup wobbled.

'I suppose so.'

The cup crashed on the table. 'My point exactly. Imagine all those missed hours we waste on commuting? Not to mention the carbon footprint of all that travel. His eyes glazed over. 'And what for? To sit alongside others in an office, sending them emails rather than talking? If we need face to face, there's plenty of efficient technology and people could go into work for one day a week or once a month?' He turned back to face Mona. 'There is another consideration.'

'Yes?'

'We mix housing with small units for craft, light industry, stuff like that and that accommodation can include more affordable housing. All my developments, planned that is, will have a small number of units for more vulnerable people, younger people and older ones.' He paused.

'I'm sure it all sounds reasonable. Why are there the objections?'

James put on an affected voice. 'Imagine all the noise and lorries and vans arriving and departing. Not to mention the type of people that might be attracted here.' He tipped the end of his nose upwards. 'Snobs. That's what we've got in a lot of these villages.'

'I'm sure people will accept when they understand—'

He didn't let her finish. 'I have an idea. Why don't you use one of my units for your art. Show people it can be done.'

'Me? I'm not a proper artist.' What was she letting herself in for?

'Those pictures look pretty professional to me,' James said.

Mona was tempted to ask what he knew about art. She didn't. Here was the chance to paint more. Who knows, she might finish enough pictures to hold a small exhibition at the end of the summer. If it flopped, it didn't matter. She was going home and might never see any of these people again. If it worked, she might be tempted to do the same back home. There was one problem. 'I can't afford much.' That was a lie. She couldn't afford anything.

'Free? Gratis? Tout libre,' James said. 'Call it an

extension of the letting agreement. One cottage and one lockup unit with heating and lighting, running water and a toilet. What do you say?'

'Where is it?'

'Come on, I'll show you.' He stood up. 'Better lock this place. Can't be too careful round here.'

'You told me this place was idyllic,' she said as she slipped on a pair of sandals and closed the door.

'It could be if there were more people around in the daytime. You could pop out to the shop for a break or a walk and the place wouldn't resemble a ghost town.'

'No. This definitely isn't a ghost town,' Mona said.

'Yeah. Sorry. There'd be tumbleweed blowing down the street and a sign board for the saloon would creak in the wind as the hero rode into town.' He looked down at his feet. 'Sorry. I spent every Saturday as a kid at the cinema. Kid's Club it was called.'

'I did the same,' Mona said.

'I've still got a soft spot for the old black and white B films.'

'Me too.'

They continued in silence, each in their own thoughts. They followed the narrow back alley off the main road and turned right at a fork. The other direction led to the playing field and the shop. They climbed a steep hill and stopped outside a three-story building with a sold sign. 'That's the house I want to make into maisonettes,' James said. 'And that—' he pointed to another building further along the road. It was a single storey with a curved frontage. Once it might have been a shop. 'That's the proposed workshop. It's an old garage. I've already started to clear it out.'

'I thought you said there would be a series of units,' Mona said as James unlocked the door and they stepped inside. Mona gazed at the heaps of rubble, dust and cobwebs. A white chipped sink stood in one corner. A tap dripped rusty brown water. Wires hung from the ceiling, and it smelt of mice.

'Got to start somewhere,' James said. 'If you were to take this on, I'd be able to show everyone how well it worked and perhaps get permission for more.'

So that was the catch. 'Take this on?' she waved her hand at the broken-down chair, three-legged table, and fridge with the door half off.

'It needs a bit of TLC,' James said. 'I promise it will be clean, with light, power and a toilet within two weeks.'

Mona stepped over some paper sacks and broken tiles. 'What was this place?' she said.

'Years ago, it was a garage. The next owner used it for storage. It's been disused for the last ten years as far as I can tell.'

Mona opened a green door. It hid a broken toilet with a cistern hanging off the walls. Chipped tiles on the floor wobbled underneath her feet. She kicked at one. It flew upwards. 'Needs a lot of work.'

'It'll be done. Say the word and this could be yours.' James puffed out his chest.

Was he crazy or a dreamer? Or was this a chance? To play at being what she wanted to be rather than what Ethan expected? If it went off beam, so what? Who was to know? She kicked at the floor again. 'As long as it's all done and there's no little furry creatures running around.' She sniffed. 'That musty smell is mice.'

James lifted his head. 'Or rats? No. They would have left this sinking ship in the last century.'

'Rats?' Mona leaped backwards.

'Just kidding,' James said.

'For some reason, I can't see anyone laughing,' Mona said and tried to regain some dignity.

James held up his hands. 'I promise, no mice, a decent toilet, working electrics, a small kitchen out the back, a lick of paint and some vinyl flooring.' He rubbed his hands together. 'That suit you?'

Mona walked slowly round the room as if she was a general inspecting troops. 'This window doesn't look too safe?' She pointed to a cracked pane.

'Consider it done,' James said and added a mock salute.

Yep. He was crazy as a hog in a hurricane. If he wanted to do all this and charge her nothing, it might be fun. Go on the voice inside her head insisted. What's stopping you except fear? The trouble was she'd been friends with fear for so long, it felt strange to push herself outside her comfort zone. What comfort zone? She'd come thousands of miles to a small village because of the link with a dead poet. Perhaps she was the crazy one. 'Agreed,' she said and held up her palm.

James hesitated. 'Oh, a high five,' he said and slapped his palm against hers.

'Shall we shake on it too?' Mona said. 'British fashion?'

James moved his hand and burst out laughing. 'You're taking the piss.'

'A bit,' Mona said. Hell, she hadn't done that in years. She'd been too scared. Ethan had made it clear a long time ago he didn't find her funny. She'd assumed everyone else would think the same. Perhaps she was wrong.

'I'd better get on with the job,' James said. 'I'll collect my van and it's a trip to the wholesalers before they close at seven.'

They walked back in silence. The sounds of children's voices floated up from the playing field. 'You got kids?' Mona asked.

'Yes. Two. Both independent unless they're short of cash. Which is a pretty regular occurrence. You?'

'No. I have plenty of godchildren and nieces and nephews.'

'Godchildren? You religious?'

'Yes. I suppose I am,' Mona said. 'Not in the "I must get to church every Sunday and when I die, there's only a choice of heaven and hell." I think there is something. Never could work out what.'

'I was educated at a Church of England school. It's odd how so many of the teachings stick. Like the parable of the talents, the ten commandments, the prodigal son.'

'Uh huh. I remember some of those stories,' Mona said.

They reached her front door. James held out his hand. 'I'll let you know when you can use the place,' he said, 'it'll be a couple of weeks.' He waved at the bus driver who was inching past his van. 'I'll be in touch.' He climbed in and was gone.

Mona watched as he drove away. She closed the door and leaned against it. What the hell had happened? She was the renter of a lock up. She went into the kitchen. 'I have a studio for my art.' She flung up her hands and spun round, like a child on a stage. She hugged her arms round her and jumped up and down several times. She stopped. Where was that parable of the talents? She fished out her laptop and typed in the search engine. There it was. She read out loud.

For to everyone who has will more be given, and he will have an abundance. But from the one who has not, even what he has will be taken away.

The message was clear. Use those talents, Mona or else. Well, here was her chance.

Chapter nineteen Sheila

I get off the bus and cross the road. I slow down as I approach Lavender Cottage. James has gone. The door is closed. If I'd known Mona better, I'd ask what he wanted. There was plenty of gossip in the village about how he is buying up properties to create holiday lets. That was all the village needed, houses left empty for the majority of the year or worse, let to hen parties or groups of youngsters who disrupted the peace with late night parties. It had happened a couple of times before when Nightingale Cottage was a holiday let. Thank goodness the owner had changed his mind and sold it to buy some caravans on a site in Skegness. Not that. At least the current owners are involved in the village, they live here.

As I pass the cottage, I sneak a look inside. There is a shadowy figure in the main room. Should I? No. I can't knock on the door. It will be too obvious. Perhaps later in the week. Or when we all go walking. Yes, that's it. I'd begin by asking if Mona had met any other villagers. The conversation was bound to turn to James sooner or later. Unless he'd concocted another money-making scheme. Didn't someone from the Parish Council say he wanted to demolish a row of the cottages and put up some flats? He'd soon find out the village was not going to be pushed into becoming a suburb of the town. Not like the small villages along the canal, swallowed up with all identity lost, except for a name.

I head for home. Tomorrow I'll take the bus again. Makes me feel virtuous. I walk up the garden path. It is still warm. The pots need a water, and the bulbs are ready for lifting. I open the front door. It is cool inside. I kick off my shoes and switch the kettle to boil. A cup of tea and a few minutes with my feet up and I'll be ready to get on again. I climb the stairs and walk into the main bedroom. It's warm up here too. I open the window as wide as possible. A faint breeze stirs the air. That should cool it down a bit. I peel off my tights and wriggle my toes on the floorboards. Bliss. However comfortable work clothes are, there is nothing like slobbing about in jeans and a sweater. I hang up my clothes, ready for the following day and pick up a stray sock (Brian's). I toss it into the washing basket. It's nearly full already. How did that happen? I'd cleared it on Saturday. Where had all these shirts come from? I pull out a pale blue one, a candy stripe and a plain white one and drop them back. Brian must have cleared them from his wardrobe. How hard is it to put a dirty shirt into the basket, rather than replace it in the wardrobe and decide later it needed washing? I close the lid. They'll have to wait.

I walk back down the stairs and pour water in a mug, add a chamomile tea bag, and open the back door. For years now this has been my favourite part of the day; my moment of peace. I sit on the patio. Contented clucking from the hen house greets me. 'Yes, girls. I'm back,' I call out. 'I'll get you some fresh water and check your feed.' It was as good as having a dog and no long walks to tie us down. I stretch my bare feet on the warm stones of the patio and look out at the view. It is beautiful here. The distant hills shimmer blue, like in an Italian Old Master. A wisp of smoke from a bonfire drifts up to the sky. The woods are flushed with light green and bird song fills the air. For a moment, I close my eyes to relish the peace.

It is eight o'clock before I've finished; I'd cooked, cleaned, watered the plants, fed the hens and replaced the straw for their bedding. I'd eaten a slice of pizza. That would do for today. For some reason I am worn out. Is it the adrenalin rush of the new job? More like old age. I curl up on the sofa to read through the notes on the cases I've taken on. I'll have to start work tomorrow and call everyone to arrange a short interview. It could be done over the phone. My eyelids droop. Damn. I shake my head and read the sentence again. It is no use. I look at the clock. It can't be nearly nine? What is Brian doing?

I stow the notes in my work bag and go up the stairs. I am in the bath when the front door opens and slams. 'Brian?'

'Who do you think it is?' The voice is cross.

I stand up and grab a towel. 'Sorry. I needed a bath to freshen up,' I say and climb out. I put on a towelling robe. 'There's a pizza, chips and peas,' I call downstairs. 'They only need heating up.'

'Where?'

'In the bloody fridge, where do you think?' I mutter under my breath.

Brian is standing in the middle of the kitchen scratching his head. 'Where?'

I squeeze past him. 'Let me,' I say and open the fridge.

'Is that all?' Brain peers over my shoulder.

My hands clench on the plate and serving dish. 'Yes. Sorry,' I say and regret it. No. I'm not sorry. 'After all the wasted food over the past few weeks, I didn't feel inclined to cook. I think I need to get in some decent ready meals for us all when we're late home.'

'For us?'

'You and Mark,' I say. 'And I may be late too.'

Brian is silent. I sense his anger. What is griping him?

'It'll have to do. I'd hoped it was toad in the hole. We often have that midweek,' he says. 'I'd been looking forward to it all the way home.'

'Sorry,' I say and feel guilty. 'Tomorrow?'

'That'd be nice. I'll get a beer and check up on the news. Can you bring the food into me when it's ready?' He disappears. I hear the click of the TV, followed by men's voices raised in heated discussion.

I wait for the microwave to finish, place the plate on a

tray, add a knife, fork, and ketchup bottle. Brian is flopped on the sofa. His shoes rest on a pale cream cushion cover. I place the tray on the coffee table and pull the cushion away. 'Shoes,' I say as if he was Mark. Why am I being such a bitch? 'Good day?' I say and sit down next to him.

'Shhh,' he says between a mouthful of pizza. 'Brexit.' He nods towards the screen.

'I'll leave you in peace.' I head back upstairs.

I close the bathroom door. The water is tepid. So much for a long hot soak. I let the water out and clean the bath. I rub cream into my now dry skin and replace the damp towels with dry ones. I get into bed and open my book. I read a few pages. It is no good. I can't get interested in yet another story of a murdered woman. I let the book fall on the duvet cover and am about to close my eyes when Brian walks in. He rummages in his side of the wardrobe. 'Have you seen my new blue shirt?'

'In the bin,' I say.

'What?'

'In the dirty linen basket. You must have put it there yesterday after I'd done all the washing.'

'I needed that one tomorrow,' Brian says.

'You've got a whole wardrobe full of shirts, wear another.'

'That one is perfect with the navy-blue suit.'

'Wear a different suit,' I say.

'I don't know what's got into you lately,' Brian says and turns to stare at me. 'Once you put the family first. You would have checked the washing as soon as you got home from work. There'd be a decent meal waiting and you'd join me in a beer instead of running off to bed to read some trashy novel.' He pokes at the book. It slides to the floor with a thump.

'If you got home at a sensible time and took an interest in something other than work and golf, there might be

108

something to talk about,' I say. I lie down in bed and pull the covers over my shoulders.

'You're different,' Brian says. 'Cold. Grumpy and petulant. Must be the bloody menopause.' He closes the door behind him and his footsteps thump down the stairs.

I sit up and grab the book. I'm tempted to throw it at the door. I don't. There is no point. As for the sodding menopause, that's always the excuse. That or hormones. If men checked their own behaviour before laying the blame at female bodies, life might be a lot easier.

When Brian climbs into bed, I pretend to be asleep. It is better that way.

'I was looking forward to toad in the hole,' he says. 'We always have that midweek.'

'Like Shirley Valentine,' I mutter.

'What?'

'Nothing' I say. 'Good night.'

Shirley would understand. Her old man kicked off when he had to have egg and chips instead of steak.

Something has to change. Soon.

Chapter twenty Mona

Remember the first meeting of the Wild Girls is on Saturday, leaving Bull's Cross at ten and ending up at the Woolpack, Slad for lunch at one. Any person requiring lifts, please let me know ASAP.

Sheila

A walk wasn't exactly what Mona had imagined. Bungee jumping? Yes. Trampolining, open water swimming? Better. It was a start. Her trainers were clean. The washing machine had done the trick. She checked the kitchen. The sooner she could get in the studio, the better. She was tired of sharing her space with art materials. To save time she'd left everything on the kitchen table. This had spread to the countertops and the utility. The only room that was clear was the lounge. For how much longer? She'd assumed she'd have plenty of time to paint and enjoy the locality. Wrong. By the time she'd been on a walk, taken a few more photos, cleaned, shopped, tidied herself up (no reason to look tacky) completed any admin, checked Facebook, answered any urgent emails and James' endless questions (How many sockets? Where? Height? Did they need covers? What type of sink? Taps? Kitchen units? Floor covering? Paint colour? Door handles?) which always required an internet search, there was little time left for painting. She'd dreamed of spending four hours a day. Three was pushing it. Two hours was more likely. It didn't seem enough somehow. She shrugged. She'd manage.

At least there was the start of a small collection of water colours. The bluebells were her favourite, followed by a cute little blue and green bird that hung upside down from the trees in the garden and chirruped at her as she walked past. The beech buds and the first horse chestnut leaves emerging from their sticky casings came next. At this rate she'd know more about English natural history than her own. She opened her sketch book. A cluster of small purple flowers nestled against a green mossy bank. Like Shakespeare.

> *I know a bank where the wild thyme blows,*
> *Where oxlips and the nodding violet grows,*
> *Quite over-canopied with luscious woodbine,*
> *With sweet musk-roses and with eglantine*
> *There sleeps Titania sometimes of night*

She spoke the words aloud. There was plenty more to be painted over the summer. When would she see her first wild rose? She'd never thought flowers would help the pain. Perhaps it wasn't the flowers. It was finding them in the outside space she was growing to love more and more each day.

'Come on, girl. You've got a lot to do before Saturday morning.' Stepping back, she looked at the painting of the bluebells. Was that really hers? She moved closer. The brushwork was smooth, the colours glowed and the perspective showed a slope. It was quite good. Mona smiled. It was as good as many prints, not quite the power of a perfectly lit photograph. Perhaps it needed something in the foreground. A bee? She picked up her pencil. Could she draw a decent bee?

Saturday morning was sunny. Mona shoved her waterproof back in the cupboard. The forecast was good. She pulled on her trainers, filled a water bottle and slung it in her rucksack. Sheila had offered to drive her and Lydia to the meeting point. She stood outside on the pavement. A chattering sound made her look up. On the wires above the road, three blue and white birds with a flash of red at their throat and a long-forked tail were preening and keeping up a constant bickering as if they were arguing.

'Seen our swallows?' Mona jumped. A car had stopped, and the window was down. Lydia wearing a white straw hat with pink and purple flowers was leaning out. 'Swallows?' Lydia pointed up.

'Is that what they are?' Mona said and shielded her eyes to get a better look.

'They arrive in April and leave in early September,' Lydia said. 'My old gran used to say they were the real signs of spring.'

'Three swallows don't make a summer,' Sheila said. 'Get in.'

Mona scrambled into the back seat. 'Three swallows?'

'Seat belt?' Sheila said. 'Unless you want to hear a beeping noise throughout the journey?'

'Beeping noise? Swallows? Am I in an alternate universe?'

'The car has so many safety warnings, I'm surprised it hasn't told me how to drive,' Sheila said. 'Lydia, tell Mona about swallows.'

'Ah yes, swallows. Hirundo Rustica in Latin, L'hirondelle in French. They winter in Africa and arrive here each spring. People used to think they slept the winter at the bottom of ponds because they were often seen skimming the surface of water. They catch insects and they make nests of mud under the eaves of cottages or in old barns. I've got some in my old shed. They won't let me near during the nesting season and if I go to the bottom of my garden for a bit of mint, they dive bomb me.' She giggled. 'I like them.'

'What about three of them?' Mona said.

Sheila answered. 'The actual saying is one swallow doesn't make a summer. It's a bit like don't count your chickens before they hatch. In other words, seeing swallows doesn't mean warm weather.'

'Don't cast a clout till May is out,' Lydia said.

'What?'

'Don't leave off your woolly vests until the May tree is in blossom,' Sheila said and swerved to avoid a pheasant who was walking along the road. 'Sorry about that. Didn't want to hit him.'

'What a beautiful bird,' Mona said and turned to gaze out of the back window as the creature strutted into the hedgerow. 'I'd like to paint one of those.'

'Come to my house one morning. I've got a male and a female strutting round my garden. I hope they're making a nest nearby,' Lydia said.

'That's very kind of you. Thank you,' Mona said and settled back to let the soothing lemon greens of new leaves bathe her eyes. They followed a narrow track with passing places at regular spaces. Cottages and what must have been farm buildings before they were converted into houses straggled along the roadside. Their gardens stretched up towards the woodland. How wonderful to wake every morning, look out and see trees towering over you, sheltering you with outstretched arms like a welcoming aunt. Dappled light speckled the road surface, and the wooded hills were taking on their summer shades. Wasn't there something about the colour green that was calming? It felt like it.

'Here we are,' Sheila said and parked between a four by four and a red hatchback. Both cars were packed with people. Sheila stopped the engine and they all got out.

After ten minutes of introductions which Mona would never remember, they set off in single file through a small area of woodland and stopped by a wooden gate next to a poem written on Perspex so that you could see the landscape through the words. 'Wow,' Mona said. 'This is so beautiful.'

Sheila walked up to her. 'I suppose it is. We're used to it. It's only when someone new comes along, we get a check

113

on reality. Not many people can boast a view like this. I feel very privileged and a bit guilty.'

'Guilty? Why?'

Sheila tuned to face her. 'So many people lead shitty lives and I have all this.' She indicated the valleys and wooded hillsides.

'I think we have to be grateful for being born in the right place at the right time and share that blessing with as many people as we can,' Mona said.

'Talking of people, you had a visitor this week... our James?'

Was there an edge to Sheila's voice? 'He owns my cottage. He heard I'd got a problem with the washing machine and changed it. No cost,' Mona said.

'So he's bought up another cottage,' Sheila said, half to herself. 'We suspected last year he was buying up places and putting them in the name of a lettings company.'

'Is that a bad thing?'

'Depends who he lets them too, doesn't it?' Sheila said.

'You talking about James Frobisher?' a tall horse-faced woman caught up with them. Mona couldn't remember her name.

"Yes. Do you know him?' Mona said.

The woman snorted. 'Offered Susy half a million to buy her cottage and land. 'It's worth a million in anyone's money.'

'Can he do that?' Sheila said.

'He does what he likes and reckons if he flashes a bit of cash at the right people, they'll go along with him. I heard he wants to buy the pub and close it down.'

'Planning won't allow that,' the horse-faced woman said. 'It's a village asset.'

The other woman shook her head. 'I don't trust him and there are plenty more who will agree with me.'

'He seemed very helpful and very interested in the local

community when I met him,' Mona said.

There was a long pause. Mona felt as if she'd goosed the pastor. 'Only if he can make money,' the horse-faced woman said.

'I agree,' Sheila said and walked ahead and caught up with Lydia who was drifting off the path in the direction of some yellow flowers.

The other two women slowed their pace. The conversation was over. James really had seemed very amenable. Could she have been taken in? Was he like a lot of con men, charming when it helped him to get his own way and a monster when anyone tried to stop him? Perhaps if she raised the subject again in the pub, others might have a different opinion? It would be worth a chance.

The gaggle of women crossed the field and headed down towards a small stream, talking, laughing and enjoying being free from any domestic or working demands for a few hours to the accompaniment of the sun, the wind and the smell of earth warming up and waking after the long grey winter months.

Chapter twenty-one Sheila

'Has anyone seen Lydia?' I scan the group, seated at a trestle table in the shadow of a vine, its soft green leaves contrasting against the gentian blue sky.

'The last time I saw her she was by the pond in the woods,' a voice calls out.

'Yes. She said she wanted a closer look and as we were the first group, we assumed she'd wait for you,' another voice chimes.

'She's got a phone, hasn't she?'

'No. She hates the things,' I say and try to stem the unease I feel.

'Is she in the toilet?'

'It was empty when I came out,' Mona says.

'I'll go and check along the road. Won't be long. You order.' I squeeze my way between the tables. Lydia had been acting strange all the way on the walk. She kept wandering off. Usually she was at the front, chivvying everyone else to keep up.

'I'll come with you.' Mona follows me. 'Do you think she's lost?'

I'm grateful for her concern. I speak softly. 'You and I know all is not well with Lydia. I meant to have a word with her but the new job's taking all my energy.' I don't mention dealing with Brian's increasing petulance and Mark's continued absence. There is a flicker of guilt; I haven't been a decent enough friend lately, too caught up in my own stuff to worry about others.

'Let's retrace our footsteps. She's probably taking her time. A few of those hills puffed me out.' Mona is upbeat. I don't feel the same. Lydia has always been a bit eccentric. Is eccentricity turning to weirdness?

We walk along Slad Road in silence and take the first fork past the houses I'd envied a few minutes earlier. Funny

I'd always wanted a bigger house with a proper hallway, an en suite and a separate dining room. It wasn't going to happen now unless Brian gets that promotion. Time to worry about that later. I can't shake off the nagging feeling all is not well. We continue towards the pond, set amongst trees. I hope no one mentioned the woman who drowned here long ago. The place is creepy enough as it is.

'God this place gives me the jeebies,' Mona says and shivers. 'I keep thinking I'm gonna see a ghost hovering over the water.'

'What's that?' There is a round, white object floating on the murky water. I stare. Flashes of purple nestle amongst green and brown leaves.

'Is it a hat?' Mona says.

'Shit, it is!' I run and climb the fence around the pond. My feet sink into the boggy area at the side. I ignore the ooze between my toes and squelch closer. Lydia's hat floats on the surface. Someone has fastened leaves in a circle around the crown. It looks like a wreath.

'If that's Lydia's hat, where is Lydia?' Mona says. 'I'll go and check the trees over the other side.'

'You don't think she's in there?' I nod towards the water. I'm frightened of the answer.

'Nope. Not unless she's wearing concrete pants. Bodies float. For a long time,' Mona says. 'Why don't you go around to the left and we'll meet up?'

'Will do.' It's good to let Mona take charge. She is down to earth. Not like me, always imagining the worst.

Mona disappears in the undergrowth at the other side of the pond. I step carefully between the holly bushes and last year's brambles. A blackbird chits a warning to its mate and a chiffchaff sings it's unmistakeable song, saying its name over and over again, chiff chaff, chiff chaff from the top bough of a silver birch. At other times I would have stopped to listen. Not today. 'Where the hell are you,

Lydia?' I say softly. I turn a corner and there she is, sitting on the bank above a small brook that feeds the pond. Her feet are bare and her clothes and legs are covered in mud. She is twisting small branches into a circle and singing to herself. I can hear the words.

There's a Friend for little children
Above the bright blue sky.
A Friend who never changes,
Whose love will never die.

'Lydia?' I speak softly in case I scare her.

Lydia looks up. 'Oh, hello,' she says. 'Have you come to help me with this wreath?'

I kneel by her side. 'Wreath? Who needs a wreath?'

Lydia continues to twist the twigs. 'That poor woman who killed herself here. I used my hat. I waded into the water and let it go. It isn't good enough. She needs a proper wreath, and it should be hung on the fence.'

I place my hand on her arm. It is horribly thin. 'Come on, we need to get you warm and dry. Where are your shoes?'

Lydia wiggles her feet. 'I lost them in the water,' she says. 'I should have taken them off. I didn't in case my feet touched her dead body.'

'The body was buried in a nice safe place years ago,' I say. 'Let me help you up?'

'What about my wreath?' Lydia holds it up. It falls apart. The twigs with their fresh injection of sap refuse to bend.

'We'll make another one,' I say. 'Mona,' I call. 'Over here.'

I place an arm around Lydia's waist. The woman is stick thin. Funny how I'd never noticed before. Another pang of guilt shoots through me. Shouldn't friends notice these things?

118

There is a crashing sound. Mona appears by my side. 'Is she OK?'

This is no time for platitudes. 'She's been making a wreath for the lady who killed herself in the pool,' I say.

'That is so kind,' Mona says and takes hold of Lydia's other arm. 'Heh, this is beautiful. Do you want me to look after it for you while we get you back onto the path?'

'It keeps springing apart,' Lydia says.

'I reckon I can fix that,' Mona says. 'I'll tie a bit of grass to keep everything together.'

'Will you?' Lydia's eyes sparkle.

'Of course. Let's get you onto the path.' Mona nods in the direction of the road.

'No. The wreath comes first,' Lydia refuses to budge.

'OK. Let me get a few grasses.' Mona climbs over the fence and pulls off a few bullrush leaves. She comes back, twists and ties them round the wreath. 'Heh. Perfect ain't it? Did you say you wanted to put it on the fence? Let's do it together.' I watch as Mona guides Lydia's hands in a semblance of a bow. She is the perfect teacher. The odd shaped collection of leaves and twigs is in place. 'Perfect,' Mona says. 'Now let's get you back home safely.'

I nod. Mona understands. Thank God. With Lydia between us and Mona keeping up a constant light-hearted chatter, we negotiate the steep path. We ignore the stares from a few gardeners and someone cleaning a car. What does it matter? We are helping a friend who's overdone the walking in the heat. No one need know any more.

Once Lydia is seated on the path off the main road, I get out my phone. 'I'm calling Brian. I want to take her to A&E. She shouldn't be left alone. She's not well.'

'Uh huh. I'll go back and tell the others…how much do you want me to tell them?' Mona says.

'Until we know what's wrong, the less we say the better.'

'I know. A touch of the sun? Covers a multitude of

illnesses. No one will worry it's contagious and it might be true. She could be delirious,' Mona says.

I'm grateful for Mona's ideas. 'Yes. A bit of heatstroke. It is uncommonly warm. We're not used to it.'

'Do you want me to wait with you?'

'Let me check it's OK with Brian?' I text him our secret word for an emergency, so he knows to pick up before I press his number. It rings five times before he answers. 'Brian, I need your help. Can you collect me from along Slad Road beyond the pub? It's Lydia. I need to take her to A&E.' I listen for a few seconds. 'He's on the golf course,' I mouth to Lydia.

'Tell him I can get your car home to you,' Mona says.

'Mona will sort my car out and I can get a taxi home,' I explain. He agrees and there is no petulance. Perhaps he likes to feel needed again.

'Shall we get Lydia closer to the main road?' Mona says.

'She hasn't got any shoes.'

Mona strips off her shoes. She hands them over. 'These socks will be fine for me. I've got feet like a buffalo, and I'll take them back at the top. She won't need shoes in hospital.' She kneels down and unlaces her trainers. 'Right, Lydia. I want you to tell me what you think of these shoes.'

We help Lydia up the slope and sit her on a small wall by the main road. 'Very nice and comfortable. Are they mine?' Lydia says as Mona takes them off.

'Not quite your size. Don't want blisters, do you?' Mona says and puts them back on her own feet.

I hand over my car keys. 'One of the other women will give you a lift back to the car park.' A new worry engulfs me. 'Can you drive my car? What about insurance?'

'I'm covered,' Mona says. 'I'll drive extra slow too as it's manual. I haven't driven one of those since I was here in 97.'

'Nothing's changed,' I say. I am reassured. it will be all

right.

'I'll tell the gang not to worry and I'll get the car back to you tonight. Promise,' Mona says.

'Thank you. I'll need to get in touch with her two sons. They must be told.'

'Are they local?'

'Dubai and Scotland.'

'Nice.' Mona stands up. 'Heh Lydia, I'm off now. See you soon.'

Lydia smiles and nods. 'Next time I'll make you a cake,' she says.

'You do that,' Mona says.

I watch as Mona walks off along the road.

'She's nice,' Lydia says. 'Do I know her?'

'Yes, and she is very nice,' I say.

'Good,' Lydia says. She cradles her knees, gazes up and down the road and sings softly to herself.

> *There's a Friend for little children*
> *Above the bright blue sky.*
> *A Friend who never changes,*
> *Whose love will never die.*

Chapter twenty-two Mona

Mona rehearsed her lines. 'Lydia's a bit over heated?' She sounded like a machine. 'Lydia's got sunstroke?' Too dramatic. 'Lydia fainted?' Yes. That's better. We all do from time to time. 'Sheila's taken her home?' No. She'd use her car. 'Brian was passing?' No. Everyone knows he has a love affair with a small white ball and a long stick. 'She's called Brian to help out in case...' of what? In case she faints while Sheila's driving. Could be dangerous? Yep. That's why she's asked me to drive her car home. In fact, if she played dumb or vague about doctors and emergencies, no one would think anything. Just someone else who doesn't understand the British systems as well as the locals. She repeated her lines. 'Lydia's fainted. Brian's taking them home and I'm looking after Sheila's car.' That would have to do.

She stepped off the road and onto the patio area of the pub and was met with a barrage of questions:

'Is everyone OK?'

'What's happened?'

'Where's Sheila?'

'Did you find her?'

Mona held up one hand. So much for English reticence. 'Lydia felt faint. Sheila's asked Brian to collect them and they're taking her home. Nothing to worry about.' Far from closing down speculation, it opened up like a gaping wound.

'The walk was too long. My head felt a bit fuzzy too.'

'Should have postponed.'

'If you ask me, Lydia's not been right for a while. I caught her wandering around barefoot in the garden last week.'

'So what? That's what I do on a hot day.'

'She was wearing a hat. Perhaps she needed sunglasses. Glare after the long, dull winter months can cause all sorts of problems.'

How come they'd all become experts? 'There really is nothing to worry about. We all get a bit overheated from time to time at our age, don't we?' Play the menopause card. Shut them all up.

'At her age? Lydia's over sixty. Must be through that years ago.'

There was a general murmur of agreement. Mona smiled and spoke brightly. 'I'm sure Sheila will let us know ASAP. What is everyone having? What's the best local food and beer? Or is it called ale? What did Laurie Lee drink?' It set off general chatter and if some returned to the drama, let them. For Mona it was job done. She'd worry about the car later. She'd allow herself one small drink. Crashing Sheila's car while being intoxicated was not something she wanted to risk.

At half past two Mona climbed into Sheila's car. She waited till all the others had gone, pretending to study her phone. How long had it been since she'd driven a manual? Ten? Twenty years? She'd spent a few months in Ireland on business pre-Ethan and she'd got used to her little Fiat. Would it come back to her? She put on the seat belt and started the engine. It purred. Music? Better not. She needed to concentrate.

She checked the pedals. Accelerator? The engine revved slightly as she pressed it. Brake and clutch? That was it. She pressed the clutch and put the car into first gear. With one touch of the gas, it lurched forward. She hit the brake. It stalled. What had she done? That was it. If you touch the brake, you touch the clutch, don't you? It had been her mantra. Time to give it a go. She tried again and the car glided onto the empty road. That was a good thing about round here. The roads were often very quiet.

She accelerated slightly to twenty-five. That would do. So, what if by the time she got home she had a convoy behind her. She was a foreigner, wasn't she? If the police stopped her, she'd play up the confused Yank.

The gods must have been on her side. She pulled onto Sheila's forecourt and stopped. Another car was parked by the side of the house. Were Sheila and Brian back already? Should she drop the keys through the letter box and go? No. She wanted to find out if Lydia had recovered. She suspected she was a very sick woman.

Mona knocked on the front door. Brian opened it. She hadn't seen him since he'd checked the radiators and sorted out the boiler. He didn't look as dishevelled as he had at that time. Underneath the grey hair and the sagging jowls was a reminder of the attractive young man he'd once been.

'Is Sheila back? I've returned her car.'

He glanced over at the car as if checking it was the right one before he looked down at Mona. 'She's still at the hospital with Lydia. They're keeping her in. I expect she'll be back later tonight.'

'Do they know what's wrong with her?'

He sniffed. 'Apart from being as nutty as a fruit cake, she's as fit as a flea.'

'As a what? Sorry. It doesn't matter.'

'Yes. Lydia is fit and well in body. Her mind is the issue except no one seems to recognise it.'

'How do you know?' Mona said. Or was this another example of the gossip she'd witnessed earlier on when suddenly everyone was an expert.

'My mother went the same way after dad died.' He looked down at the floor. 'Poor old bugger, he'd hidden her increasingly erratic behaviour from everyone. What he went through, I dread to think.'

'Let's hope she can get the help she needs,' Mona said and held out the keys.

'I doubt it. Care in the community and all that.' He ran a hand through his hair. 'I'm really sorry. I should ask you in. Come in and we can talk more. '

'If you aren't too busy?' Mona hesitated. Should she? Could she trust Brian? Hell, she was her friend's husband, he'd behave himself, especially if she gave him no encouragement and she did want to know more about poor Lydia.

'Come in. I'll make coffee or would you prefer something stronger? I was about to have a glass of wine on the patio. It's warm enough and there's no point going back to the golf club.'

Mona stepped inside the house. 'Why is that?'

'Everyone will be ending their rounds, not starting them,' he said. 'Go through the doors and I'll be out in a minute.'

Mona walked across the lounge floor. It was a homely place with books stacked up on either side of the fireplace. One wall next to the staircase was hidden under photos in silver or wooden frames. Some were black and white? Parents? Grandparents? She moved closer and stopped. Was it done to snoop at photos? Did you ask first?

It was odd being in someone's house. You learnt so much about them. There was a hessian bag with knitting poking out the top. A dog-eared book of Sudoku sat next to the remote controls. The shelf under the coffee table had this month's copies of *What Car* and *Homes and Gardening* and a small collection of ornaments clustered on the mantelpiece. One was a snow scene. There was also a figurine and a small misshapen pottery hedgehog. A child's artwork?

A clatter from the kitchen made her jump. She didn't want Brian to catch her acting like Miss Marple. She slid open the patio doors and sat on a chair with a green and white checked cushion tied to the back and the seat. She crossed her legs and waited.

Brian emerged from the side of the house. There must

be a separate entrance to the kitchen. He handed her a glass of white wine. It was cool and the colour of lemons. 'Semillon. I like a fresh, dry wine at this time of the year.'

'As long as it isn't rosé,' Mona said. 'It might look and taste like fruit punch except it has a kick like a mule.' She took a sip. 'Very light and dry.'

Brian took the seat opposite her. 'How are you settling in?'

'Yeah. Good,' she said. 'There's plenty I don't understand. Like this care in the community? What's that all about?'

'The idea people should be cared for in their own homes.'

'Sounds great? Who by?'

Brian pulled a face. 'That's the problem. It means a poorly paid carer rushes in three times a day for twenty minutes. Care? It's like feeding and cleaning an animal. Where's the companionship? Where's the concern? Where's the support?'

'Is that what happened to your mom?'

Brian smiled. 'I like the way you say that. Mom. She'd have liked it too.' He paused. 'The trouble is no one knew how sick she was. Dad did his best. We didn't realise how tough it must have been for him and we only found out from the neighbours when he'd died. He couldn't care for her. She wandered off at night. She needed continual watching or she'd do something like fill an electric kettle and set it on a live gas flame.'

Mona shuddered. 'She could have killed herself.'

'Yeah, and the people around her in the flats where she lived. She had to go into a residential home. She died a few months later.'

'That's sad.'

'Yeah. I hadn't realised at the time how much it had hit me. I do now.'

'It will get easier. The sadness I mean. One day you'll remember her or them both with happiness.'

'You think so?'

'I know so.'

One glass of wine stretched to another and by the time Mona got back to her cottage, it was nearly five o'clock. Should she text Sheila? Why not?

Car delivered safely. How are you all doing?

The reply came back instantly.

Lydia might be in for a few days for tests. Will speak later this weekend. Should be out of here by six and home soon after.

Mona switched off the phone. God she was tired. She wanted to talk to someone, tell them what had happened. Who? There was no one. At least Sheila had Brian to talk to. Lucky lady.

Chapter twenty-three Sheila

Brian arrives. 'What's she done this time?' he mutters to me. Lydia doesn't hear. She is in her world. I know what he thinks. He's never really liked Lydia. Reckons she was too hippy for him, with her candles, crystals and belief in Ley Lines from Glastonbury Tor passing close to the woodland behind the village. Once he'd left us at Gloucester Royal, he'd driven off as soon as he could. I don't mind. I feel guilty no one has realised how bad things were getting. Or am I overreacting?

Lydia is sitting smiling and singing to herself. Should I get a coffee? 'Lydia, would you like a drink?'

'Yes please,' she beams.

'Promise me you'll stay right here?'

She nods.

I scurry off and get back as soon as I can. Thank goodness she is still sitting quietly. I hand a cup of coffee to Lydia. Black with no sugar is how she likes it.

'Why are we here?' Lydia says, taking the cup.

'You had a fainting turn and might have hit your head,' I say. 'We're going to get you checked out.'

Lydia nods. 'I do feel a bit achy.'

'Sit quiet and we'll soon have you back home.'

Three hours later I am standing outside the cubicle where a doctor and a nurse are attending to Lydia. The curtains swish back.

'How is she?'

'There's no sign of head trauma. It might be dehydration, possibly poor nutrition. We'd like to keep her in for a few days for observation. She struggled to answer some of the questions.'

'Malnutrition? Lydia is one of the best cooks in the village. She's always baking for events and the local shop.' What are they talking about?

128

'She is very thin.'

He's right. The sensation of lifting Lydia was like lifting a bag of twigs. 'Could it be anything else?' I say.

He's hedging. 'We don't know. Are you next of kin?'

'No. Her eldest son is in Dubai. I can contact the one in Scotland. I have his number so if there is a problem with the house when Lydia is away on holiday, I don't have to disturb her.'

'It would be a good idea if someone could come and stay for a few days, especially when we get the results of the tests.'

'Tests? You know something don't you?'

'I never speculate. I act on data. That's what we need now. Information before we can make any decisions or diagnoses.'

That's all he'll say. Patient confidentiality and all that. 'I'll call him, and he can let the other son know what's happened. Can I see her?'

'Yes. Of course. She will be taken up to the ward in a short time.'

'Right. I can pop to the shops, get her some stuff and call the boys.'

'Excellent. I'll check on bed availability,' and he walks off along the corridor.'

I pull aside the curtain. 'You gave us all a fright.' Lydia is swamped in the bed. She looks so frail and so vulnerable. 'I've told the doctors and the nurse I'll contact Tom in Scotland and he can get in touch with Chris.' I hold out my phone. 'Do you want to talk to them?'

'Why?' Her eyes take on the look of a startled deer.

'The doctor thinks you need a bit of TLC and when they've got the results of the tests, it'd be useful if one of them is here.'

'I don't need them. I want to be out of here and back in my own home,' Lydia says as her eyes fill with tears.

'It really is better to let them know. You need a bit of building up,' I say. 'A bit of muscle on those arms and you'll be fighting to get out of here.'

She ignores my pathetic attempt at a joke. 'I don't want to be a bother,' she says.

'It's no bother. We all need a bit of TLC from time to time. Perhaps this is yours.'

'Are you saying I can't look after myself?' The anger flashes in her eyes.

'No. Nothing like that. It's a precaution,' I say.

'You do it then,' Lydia says and turns her face away from me.

I walk to the car park. It's quieter and there's chance of a better signal. 'Tom? It's Sheila, your mum's friend. She's had a bit of a turn. The doctors are keeping her in for some tests. She's with me in A&E.'

I keep my comments as positive as I can until I get to the part that the doctor wants to speak to next of kin when the test results are back. Tom says he'll call Chris in Dubai and let him know and will be in touch in a few minutes. I rush to the small shop in the foyer and buy a dressing gown, a wash bag, toothbrush and toothpaste and a small comb. That will do for tonight. I'll collect Lydia's stuff tomorrow. For some reason, I am exhausted. The thought of going to Lydia's home, coming back here and then going home is too much. Far better to get Lydia settled and come back tomorrow when I feel stronger. Ten minutes later my phone goes. Chris is already heading to the airport in Dubai for an overnight flight and will land at Birmingham in the morning. He'll get a train to the station and a taxi to the hospital. He hoped to be there before two o'clock. Tom will follow on Monday.

'Chris will be here tomorrow and Tom sends his love,' I say as I pull up a chair next to Lydia's bed. She is in a small room with three other beds and a large window overlooking the car park.

Lydia smiles. 'It will be nice to see him,' she says 'Although I don't know what all the fuss is about.'

'The doctors and nurses are being careful. That's all.'

'Waste of resources if you ask me.'

'Nonsense.' I bustle round and plump up pillows.

Lydia grasps my hand. 'I am very grateful for all you've done. I won't forget it, you know.'

'Lie back and get some rest. I'll be in to see you tomorrow with your clothes and I'll pop round to the house to check there's some milk and bread for Chris.'

'That's very good of you. He's a dear boy. You'll like him.'

I place my fingers over her lips. 'Shhh. No more. Get some rest.'

It is eight o'clock before I reach home, thirsty, tired and hungry. My car is on the drive. Good old Mona.

I open the front door. The remains of a takeaway is cooling on the coffee table. Brian is stretched out on the sofa asleep. An empty wine bottle and one glass shows how he's spent his evening. I collect up the dirty dishes and the food and go into the kitchen. Has he ordered enough for two? I fancy something spicy.

An empty brown carrier with the tell-tale grease stains of a takeaway has been plonked on the counter. I peer inside. No. From the empty containers, he'd ordered one main, one rice, a couple of onion bhajis and a naan bread. All that is left is a soggy piece of naan bread. I take a bite. Urgh. I hate plain ones.

I go back into the lounge and rattle the bottle. 'Wassup?' Brian stirs. 'Oh, it's you?'

'Who else would it be? Genghis Khan?' The humour is lost on him.

'Eh? How's the invalid?' he says, sitting up and scratching his head.

'They're keeping Lydia in for a few days and Chris is coming over from Dubai tomorrow.'

'Sounds serious,' Brian says.

'No. It's precautionary,' I say between tight lips.

'I reckon the old bat's off her trolley,' Brian says. 'Always has been. Always will be.'

Something inside snaps. 'How dare you say such a thing.' I want to slap his smug face. 'I've spent the afternoon helping a neighbour and a friend and all you can do is slag her off?'

'Heh, sorry and all that. Didn't know it was such a touchy subject.'

'That is not the point.'

'What is the point?' Brian stands and rests one arm on the mantlepiece as if he is in charge.

'A bit of understanding would have been nice. Perhaps a bit of thoughtfulness. Brian's hungry. Brian can't be bothered to cook. Brian orders himself food.' I emphasise the word himself. 'Sod everyone else.'

'If all it takes to keep a woman happy is a biriyani from Curry and Go, I should have bought shares in it.'

I want to wipe the smirk from his face. 'That's not what I'm asking.' I escape into the kitchen.

Brian follows. 'Go on, run off, bury yourself in being the perfect housewife and mother.' He puts on a mincing voice. 'Ooh must do this for the children. Must make sure they're happy with the holiday, the furniture, the garden, the food, the days out, even the bloody washing powder. In my childhood, we fitted into our parents' lives. We weren't the epicentre.'

I throw the empty bottle into the recycling container and lean on the sink. He is questioning me as a mother. 'I did what I thought was right for our children. I always have done. Are you telling me I've been wrong?' I say trying to control the tremor in my voice.

'No. You did what you thought was right for you so that everyone believed you were the perfect mother.'

'What's the harm in that?'

'Fine if that's all you want to be. The woman I married was a person too. A decent wife, a good friend to me, a laugh, someone I could talk to.' His voice drops to a husky whisper. 'She's gone.'

I stare out at the darkening sky. The crescent moon has risen above the church. Its beauty eludes me today. Does Brian resent all the time I've spent with the children? Is he jealous of the attention? Or is he right? 'I thought you agreed with me on the way to bring up the children,' I say and wait for reassurance or some agreement.

'I didn't really get a look in, did I? You called the tune. I was only the one who paid the piper,' he says. 'I'm off to the pub.' The front door slams and I'm left alone.

Chapter twenty-four Mona

Mona read the text.

> *Lydia's OK. Her son is coming over from Dubai to stay for a while. I'll let you know as soon as I hear anything more. Sorry about your first experience of the Wild Girls. It has to get better. LOL*

She smiled. Can't you be *wild* without doing *wild* things?

There was a knock at the door. Who on earth? She prayed it wasn't Brian. There was something creepy about him and two glasses of wine in his company was enough for the next six months. He'd talked as if no one had ever listened before. The knock was more insistent this time.

'Yeah. Coming. Where's the fire?' She opened the door.

'Heh, Mona, do you want to see the finished studio?' It was James. A set of keys dangled from one hand.

'Is it ready?'

'As Freddy,' he said. 'Sorry.' He did a mock salute. 'As we Brits say. It means it's OK to go.'

She ignored his fake accent. Why did so many people assume she was from the Wild West and put on a weird twang that had suited 1960s spaghetti movies and nothing else? 'I'd love to,' she said. 'I've run out of space for my paintings and I fancy doing a really big canvas of the valley in summer.'

'No time like the present,' he said.

Mona closed the door behind her. James was in his Sunday best, if he had any. On his feet he wore clean trainers and he'd replaced his cords with navy chinos and a pale mauve polo shirt. It suited his greying hair and freshly shaven skin. If she'd been on the lookout for a replacement Ethan, she could have done worse. As it was, the thought of any man in her life gave her goosebumps. And not the nice type.

James set off at a fast pace. Mona struggled to keep up. 'Heh, what's the rush?'

He stopped. 'Sorry. I've always been ready for tomorrow, today,' he said and smiled. 'I'll try to slow down.'

'Good thing,' Mona said. 'I was out walking yesterday, and my city legs still aren't used to soft grass.'

'How was the walk? I heard someone was taken ill?'

How the hell did he know that? He answered her unspoken question. 'It's a small village. People talk.'

'Or should that be gossip?'

'People in this place are interconnected in more ways that anyone new to the village realises. My housekeeper's daughter was on the walk too.'

'Housekeeper? You don't do your own washing and cooking?'

'I can heat up ready meals and stick stuff in the washer and I am a dab hand with the hoover. If I can pay someone to do what I dislike, it gives me more time for my business and it provides a small income for someone.'

'She works on a Sunday?'

'No. She was delivering my clean washing back to me yesterday afternoon.' James stopped in front of the doorway to the studio. 'Close your eyes,' he said.

Mona did as she was told. He took her hand. It was cool and firm, the way she liked a man's hands to feel. He led her inside and stopped. 'Open them.'

'Wow. This is fabulous.' Mona spun round. Over the past week, she'd often wondered if she'd done the right thing. Her memory of the place was that it might be too dark and gloomy for a decent studio. She was wrong. The whitewashed walls, the clean windows and new skylight filled the room with spring sunshine.

James opened the top half of a stable door. 'Kitchen area and through the next door is the toilet and store cupboards.

What do you think?'

He'd added a table, a small bookcase, a couple of upright chairs and a two-seater sofa with yellow cushions. 'It's perfect,' she said and twirled around. 'I can set my paints there.' She pointed to the bookcase. 'There's space for a proper easel if I need it.' She touched the walls. 'Do you mind if I put up a few picture hooks?'

'I have a better idea,' James said. 'What if I put a picture rail about this high.' He indicated a space a couple of feet from the ceiling. 'You can hang any number of pictures from it. Like a proper gallery,' he added.

Mona clapped her hands. 'That would be perfect. When can I move in?'

James handed her the keys. 'The place is yours,' he said.

'I'll make a start today.'

'I've got my car. Do you want me to help? We could do it in one journey?'

Mona was about to refuse when she caught sight of James' eager face. Why did people have such a bad opinion of him? Or was he like Ethan? The master of control and influence when he wanted something. He seemed genuine. What the hell? She wasn't going to be here long enough for him to be a problem. 'I'd really appreciate that,' she said. 'In return, I'll paint you a special picture. What will it be? Your house? A pet? I'm not so good on people.'

'Let me think about that,' James said. 'If we get back to your place and load up, I can drop everything off here and whizz down the DIY store to get the picture rail. It'll be up by the end of the morning and you're really ready to go.'

An hour later Mona was sorting her paints and brushes and arranging them on the shelves while James drilled into the walls. Two hours later she'd pegged some of her earlier work to wire coat hangers and hung them from the rail. The place looked lived in. She stood back to admire her work. 'I'd offer you a cup of tea or coffee, but I don't have any,' she said.

'Oh yes you do,' James said. 'Check in the first store cupboard.'

Mona opened the pale grey door. Inside was a kettle, six mugs, plates, assorted cutlery, including teaspoons, a pile of tea towels, washing up liquid, a bowl, rubber gloves, a broom and a dustpan and brush, a mop and bucket and in the centre of the middle shelf, a jar of coffee, a cafetière, a packet of sugar and a container of ground coffee and a glass jar with tea bags. 'You think of everything,' she said.

'Milk in the fridge.'

'How come you got all this sorted? Not bad for someone who needs a housekeeper,' Mona said and filled the kettle.

James perched on the edge of the table. 'I asked myself what my old mum would want as basics and that is the answer.'

'She sounds like a great lady.'

'She was.' James said. 'She died two years ago.'

'I'm sorry,' Mona said.

'She was in a small flat and had a carer going in once a day. Except over the weekend, the carer didn't turn up. Mum fell. She was dead by the time someone checked on her on Monday. So much for care in the community.'

Mona handed him a mug. 'Milk?' He shook his head. 'Was that the spark for this idea of yours about having people live and work in the same place?'

James sat down on the sofa and cradled the mug between his hands. 'I suppose so. People would get to know if Mrs Jones hasn't drawn her curtains, or Bill from number twenty-two hasn't put out his rubbish. They'd be around during the day, walking the dog, hanging the washing, mowing the lawn rather than leaving at the crack of dawn and arriving back in the evening. If there were enough small cottages or maisonettes for more vulnerable people, set close together, they could share resources. A carer could be assigned to a group. It makes sense.'

'Sure does,' Mona said. 'I wish you luck with your plans.' She lifted her mug to toast him.

James looked down at the floor. 'That's why I wonder if I could bring someone round to see this place at the end of the week? The meeting to consider the planning application takes place Monday week. If the Councillors could see a business unit like this in action, it might squash some of their fears.'

That was the catch. She knew it all along. For a moment she was proud off her assessment of human nature. It was replaced by disappointment. James was like everyone else. What's in it for me? 'I see.' She was going to get to the bottom of this. 'Is that why there was the breakneck speed to get me in place and ready for action?'

James looked back at her and a grin spread across his face like a naughty school boy. 'I'm a great believer in good for you, good for me, good for the planet. Aren't you?'

For a moment, Mona was tempted to be cross. Had she been taken in by him? People had said he was devious. Or was he simply on a mission? She had a choice. Accept his explanation or assume he was on the make. She chose the former. This time. 'What a coincidence,' she said. He squirmed. She'd hit the mark. Did it matter? She'd got her place to paint after all. 'Actually, I quite like coincidences.' She lifted her mug. 'Here's to us and whatever plans we have, may they come to fruition.'

'I'll drink to that,' said James. Did he wink? Or were his eyes slightly screwed up against the sunlight coming in through the open doorway?

She refused his offer of a celebratory drink. And lunch. She wanted to get started on her new idea and she needed to make a few preliminary sketches. In her head was a landscape of the valley. Up close you could make out individual plants, birds and insects. In the background, the

138

hills stretched away in shades of blue until they merged with the sky; fragile images of nature set against the strength and permanence of the landscape.

Chapter twenty-five Sheila

I open the front door of Lydia's cottage and recoil. The smell is overpowering, rotten fruit or cabbage, stale air and the muskiness of mice. In the darkness, there is a scuttling and rustling. As long as it isn't rats. I take a step forward. Mice I can handle. Rats. No. They're creepy. Or is that a legacy from school history books and the stories of the plague?

My eyes are becoming accustomed to the dim light through closed curtains. Clothes festoon every surface, and the floor is littered with newspapers, plates of half-eaten food and mugs with the remains of tea or coffee. A biography of Virginia Woolf is propped open, its spine split, and the pages smudged and greasy. What has got into Lydia? She was always so spotless. And her cooking? Had we eaten food prepared from here? I cross to the window, trampling papers and newspaper cuttings and pull back the curtains. The red velvet is greasy to the touch. I open one vent as wide as the warped wood allows. What will her son think? If I clean it, he won't realise how Lydia has been living and concealing it from everyone. Why hasn't any of us spotted the warning signs? Were there any? I'd always met Lydia at events. This isn't a village where people popped in on the off chance. Most lives were so busy, advance warning of weeks was often needed for the simplest of meetups.

I can't leave it like this. I suppose I could make sure the kitchen is tolerable. I push open the latch. Bloody hell. This is worse. Dirty plates and dishes adorn every countertop. The sink is full of stagnant washing up water where a series of burnt saucepans are in soak. Lydia had been so proud of her new kitchen. It was the last time I'd been here. That must have been two, no three years ago. Shortly before Alun died. Her boys had already set up home elsewhere.

She must have been so lonely. I'm wracked with guilt. There had been an unspoken sense of relief as Lydia continued to throw herself into her voluntary work and the church. We should have been there. Done something. I fill a kettle with water and am about to switch it on. I stop. The base is blackened as if someone has put it over a gas flame.

I fight back the tears. Lydia could have been killed. Nobody suspected a thing. How could this have happened? I run the hot tap and roll up my sleeves. Soapy water and elbow grease will clean up a bit. Enough so it's hygienic. I get out my phone and take a few photos. I'll have the evidence for Chris to make his own mind up. Lydia will need a lot of support.

I set too and scrub the work surfaces, tidy the worst of the mess away and hoover the lounge carpet. I wash the kitchen floor and fill a bag of rubbish for the non-recycling bin. With another window open and the back door ajar, the warm breezes from the south take away a lot of the smell. I open the fridge. Half opened packets of food spill off the shelves. I pick up a packet of bacon. I don't need to check any dates. The green colour tells me all I need to know. It joins the rest of the food or what was once food in a spare black sack. A quick wash with soapy water removes the grime. The smell is something else. Lydia had been a cook, hadn't she? Bicarbonate of soda will take away a bit more of the smell. I check the cupboards. Each one is full of packets and tins. Some have been opened. Some are still in their plastic wrapping. Behind three half opened bags of plain flour I find what I'm looking for: six packets of bicarb. I empty the one packet into a small pudding basin and place it in the fridge. That will have to do for now. I'll pop to the supermarket and get a new kettle, bread, milk and a pizza. I'll leave a note for Chris telling him to call as soon as he arrives. It will be brutal. Perhaps that's what is needed.

Sunday afternoon is always an odd time. I'd hated the

dullness as a child, the creeping dread that another week of school was beginning, to be followed by the same feeling at work. No matter how much you enjoyed the job, Sunday evening means the loss of freedom. I'm sitting on the patio. My phone is next to me and I'm trying to concentrate on the latest news about Brexit. It's all opinions. No one really knows what is going to happen or not happen. I start the article again. It promises in depth, incisive discussion. It's as dull as a wet February. Brian is out. Golf again. It's his escape. That and work. Anything except face the issues between us. Is that why he is so intent on getting this promotion? It will keep him in work and away from home for the next few years. Or should that be away from me? His words had hurt. Had I really put the children first? I thought I'd always involved him, talked to him about any worries and fears. Had I forgotten I'm wife as well as mother? I'd made sure he had a decent home, good food, clean clothes, sex when either of us could be bothered after the children had been born. Had I become mum to him, too? We need to talk. Except if he isn't open to any discussion, what can I do?

The phone rings. 'Mark, where are you?'

'Hi, Mum. Just ringing in between shifts to ask you a favour.'

'Shifts? Are you at work?'

'Yeah. I'm working at a really cool bar. I do mornings from midday till four and start again at six. It's a great place and the boss reckons if I carry on as I am, he's going to let me take charge of a new venture closer to the sea front. Should be fun.'

'You are working in a bar? What sort of bar?' Visions of strippers fill my head.

'The focus is on entertainment. Monday is comedy, Tuesday is buskers, Wednesday, my idea,' he says proudly, 'an open mic for poetry and prose. It attracts students and local writers.'

'I see.'

'Heh, Mum. I recognise that tone of voice. You don't approve, do you?'

'It's not that…after the expense of your degree, I hoped you'd get something a little more—' What can I say? I'm disappointed? I am.

'Entertainment is very lucrative,' he says. There is a catch in his voice. 'I could end up working for a really big company. We're a leisure society today, remember?' The voice is stronger once more. 'Nothing gets in the way of going out and eating out.'

'Yes. But bar work?'

'It's great fun. Anyway, can you pack up my uni stuff, you know the saucepans and the duvets, towels? All that crap. I'm moving into a flat next weekend. Elroy will drive me back on Thursday to collect it all. If you leave it in the front room, I've got my key.'

'What sort of flat? Who with?'

'Some mates. Sorry got to go. I'm auditioning a transvestite cabaret for the first Saturday every month and the ladies have started to arrive. Love you,' he says as the phone goes dead.

A bar? I need to tell Brian. My call goes straight to answer mode. 'Sorry. Leave a message and I'll be in touch ASAP.'

'I've just had a very garbled conversation with Mark. He's got a job in a pub and wants to stay in Brighton. I need to talk to you. Please call back.'

I replace the phone on the table. Why does it bother me so much? Mark has finally shown some initiative. He's got a job. He's found it for himself. He's moving out into a flat share that is not a student dive. He hasn't asked for a deposit. He is setting out on his own. I should be happy. I'm not and I know why. I'd imagined something better.

Even retail might be better. People love to shop. He could become manager of a huge store, something with a future and plenty of opportunities. I'm ashamed I'm disappointed. A pub? He says it's a bar. What's the difference? Am I a snob? Yes. I think I am. And there's another thing. This hurts even more. He's leaving home. For good. I might moan about him. At least he's here to moan about.

The phone rings again. Brian? It is an unknown number. 'Hallo?'

'I'm Lydia's son Chris. I've just got in and read your note.' His voice is shaky.

'How's your mum?'

'Sitting up in bed and demanding to come home.'

'That's a good sign,' I say.

'Is it? You've seen the place. And thanks for cleaning up downstairs.' He's come straight to the point. I like that.

'I think she's going to need a bit of support.'

'Bit? I don't reckon she'll survive on her own.' The voice cracks. 'I'm already in discussion with my boss about taking a sabbatical for six months while Tom and I can get something sorted for her.'

'You mean carers?'

'Whatever is best for Mum. At the moment we don't know what that is. I spoke to a doctor today. They're doing tests. They don't need to. I know she's got dementia. She has good days and, as this place shows, very, very bad days.'

I know he's right. I still have to ask. 'Are you sure?'

'My boss's wife was diagnosed last year. I've had plenty of first-hand experience.'

'Could it be something else?'

'I hope so. I mean, I hope I'm wrong. I don't think so.'

We both know he's right. 'When will she be home?'

'As soon as they've completed the tests and if it is dementia, I'll need to get a care package in place to tide her over until we can sort something out permanently.'

144

'Do you need anything from me?' This time it's my voice that wobbles.

'No.' The voice on the phone is calm and clear. 'I ranted a bit when I got here. I suspected when I saw her, all was not well. This confirmed it. All I can do is to be the support she always gave me as a child. I owe her that. It's what Dad would have wanted too.'

'Thank you for letting me know. Please keep me informed.'

'Yes, and until we get a proper diagnosis and Mum wants people to know, can this be between us?'

'Of course.'

I switch off the phone and place it back on the table. Tears splash off my face and onto the warm tiles on the patio. They soon dry and leave no mark.

Chapter twenty-six Mona

The days fell into a comforting, reliable pattern of her own making. Wake up, go for a walk in the early morning before the rush of dogs and riders, come back and eat something, usually in the kitchen or on warmer mornings which were increasingly commonplace, on the patio. She'd hear the chatter as children ran to school, the warning clang of the bell and silence as they fell into line. Vans arrived and disgorged tradesmen of different sorts outside the cottages and houses spread over the valley and the hillside. Dog walkers, poop bags in one hand and a ball or a lead in the other greeted fellow dog owners. And always the screech of the swifts and the chatter of the swallows was a constant accompaniment. It was the blackbird that thrilled her most. He'd find the top bough or a chimney stack and sing, puffing out his chest and opening his yellow beak wide as a torrent of liquid velvet notes joined the squabbling of the sparrows.

At about ten, she'd head to the studio, stopping to buy a sandwich or a roll at the village shop. That would keep her going till late afternoon when she'd lock up, go home and make a salad or a simple dish of pasta and spend the evening getting acquainted with English TV. It was all so quaint and homely. With trips to the shops, the occasional coffee break with Sheila or a pub quiz at the local, she had enough social contact and she was keeping in touch back home with snippets of information to keep them happy and not enough for anyone to pinpoint where she was. She felt safe for the first time in years. May and the first part of June flew past, and her collection of paintings was mounting.

James' meeting with the housing association had been postponed. That had all been a dream of his. Thank goodness. Or so she thought when she was disturbed by a knock on the studio door one morning in mid-June. She opened it. James was standing there with a woman in black trousers and a pale pink shirt and younger man in a similar colour scheme. Both had pink and black lanyards round their neck.

'I'm so pleased you're in,' James said. 'I know this is an imposition, but could these people have a quick look at the project we've undertaken here?'

'Project?' Mona said.

'Yes. The studio?' He ran a hand through his hair and left a bit sticking up. He looked like a tufted duck. 'I'm sorry I couldn't warn you, the meeting ended sooner than we'd expected so I thought why not take the opportunity to visit. Sorry we had to cancel last time,' he added and smiled.

'If it's inconvenient, we quite understand,' the woman said. She spoke with a slight accent, like Dylan Thomas.

'No. Come in,' Mona said. 'Anyone like a tea or a coffee?'

'A glass of water for me,' the man said. 'I can't remember heat like this.'

'Tea would be fine,' the woman said.

'I tell you what, I'll make it and you sit down and tell these people what we're doing,' James said.

'By all means,' Mona said and pulled up two chairs next to the sofa.

'I'm Karen and I work for the Perkins Alternative Housing Association. This is Brad.'

'Brad's a nice American name,' Mona said.

'I'm named after Brad Pitt,' he said and looked at the ground.

'A great actor,' Mona said.

'Are these all yours?' Karen said.

'Yes. These are my paintings.'

'They're lovely.' Karen got up and went across to the series Mona had completed of hedgerows and sheep grazing nearby.

'Thank you. I want to capture the environment as I see

it in the spring and summer.'

'You certainly have done that,' Karen said. 'Is this one for sale?' She pointed to a painting of a Hawthorne tree, smothered in white blossom with two sheep underneath grazing on a buttercup-filled field.

'I haven't thought about it,' Mona said.

James poked his head round the kitchen door. 'Didn't you say you were planning on having an exhibition later this summer?'

'It was an idea,' Mona said and felt her cheeks go pink. Her work wasn't good enough.

'Great. Tell James when it's on and I'll place a reserve on that one.' Karen sat down.

'Really?' Mona said.

'Yes, as long as it's under one hundred. Most artists round here charge about that for a small landscape.'

'How do you know all this?' Mona said.

'Open gallery week in October is a great place for picking up presents for some of my more difficult aunts and cousins,' Karen said and smiled. 'That would suit Aunt Glenda. Her birthday is in early May.'

'I'm not a professional,' Mona said.

'All the better. I can tell Aunt Glenda you're an up-and-coming American artist in love with the English countryside.'

'She is all of that and more,' James said as he handed out the drinks.

'Do you have a website?'

'Er no. Not yet.' Karen didn't look the sort of person who played games. If she liked the artwork, perhaps Mona wasn't so talentless as Ethan had made out. 'I'll think about a website.'

'Tell me how all this started,' Karen said and took a sip of her tea.

James settled himself on a small camping stool Mona

had brought from the cottage. 'This is the idea,' he said and wafted a hand round the room. 'A small work unit in a village environment. No smells. No noise. No disruption. A family friendly alternative to everyone heading off to the nearest town or city.'

Karen raised one eyebrow. 'This is a simple art studio. How would it be if this was a pottery? That needs a kiln. Or a metal worker? That might create noise?'

Her words were cut short by the piercing wail of a chain saw in the woods above the village. 'Quietness doesn't imply silence,' James said. 'When the cattle lose their calves in June or July, everyone hears it for miles around.'

'Point taken,' Karen said. 'They are part of country life. Industry is not.'

'I'm not imagining large-scale production units,' said James. 'There's plenty of opportunities for distribution, crafts, small-scale options. There's a woman who makes soap in the next village, all from natural products and a couple who are running an online cosmetic company from their kitchen. As this was an experiment, we thought we'd begin with something simple.'

'Have there been any complaints?'

'Not to me,' Mona said. 'I go to the shop every morning to get a sandwich, and everyone knows what I'm doing. They seem to think it's nothing unusual.'

'We do have a tradition of writers, artists and creative people in the area,' James said. 'In fact, I've been told per head of the population, there are more creative types here than anywhere else except London.'

Karen nodded. 'As it is an experiment, I think the idea of creating studios is excellent. How it would work with more traditional activities, I'm not sure.'

'Isn't that what this is all about, challenging traditional working practices?' Mona said.

'Go on,' Karen sat back and sipped her tea.

'Like back home, I get the sense manufacturing industries over here are in trouble. New work is being generated using IT and you can set up a screen anywhere. There's also a market for small-scale creative items that are not mass produced. This set up is perfect,' Mona said.

Karen nodded. 'I think this is a good model that has some opportunities and should be explored in greater detail.' She paused.

'Go on, what's the *but*, 'cause sure as hell there's gonna be one,' Mona faked her accent a bit more. Somehow it never ceased to amuse the English.

'Only that we would like to see a similar set up with a manufacturing basis somewhere.'

'Like what?' Mona said. 'Candle making? Macramé pot holders?'

'I'll leave that to you,' Karen said to James.

'Certainly. I actually do have a local person who wants to set up a small distribution centre for beeswax products and a knitwear designer who wants more space.'

'That would be very suitable.' Karen stood up. 'In the light of positive feedback over the next six months, the association will be very keen to enter into discussion about the proposals for any future supported housing alongside the business venture. It could make for a very inclusive community.'

'Thank you,' James said. He turned to Mona. 'We'll leave you in peace. Perhaps I can pop over one evening and get a full update on how it's going?'

He winked. What was it with these British eye twitches? 'Anytime,' Mona said.

'When you have the exhibition, remember that painting is mine,' Karen said. 'Come along Brad, unless you have any questions.'

The young man blushed. 'No. All very clear,' he said.

'Brad is our newest trainee. I'm taking him out on sites

to get him blooded.' Karen's eyes sparkled. She was a tough lady with a soft heart underneath. Mona liked her. God she was missing the rough and tumble of work.

'Good luck,' Mona said to the young man as she shook his and Karen's hands.

As James closed the door, he poked his head round and whispered. 'Nice job. I owe you.'

The door closed and he was gone. Mona went across to the painting Karen had admired. It wasn't one of her best. It did have a softness about it, a quality of old-world charm with its pastel blues, greens, yellow and the chalk white of the sheep which mirrored the clouds and the blossom. She tore off a piece of paper from her pad and wrote SOLD in red before she fixed it to the metal coat hanger.

She'd sold her first painting. She looked at the others. How many did you need for a one-day exhibition? Could she hold it here? Like an open day? Who would come? Or an open studio, like the ones Karen mentioned. It might make her a bit of money and save her taking everything back. She stopped. The thought of going back hadn't entered her head for a while. She counted on her fingers. She was nearly halfway through her time here. She sat down at the table. She was a visitor. This wasn't her home. Except it felt like it. And she had to sort out the mess between her and Ethan. He owed her half the cost of the house and the furniture. Even though she hadn't been in touch for a while, she couldn't pretend he didn't exist. She had a right to that money, and she'd get it. There was a slight tapping sound. She looked down. Her hand was knocking against the table. If the thought of meeting Ethan did that to her, how on earth was she going to face the real thing?

Chapter twenty-seven Sheila

At five o'clock a few days later, I knock on the door of Lydia's house. A male voice calls 'Coming. You sit there, Mum.'

It opens to reveal a tall dark-haired man. If I hadn't known Alun was dead, I would have thought he'd been brought back to life, years younger. 'Chris?'

'You must be Sheila? Mum's told me so much about you. Come in.'

I walk into a spotless lounge. All traces of the debris and dirt have been cleared away. Lydia is sitting in an armchair in the corner, surrounded by books and magazines. Her hair is neatly cut, and her make-up is perfect. She is dressed in a pink silk blouse and black jersey trousers. On her feet she wears black patent loafers. Even her nails are the usual shade of pearly pink. 'Sheila? Lovely to see you. How's Brian?'

I sit on the sofa opposite the fireplace. 'He's fine. Getting ready for a big interview next week.' I don't tell her we've hardly spoken since the argument or that he is becoming more and more tetchy and morose by the day and resents the time I spend working rather than running around at his beck and call.

'Can you make us some tea, Chris?'

'Tea coming up,' Chris says and disappears into the kitchen.

'What about you?' I say and wonder what her reply will be.

'Me? Load of fuss about nothing. It's tests after test after test. And blood? I've had so many samples taken I'll need a transfusion soon.'

'Any results?'

Lydia folds her arms. 'They think it's my memory. Go on. Ask me something. Anything.'

'Er. When did England win the world cup?'

'Easy and I know today is Thursday, Theresa May is prime minister. Jeremy Corbyn is leader of the Labour Party and we're doing well with the football under that nice man with the waistcoat, Gareth…thingy.'

'You know more about what's going on than me,' I say. 'I try to avoid the football.'

'Chris has been telling me all about it,' Lydia says. I've told him he can wear one of Alun's waistcoats, like that nice man…'Er who is it?'

'Tea and biscuits,' Chris says and places a tray with cups, saucers, a milk jug, and a tea pot on the small table under the window. 'I'm sorry they're not home-made. Unless Prince Charles or Camilla personally stir the mix for Duchy Originals.'

'I'm very impressed,' I say. 'Lydia was always more organised than me. I'm a tea bag and mug person now.'

'Mum is a stickler for tradition,' he says and hands her a cup.

'Traditions are important. Now tell me all the village gossip,' Lydia says.

'There's not much to tell. Mona has an art studio and is painting. Three cottages along the High Street have been snapped up. No one knows who by and my Mark is running a bar in Brighton.' He is a bartender. It is a small distortion of the truth. Does it matter?

Lydia nods. 'Excellent. I can't wait to get back to the shop and the church.'

'All in good time, Mum. You mustn't overexert yourself which is why I'm getting on with supper while you chat to Sheila.' He goes into the kitchen.

I stay for an hour. Lydia chatters on and listens. Is this dementia? She seems more clued up than a lot of people I know. Before I leave, I want to talk to Chris. 'I'll take these cups into the kitchen,' I say.

I close the door behind me. Chris is stirring a saucepan of tomato sauce. 'Thanks for coming over,' he says

'She seems very bright.'

Chris stops stirring. 'Today is a good day. I just never know what to expect. Tom's coming down for a month once term ends and I'll be back full time from the end of August. I think there's only a fortnight when one of us won't be here and I'm in the process of arranging support.'

'It really is Dementia? Alzheimer's whatever they call it,' I say.

'I've learnt a lot about the brain over the last few weeks. Mum won't get better. The good days will fade. She will become increasingly frail and needy. At some point she will require residential care. As I told you. I've seen it before. It's tough when it's your own mother but somehow I always expected it.'

'What do you mean?'

He adds a pile of chopped mushrooms to the sauce and continues to stir. 'Mum was often a bit odd. We just thought it was her. You know, forgetful, losing her keys, not switching the oven on one Christmas Day so we ate at eight o'clock at night. Dad covered up a lot in his later years.'

I steady myself against the countertop. How come I never realised? No one did. 'I see.'

'You're shocked, aren't you?'

'I suppose I am. At Lydia's illness and how strong you are.'

'I have to be, for Mum.' He looks at me. 'Remember the old corny phrase from the cowboy films, "A man's gotta do what a man's gotta do"?'

'I remember it well,' I say. 'I always thought it was sexist.'

'I took it to mean sometimes you have to grit your teeth and get on with the task in hand, no matter how hard and not whinge about how terrible or unfair it is. Just get on with it.'

'What can we or I do?'

'Be as normal as you can,' Chris says. 'Invite her for coffee. If she's not up to it, we'll let you know. The vicar has said she'll make sure Mum gets to and from church and there's someone in the same pew as her in case of…you know.'

'Be there but not in your face. Helpful and accommodating, not intrusive.' The words come easily. Will the actions be as easy?

'You got it.'

'Right. I'd better be going. Nice to see you.' I hold out my hand.

Chris comes over and puts his arms round me. 'What makes it easier is knowing how much Mum was and is loved and admired by everyone. Thank you.'

I break away. 'I'll see you again soon,' I say and sniff.

'You bet.'

I go back into the lounge. Lydia is staring out into the garden. 'Have I missed Midsummer's Day this year. Still, it'll be the fourth of July and Bastille Day soon. Perhaps I can celebrate those instead.' Is she talking to herself or to me?

'What a good idea.' I walk towards the window. 'Such a lovely view here.'

Lydia looks up at me. 'How long will I be able to enjoy it?' she says.

'Years and years,' I say. 'You'll outlive us all.'

Lydia turns back to the window. 'What if I don't want to?'

'You'll feel more like your old self when you're back at the shop and going to church. No one likes hospitals, doctors and tests.' I speak firmly. As I'd done when the children were moping over something. It always worked.

'Yes. You're right,' Lydia says and smiles brightly. 'I'd better start my knitting for the Christmas sale of work. I'll have to ask Chris to help sort out my patterns.'

'Good idea. I must go. Take care of yourself and I'll pop in again soon. Perhaps you can come for supper one evening?'

'Oh yes. Chris is very good, but we do seem to eat a lot of pasta,' Lydia says in a hushed voice.

'I understand. If Brian cooked for us, we'd be having a barbecue in the middle of winter.'

'I like barbecues,' Lydia says. 'All that crispy meat and loads of ketchup.'

'I'll check if he's available,' I say and smile. Lydia is her usual self. Those doctors had jumped to the wrong conclusion. They'd soon find out. 'If there is anything you need, you have my phone number.'

'Do I?' Lydia says. 'Oh of course. It's your mobile I don't know.'

'I'll leave it for you.' I look around. Underneath a retro style phone is a small pad with a pen attached. I write my name and number. 'All done.'

'See you soon,' Lydia calls as I close the front door.

What could I do? A party? Lydia said she like midsummer. Too late to arrange anything for that. Bastille day? With Brexit dividing people, that was not such a good idea. July 4th? American Independence Day? It would be an excuse to get Mona involved. It might help her if she is feeling homesick. The food will be easy. Burgers. Ribs. Hot dogs. With ice-cream sodas to follow, or was there a special dessert? Mona will know. Except it wouldn't be a surprise for her and she might want to help instead of being a guest like Lydia. No. I'd sort something out. Red, white, and blue, plenty of American flags and simple food. And fireworks. Every decent party has to have fireworks.

By nine o'clock that evening I have sent out invitations to twenty people, including Lydia and Chris. Tom and his family might be down by that weekend. I add them to the list too. The last person to contact is Mona. I call her number.

'A 4th July celebration? How exciting! You must let me help.'

'I rather hoped you'd be the guest of honour,' I say.

'Me?'

'Yes. Any advice you can give, I'd be grateful.'

'Fireworks,' Mona says. 'There have to be fireworks. Let me buy those. It's my way of saying "Hello England".'

'Are you insisting?'

'Betcha life I am,' Mona says.

'Agreed.' I'm pleased as I don't want to bother Brian and I know nothing about fireworks. 'Saturday 7th July from seven till eleven. A special 4th July party and it will end with fireworks. Not too many banging, whizzy ones. Might upset the pets and keep the children awake.'

'They'll be full of stars,' Mona says. 'In as many shades of red and blue as I can find.'

I put the phone down and check the clock. It is gone ten. Surely Brian isn't still working? Or perhaps he's stopped off at the golf club…The party will be after we know the result of the interview so either he'd be celebrating or commiserating. Which one would I prefer? God knows. Either way he'll be impossible to live with.

I open the back door and look out at the darkening sky. Where the hell is he?

Chapter twenty-eight Mona

Heh, everyone. How are you? I've been painting again and this one's sold already. I've nearly got enough for a one-woman show. I'll let you know what happens and I'll be celebrating Independence Day as usual although it will be on the 7th.

Mona posted a photo of the painting Karen wanted. It could be anywhere in Europe, couldn't it? If Ethan was snooping round her FB feeds, he'd make of it what he wanted. She was safe. He'd never find her. She'd return when she was ready. The Independence Day party was going to be cool. A selection box or two of fireworks would be a perfect end to the evening. A couple of hundred bucks wouldn't break the bank.

If she was going to hold an open studio at the end of August, she'd need plenty of stock. Not everyone would want a painting. What if she did a series of cards and left the inside blank? Twenty at a couple of dollars each would be a start. She'd have to get a move on, and she'd need card and envelopes. She'd pop into town.

Mona parked in the car park by the church. It was her favourite place. From the high point she could see the valleys spreading out in four directions. Beyond were the hills and in the distance, the blue tints of distant forests and the mountains of Wales. She had had so many plans to explore. What happened? Community. She'd got sucked into the ties of a small community. As a city dweller, she'd been used to anonymity. Not here. Every morning as she walked to her studio, she'd got used to saying good morning to the milkman, the man with the Alsatian called Rusty and the lady with the two whippets, Bill and Bella, exchanging a few words with a keen gardener and waving to the lady doing her yoga. She didn't know their names. So what? She was acknowledged and that was priceless.

Mona locked the car and walked towards the steep High Street. The tinkling sound of the busker playing the keyboard greeted her. It was already hot and promised to stay that way. She purchased fifty sheets of card in assorted creams and whites and some A5 envelopes. Paint? If she stocked up, she could press ahead. She stood for a few moments admiring the paintings in the window of the art suppliers. Could she have a go at oils? The large canvases with their bright scenes of the town looked easy enough. Perhaps she'd take a course when she was settled back home. She collected an assortment of acrylic colours, some thicker papers and a palette knife. She could have a go. She reminded herself to get a couple of bottles of white spirit later to clean up any mess.

'Mona?'

It was a man's voice. Her stomach lurched. Ethan? She spun round. She let out the breath she was holding. Ethan? No, it was James. He had two large bags, one in either hand. 'Supplies,' he said in answer to the question she hadn't asked.

She pointed towards the one in his left hand. It had a picture of a dog on it with a red lolling tongue. 'Not yours. I hope?'

He lifted it up. 'No. Must keep the hound happy.'

'That's good or I might be tempted to throw a stick and shout fetch.' She liked teasing him. It was something she'd never dared do with Ethan. He either took offence, told her she was stupid or got jealous if the remark was addressed to anyone else. She fought back the irritation. He was a long way away.

'I was about to stop for a coffee or a cold drink. Would you care to join me?'

'Why not? Any excuse to get out of the heat.'

'I thought you were used to it?'

'Heat yes. Lack of air conditioning, no.'

'I know just the place,' he said. 'This way.'

She followed him along the cobbled High Street and down an alley to a shady courtyard. 'I didn't know this was here,' she said. Tables had been set out. The air was cool, shaded by the buildings on either side which created a buffer from the sun.

'Coffee or something else?'

'Do they do iced coffee?'

'That's what I was planning to have. Shot of flavoured syrup?'

She shook her head. 'I'm a purist. Iced coffee should taste of coffee.'

James dumped his bags on a metal chair. 'I'm not,' he said. 'I've got such a hazelnut addiction, my family reckon I'm half squirrel. One plain, iced coffee coming up.'

Mona sat down on another metal chair. James was in a very happy mood. What had happened?

'The coffees will be here in a few minutes,' he said. The chair rattled on the stone slabs. At least he wasn't wearing shorts and sandals. It was something she'd noticed. So many men wore shorts, sandals, and socks, sometimes the socks were brown. Why didn't they wear trainers and bare feet? And the legs...pale white, hairy and with tattoos. What was it about tattoos? Ethan had called them tramp stamps. She shivered.

'Cold?' James said.

'No. Just thought of something I'd rather forget from my past,' Mona said.

'We all have them,' James said.

'I know it's probably none of my business, except you seem very happy. Is business going well?'

James looked at her under hooded eyelids. 'Well spotted.' He leaned forward. 'Karen was very impressed with the studio idea and likes the thought of the supported

160

housing project. I've got the go ahead for a unit the other side of town. When it goes well. I should be able to create some in the villages.'

'In my village?'

'That sounds as if you're thinking of staying?'

The waitress placed two thick glasses of iced coffee. Each had a paper straw. 'Red one has the syrup,' she said.

'That's for me.' James pointed to the space on the table in front of him. 'Are you?'

Mona took a sip of the chilled liquid. It was creamy and sweet with the tang of strong coffee. 'Good,' she said. 'Am I staying?' She smiled. 'I feel at home and yet it's not my home. Let's say the jury is out, for the moment.'

'Yes. I came for a year's secondment. That was in 1998.'

'Should we toast the success of your plans so far?' she said.

'I'd like to. Except there's a small fly in the ointment.'

'What?'

'A slight problem,' he said. 'Or it might be.'

'What's that?'

'There's a new woman in the department I have to deal with and I'm not sure she's on board. Yet,' James said.

'Why is that?'

'I don't know. I think it's because I'm offering something new, and people are scared of new things. That and she lives in the village. Probably scared I'll change the plans and build a few high-rise blocks.'

'Tell me about it,' Mona said.

Half an hour later, Mona checked her watch. 'Sorry. I'd better get going. My parking runs out in ten minutes, and I want to check the party shop for flags and banners for Independence Day.'

'Are you celebrating?'

'Not me. I'm helping someone to make their party a real Yankee occasion,' she said.

'Wow. That will be very special. I'd like to see that.'

'Come as my guest,' she said. What the hell? One more wouldn't make a difference, would it?

James' face flushed. 'I didn't mean to wangle an invite.'

'Crap. You're not,' Mona said. 'I'm providing the fireworks. You can help set them off.'

'What about the host and hostess?' James shifted slightly. 'Won't it inconvenience their catering?'

'We're all entitled to a plus one and burgers and hot dogs aren't exactly haute cuisine,' Mona said. Sheila wouldn't mind. Especially if it meant she could sit back and enjoy the fireworks and not be responsible for them. 'Give me your number and I'll text you the details,' she said.

'If you're sure?'

James seemed uncertain. Was this the same misery she'd met a few weeks ago? Either he'd had a lobotomy, or something had changed. 'It'll be fine. Trust me.'

They exchanged numbers and Mona headed to the party shop and ordered enough stars and stripes flags and banners to decorate a small state. She texted Sheila.

Got the fireworks, flags, and banners on order. Hope you don't mind if I bring a friend.

She stopped. Hadn't Sheila said something about James, and he wasn't to be trusted? Or had she imagined it? Well, if there was an issue, perhaps this was time to put it to bed. James seemed an OK guy. A friend said enough, didn't it? She wasn't really sneaky. Was she? No. It'd be fine. At parties, you're often so busy, you don't have time to fuss over who is with whom.

That was enough. She hit *send*.

She'd get home, go to the studio, and make a start on the small cards. Roses were popular and they were in such pretty colours. Tonight, she'd take a walk through the village. Would people think she was crazy if she asked if she could photo their flowers? Did it matter? She'd stick a few on FB. As she was about to get into her car, she heard a screeching sound. Delta shaped birds were wheeling round the church spire and screeching, like children playing chase. She got her phone and videoed their antics. That would be fun to post.

Chapter twenty-nine Sheila

'What's up?' I sense something is wrong as soon as Brian walks through the door. He slings his laptop bag on the floor. There is an ominous crash. He flops onto the black leather armchair by the side of the fireplace. I wait. He sits forward, rests his elbows on his knees and covers his face with his hands.

'I've resigned,' he says. 'There is no way under the sun I am going back or eating humble pie and apologising.'

'What happened.' As if I can't guess.

'They gave the post to some woman, barely out of Harvard Business School with no more understanding of the company than the local bin man.'

'Did they tell you why?' I'm treading on dangerous ground, yet I want a proper explanation. Brian has always been vague about the truth from time to time.

He lifts his head. 'Oh yes. All about needing someone who understands new challenges, new attitudes, new expectations. We're in the money business. That's what I know, and the questions were all about diversifying, acquiring new products, new markets.'

I go across to him and kneel by his side. 'Did they offer you an alternative?'

'Oh yes. At the same salary, less resources, and more responsibility. It's an impossible task, designed to make me fail and get out. I told them as much and walked away. I've resigned as from this moment.'

I take a deep breath. 'What about giving them proper notice?'

The face that turns towards me is twisted with anger. 'You don't fucking care, do you? I've put my heart and soul into the job and this family for decades and when I need some support, it's kicked back at me.'

'I didn't mean it like that. I meant—' I move away

164

slightly. The strength of emotion unnerves me.

'I have gone. I won't be going back. They can collect the car, the phone, and the laptop. I have three weeks holiday due and last month's salary. I will not be humiliated.'

'Who has humiliated you?'

'The board. People I trusted. People who encouraged me to apply, led me to think…oh I don't know.' He pauses. The contorted face softens, and the voice is quieter. 'Was I wrong?'

I stand up. I need to do something. 'I don't know. I'll make some tea.' It's pathetic but it's what we always do, isn't it?

'As if that'll change things,' Brian says and sits back, his eyes close.

I go into the kitchen and fill the kettle. Brian will get another post. There must be plenty of places where his experience would be welcomed. Yes, it's a blow. Probably more to his ego than anything else. I make the tea and carry two mugs back into the lounge. I draw up a small glass topped table and place a mug of tea on a slate coaster. Tears are running down Brian's face and he is letting them fall. I place a hand on his. 'Don't let it get cold,' I say. He'll come around. I've never known him to be down for long. His old spirit always bounces back. It may take time. All I must do is be understanding and not push him or make demands. I place my arms round his head, like I did the children. He'll tell me everything in his own time. He needs me. It feels good.

The following morning, I set off for work as usual. Brian is already up and studying job sites. 'I need a decent CV,' he says. 'Haven't had to create one for years. All you do is post a current version and companies and businesses trawl through and search for the best candidates.' He looks up from the desk in the small study.

I smile. Last night's discussions have encouraged him,

165

and me. 'You'll be fine,' I say. 'Take it steady. Rome wasn't built in a day and all that.'

On the way to work I stop to get a coffee. It has become a bit of a habit. Don't I deserve it? Although if we have to rely on my salary for a while, things might be a bit tight. I text Mark.

Dad didn't get the promotion he wanted. If you can cheer him up, he might appreciate it.

I don't expect a reply. Not yet. Mark is probably still in bed.

I call Claire. 'Hi, Mum. How are you?'

'Good. It's Dad. He didn't get the promotion he wanted and he's feeling a bit down. Any help in cheering him up would be welcome.'

'Oh.'

How can anyone pack so many syllables into one sound? 'Is there anything wrong?'

'No. Not really.' Claire's voice is hollow.

'Go on, what's up?'

'It's just we were hoping if Dad got this promotion, he could lend us twenty thousand for a new kitchen. This one is not suitable.'

'Not suitable?'

'The countertops should be marble, and everyone needs a moving gondola, not to mention a double temperature oven so you can cook different meals at the same time.'

'It's a new house with a new kitchen. You've only been in there a couple of years. It can't be that bad.'

'It's not that.' There is a distinct sound of petulance in her voice.

'I think it is, young lady. I call you to ask you to do something for me and your dad and all you can think of is replacing a state of the art two-year-old kitchen with a new model. What about considering your father for once?' I haven't felt so angry in years. Or have I? And had ignored it. There is something familiar about the irritability I am sensing. Have I hidden it away or deliberately ignored it?

'Other people's families help them,' Claire says. The petulant tone has not gone away.

There it is again. The same old chestnut. Everyone else is doing it, so we must too. 'Lucky them. I think we have been more than generous.'

'I'll see what I can do,' Claire says. 'I must admit I feel a bit let down.'

'Thank you. Love to the twins.' I switch the phone off. There is a twinge of guilt. Why? Is it the comment about other people's families? My own mother and father had never given in to what was emotional blackmail. I'd tried it often enough as a child. All children do. The response was always the same. 'Good for them' and the subject was closed. Any more whines and I'd be told to go to my room and come down again when I was in a better mood. Too late to take that stand with Claire. She is what Brian and I have made her. I finish my coffee and climb the stairs to the office on the fourth floor.

'Morning, Karen,' I call through to the small side room.

'Good. I'm glad you're here. I have a small favour to ask from you.'

'Go ahead. I'll do my best.' I plonk my bag down and perch on the edge of the chair opposite Karen's desk.

'James Frobisher. Does that name ring a bell?'

'We all know that name round my way. He's a local man, always on the make as far as we're concerned and no one in the village has a good word to say about him. Why?'

'He's cosying up to the Council. Reckons he has some suggestions for changing how we allocate people to our properties. Vanessa from Social Services wants a meeting with him and us on Friday morning. I have to be in

167

London. Could you go along and hear what he has to say? I quite understand if you feel compromised. I can send Sarah.'

'No,' I say. 'I'll be perfectly professional. It's only gossip after all. I prefer to make up my own mind.' I don't add that as far as James Frobisher is concerned it's a case of keep your friends closer and your enemies closer still.

'Good. I hoped you'd say that.' Karen swivels round and pulls a file from the top drawer of the cabinet. 'These are his plans. I like them. I'm concerned he and the Council might want to cherry pick the tenants. Show what a brilliant idea it is and bang, bang, the community is expected to provide support. I suspect it could lead the way to further cuts in services.'

'That's what we don't want,' I say.

'Exactly.' Karen slams the drawer shut. 'Go through the file with our list of possible tenants. We know who is desperately in need. You might want to challenge him and the Council on their expectations.' She pushes the file across the table. 'I'll email to say you will be attending in place of me. I know you don't usually work on Friday. We'll pay overtime,' she adds.

I take the file and sit down at my desk. Friday? That's the day before the party. Damn. I've got loads planned. Brian will have to lend a hand. I'll arrange as much as I can on Thursday, and he'll have to help out. I'll go through the file straightaway and over lunch I'll make a list of everything to do before Saturday and when it has to be done. It might work out a good thing for Brian to help and not let me take responsibility for everything to do with the house and home.

I sit back and open the file. Why is every case so desperate? It breaks my heart. How can a decent society let people end up in such terrible circumstances? Where is the support? If the Council thinks it can foist the neediest people into rural areas devoid of doctors, dentists, shops, bus routes, decent pavements for buggies and disability scooters, they are wrong. They have a duty to everyone, and I'll make sure I fight for them too.

I gaze out at the sky. The sun has bleached it pale blue. Despite the sapping heat, I'm energised. What is happening to me? Whatever it is, it feels good; scary but good.

Chapter thirty Mona

Mona opened her emails. 'Spam, spam, crap, crap,' she muttered and stopped. What the hell was this one? She didn't recognise the name. Not another of those doing the rounds, telling her she'd been spied on and her interest in certain porn websites had been noted and videoed. 'Fat chance,' she'd said and laughed after the initial shock. No. It was worse.

> *Please don't delete this. We need to talk. I've heard from friends you're safe and exploring Europe. If you wanted to discover the world, you could have said. We'd have gone together. If you needed to find yourself like some latter-day hippy, that's fine by me too. As it is, everyone is accusing me of not understanding, being the cruel husband. Since when? I thought we were happy enough.*

Happy enough? That might be all right for Ethan. It wasn't for her. One finger hovered over the *delete* button. What else was he saying? She scrolled down.

> *I know we have had some troubles. This is not the answer. If you don't get back to me, I'll keep trying. I don't give up easily. Not like you, obviously. Our marriage and our life together couldn't have been worth that much. If you want a divorce, you'll have to wait. I'm not doing anything over email or the phone.*

As if she'd call him. He always had an answer. He always had an excuse. Somehow whatever happened he made it out to be her fault. He'd never change.

> *I know you're in England. That photo of the flowers by the tree was a big clue. In the background was a signpost. It said*

footpath. As far as I know, only the Brits use English on signs and the green colour was a symbol of important footpaths in walking areas. How many are there? Perhaps sixteen? I don't think you're in a coastal area. The Pennine Way? The Cotswold Way? Who knows?

Mona's hands froze over the keyboard. Delete it. Delete it her mind insisted. She couldn't. She had to find out more.

Please get in touch. We need to talk. I promise I'll listen. I won't let all we've gone through be discarded like a turkey after Thanksgiving.

It was signed with much love, your husband Ethan. She read it through again. Fear had been replaced by irritation. He'd never find her. Those trails were huge. She could be living anywhere along any one of them. Or even further away. Yet he was determined. Should she give in to the same old pattern of wheedling and accusation? One email wouldn't matter, would it? It might deflect his attention, at least temporarily.

Hi Ethan,
Yes. I am well and I'll be back in the States in the fall. We can talk then. Please don't try to contact me again. Give me some space.
Mona

That was enough.

She closed the laptop. What if he was already over here? What if he knew where she was? What if he turned up? No. He'd never take leave of absence. Someone might think everything was less than perfect. A private detective? Cost too much. Unless he remortgaged the house. Would he do that? She'd be in debt, rather than have a bit of equity once the sale went through. No. He was mean too. He'd put his own leg in plaster rather than claim on the insurance.

She went into the kitchen and collected the studio keys. She'd never paint today. She'd be on the lookout for unusual cars or men in long macs and Homburg hats. She giggled. That's what comes from watching so many cartoons and B movies as a child. Didn't they all wear black leather jackets, jeans and black turtlenecks? With shades?

She could take the fireworks round to Sheila's house. It would save time tomorrow and after a breath of fresh air, she might be in the right frame of mind for painting. The cards were looking good. Should she have a go at some winter scenes? They might make perfect Christmas cards.

She collected the boxes of fireworks and piled them in the back of her car. On top was a bag of stars and stripes flags. She dumped packets of paper napkins and balloons on the front seat and set off. There was enough space for her to pull up close to Sheila's house so she wouldn't have to carry the stuff any distance. If Sheila needed any help, it would take her mind off Ethan.

No car was parked in the drive. Did they have a garage? The downstairs window was open. Sheila must be in. Mona stopped the car on the driveway and got out. Sheila had said she shouldn't bother to knock, just go straight in. It wasn't her way. She knocked on the door and stood beneath the porch, grateful for the overhang which protected her from the sun.

'Yes?' It was Brian. What was he doing home?

'I've brought the fireworks for tomorrow and some American themed bits for the party,' Mona said.

Brian looked over to the car. 'I'll give you a hand,' he said.

He stacked the boxes of fireworks on top of each other. 'Thanks,' Mona said. 'I can bring the rest.'

'Better not put the fireworks in the kitchen. We'll use the

outhouse,' he said and walked onto the patio. A small brick-built structure stood next to the henhouse. It was like the one in Mona's garden, except there was no old oil tank, rusting in the corner. 'Can you get the keys?' he nodded towards a series of hooks by the kitchen door. 'The one with the red tag.'

She picked the key off the hook and followed Brian along the garden path. Someone had watered the garden. The hose was lying curled on the patio and the earth was still damp. He stood aside as she unlocked the door. It swung open. Inside was a work bench. Around the walls different tools were hanging up. There was a smell of sawdust and something else, like walnuts. Or was it the smell of wood? Behind the bench, planks of old and used wood waited.

Brian placed the boxes of fireworks on the bench. 'We used to hide the children's presents in here,' he said. 'It's always nice and dry.'

'Whose workshop? And what are these tools for?' She ran a finger along the shiny handle of a saw.

'Mine,' Brian said. 'Some of these tools belonged to my grandad,' he spoke proudly and wistfully. 'I used to make frames for the children's artwork. They made cheap presents for the relatives when we were first married.'

'Do you still use them?'

'Not now,' he said. 'I made Claire a doll's house and a doll's bed. Mark wanted a garage. I made him a farm too. I wonder where it is?' He scratched at his unshaven chin.

'Is Sheila around?' Mona said.

'No. She's at work,' his voice changed. 'As you see, I am not.' There was a slight edge to his voice.

Mona changed the subject. 'I was going to ask her if she needed any help today.'

'She doesn't. She's left me a list of things to do.'

'Do you need any help?' Mona said and willed him to

173

refuse.

'She's left me with a list of food to buy. I'm waiting for a call, and I don't want to be in the middle of the supermarket when it arrives.'

'Business?'

'Yes,' Brian said. The way he said it, Mona knew not to continue that line of questioning.

"Give it to me. I've got to go into town.'

'Are you sure?' Brian looked relieved.

Mona held out her hand. 'Give it here,' she said.

'Payment will be difficult,' Brian said. 'I tell you what, let's do it together. If the call comes through, I can disappear back to the car.' He tapped his pocket. 'Credit cards at the ready.'

She said she'd help; she couldn't back out. She took a deep breath. 'I'm pleased to be of help.' No. That was wrong. She felt safer with people rather than being on her own. Ethan's words had spooked her. She'd get over it. She needed a bit of time.

'We'll have to go in your car,' Brian said.

'Fine by me.' His must be in for a service or repairs.

At least he didn't point out the speed limit, tell her which lane she needed to be in and if she was too close or too far away from the car in front of the kerb. Ethan had an unnerving way of pretending to be helpful. In reality it was simply criticism and making her understand that no one did anything as well as he did.

It was the same while they were shopping. Brian had a list and he kept to it with minimal fuss. No checking the sell by dates, comparing prices per pound and the list of ingredients in case there was too much salt, not enough seasoning, too much fat, not enough meat and so on. Shopping with Ethan had been a lesson in micromanagement.

They got back to Sheila's within an hour. Mona helped

Brian unload her car and they filled the fridge and the freezer. 'There's plenty to eat,' Mona said.

'The meat will be delivered tomorrow,' Brian said. He ticked off on his hands. 'We have sausages, burgers and ribs. The miserable veggies can have a bean burger,' he grimaced.

'You're a carnivore too,' Mona said.

'You bet.'

'Good man,' Mona said. 'I'll be getting along, and I will see you tomorrow. You're back in plenty of time for that call,' she said.

'Yes. If it happens.' As he said the words, he seemed to shrink, the lines on his face were more deeply etched and he slumped.

Mona put out her hand and touched his arm. 'It must be important,' she said.

'It is,' Brian said. 'Very important.'

'Well, if it's meant to be, it will be,' Mona said. 'See you at the party?'

Brian nodded. 'Yes. See you at the party and thanks for the help and the company.'

The sadness was back. What was happening? Did Sheila know? Or was that the problem? Mona returned to her little cottage, grateful to be single at least in her mind, if not in her life.

Chapter thirty-one Sheila

'Good luck,' Karen calls as I leave the office. 'I reckon James Frobisher is a real charmer. I hope he hasn't got the Council wrapped up in any of his schemes.'

'What schemes might they be?'

'Exactly. That's what we want to know. Have fun.' She bends her head over her desk.

I close the door and check I have everything. 'Laptop, minutes of last meeting, notes on Karen's meeting with Social Services, diary, pens, phone. Done.'

I'd learnt the lesson a long time ago that in any important meeting, have a hard copy of all the notes, agendas and minutes. It's easy for a system to go down, battery failure when you haven't got the correct leads or even a deliberate omission so that people can claim they knew nothing about a particular point of order or request for information. 'It didn't come through on my system,' would be the bleat. Much better to be able to whip out a copy, highlight the point and pass it round. Devious? You bet. So are others.

My meeting is for two o'clock. Should I call Brian to remind him about the shopping? He wasn't that keen and kept saying he had the chance of a job. I'm not convinced. He's been quiet for the last few days. Too quiet. It isn't like him. I'm sure he's doing this deliberately. And he'd avoided any conversations about the future. Probably so we can't have one of the 'we need to talk' talks. Yet we do need to talk and seriously. This is a chance to get back together, the way we'd always been, doing the best we could for the kids, making ends meet as my gran used to call it. Budgeting. We hadn't done that for a while. Not that we're rich. We're comfortable. More comfortable than my parents had ever dreamt of being. I climb into the car. The steering wheel is like a hot iron. I manoeuvre onto the main road. Beads of sweat form on my top lip. I switch the air flow to max. It's warm. Brian's car had air conditioning. 'Better get used to this,' I say out loud. If we downsized, we could buy a new electric run around. Better for everyone. I fan my hand in front of my face. Still too warm. I wind down the window. Sticky, fetid air, tinged with diesel blows in. I close it again. Better to be hot than gassed.

It is quiet on the roads. Too soon for the school run and too late for the morning shoppers. I turn in to the Council car park and wait as a young woman in a red sports car eases her way out. The roof has been withdrawn and she has sunglasses on. Do electric cars have sunroofs? It would be nice, for once to drive something stylish. No. Sexy is the word that springs to mind. Me? Sexy? After two kids, the menopause and the creaks and groans of middle age? That Greek sailor fancied Shirley Valentine, stretch marks and all. I can dream, can't I?

I get out, slam the car door and head across the hot tarmac to the main offices of the Council. Why here? It's simply a preliminary meeting, isn't it? I give my name at the desk and am escorted through the plate glass security screen, up a series of stairs to a corridor. The door of one room is already open. There he is. Mr Big Shot. James Frobisher and several people I don't recognise. It is clear this is more than a preliminary meeting and as the discussion ranges over the costs, the value to the community, the support for the project from everyone including the police, although why they had a finger in the pie, I have no idea, I am convinced this is a set up. What the hell can I do?

'I wonder if the representative from Perkins Alternative Housing Association would like to comment on what is being proposed?' A small round man with a pink and white face which blends with his white shirt and pink tie speaks.

What had Karen said about this scheme cherry picking the best tenants? I clear my throat. 'As you know, we support some of the most challenging, vulnerable and needy in the community. Can we be assured that we can put forward names for this scheme and they will be taken seriously?'

Mr Pink and White looks around. 'Absolutely,' he says.

'Can that question and the answer be minuted?' I address the young man taking notes.

He glances around. Mr Pink and White nods.

'May I ask what extra provision will be made at the lower end of the housing market if these small places are bought up by developers? It is common knowledge that with the increase in student numbers, dwellings at the lower end of the market in both letting and purchasing are in short supply.'

James folds his arms. 'A few run-down cottages is hardly making a dent in the market,' he says.

'I disagree,' I say and stare at him. 'These so-called run-down cottages could be just the thing for lower income families, trying to get a foot on the property market.'

'I assure you; I am not about to become some mega developer.'

'How many cottages have you bought already and how many more are in the pipeline?' I am warming to the subject.

James' neck is turning blotchy under the blue collar of his polo shirt. 'Is this reasonable? I didn't come here to be questioned on my private business dealings,' he says.

'All I want is a reassurance that whatever is planned will fit in with a mixed community, where everyone has equal opportunity to purchase property and it is a level playing field for all concerned; developers, renters and purchasers,' I say.

'I believe that all those items have been taken into consideration.' Mr Pink and White shuffles his papers. The pink blotches on his face and neck are deepening to a shade of red.

I fold my hands on the desktop and look at each person in turn. 'Could we table an agenda item for the next meeting in which we hear how many units are planned, where and how they have been acquired? I would also like to know exactly how tenants will be allocated and whether all associations, like Perkins, will have equal access.'

There is silence. James speaks first. 'I have no objection to letting you know already I have purchased three cottages in…' he reels off a list of places and what he had acquired. Four are in my village. Am I being unfair? No. The village needs low cost housing. Is this a solution?

Mr Pink and White looks at his watch. 'I feel we must draw the meeting to a close. The notes will be circulated with a report on how a small studio project is working out as well as the first sheltered maisonettes in the centre of Frampton.' He stands up. 'Thank you, everyone.'

I pack up my papers and go out to the car. 'Heh, can I have a word?' James runs after me

'What is it?' I am on my guard in case he thinks he can get me on his side before I've got all the reassurances I need.

'You don't like this idea, do you?'

'I think the idea is very good. As with all good ideas, the devil is in the details.'

'What details might they be?'

I lean against the door of my car. A waft of hot air drifts out. I shield my eyes against the sun as I look up at James. 'I don't like the idea of small villages with no facilities being a dumping ground for vulnerable people. I don't like cottages and outbuildings bought up, refurbished and sold to the highest bidder, usually from the city when local families could have done that and stayed closer to where they were brought up. Finally, what is to stop any developer renting these out until there is a spike in the housing market, selling and making a killing?'

'I assure you, none of that will be of my making,' James says.

'Really?'

'Give me a chance, will you?' James says. 'This is new. Some of it is bound to have a few teething problems.'

'That's fine. Except it will be people like me and the people I work for who have to pick up the pieces or villages like mine which are depleted of decent affordable homes.'

James holds up his hands. 'Whoa. That's not the plan.'

'No,' I say. 'Except we've come to realise it is always the most vulnerable who lose out and it is always the shareholders of the outsourced services who benefit.' I get into my car, close the door, and drive off. In the rear mirror I can see James mouthing words after me. Pity I can't lip read.

'Brian?' I open the front door and kick off my shoes. The bare floor is cool to my sticky feet. Perhaps it is too hot for tights. 'Did you get the shopping done?'

Brian is sitting on the patio. An open beer can balances on his stomach. He raises an eye towards me. 'Hallo, Brian, how are you? How was the most important phone call? No. All you bloody care about is the sodding sausages.' He takes a drink from the can.

I'd forgotten about that. 'I'm sorry. I forgot. It's been a pig of a day. Is it good news?'

Brian shakes his head. 'Good news? It was an outside chance. I suppose I was in cloud cuckoo land. I am out of a job, and it is highly unlikely I will get another unless I take a major hit in salary and responsibilities. Over the hill? See? Past it?'

'Oh Brian.' I sit on the chair next to him and hold his other hand. 'Something will turn up. You know it will.'

Brian takes another long drink. 'Yes, but what will it be and when?'

Chapter thirty-two Mona

Was she right to ask James to meet her here so they could arrive together? Did it seem too…? What was the word? Too cosy? No. Too affectionate? No. Too much like a special relationship? Perhaps. Whatever it was, it was done. If James had got the wrong idea, she'd soon put him right.

Mona opened the bag and pulled out a dress wrapped in tissue paper. It was a bargain. She hadn't bothered too much with dresses back home. It seemed right here. She'd seen it in the shop window, tried it on and fallen in love. How could you fall in love with a white shift dress with huge splashes of colour? It reminded her of tropical flowers, and it fitted. Had she really lost weight? There were curves where previously there had been bulges. It must be walking up the hills or the food. Portions were half the size they were back home. Mona opened her small collection of jewellery. There wasn't much. Ethan disapproved of display. That didn't include his personal watches of course.

She picked out a small gold chain with a single pearl drop. Her mother had bought it for her for her twenty-first birthday. She fastened it round her neck. The pearl nestled in the hollow of her neck. Small gold studs sat on her earlobes. She rubbed the space where her wedding and engagement rings had been. It was strange to be without them. She selected a small gold band with the letter M engraved on a heart. Another present. This time from her father. She'd been sixteen. It still fitted. That was enough. She skipped down the stairs, sandals in hand. Would James be late? There were still a few minutes to go. She bent down to fasten her sandals. The bell on the front door rang.

'Coming,' she called out and slipped on the other shoe. She reached the door before the bell rang a second time. Was that a sign of desperation or good manners? She opened the door.

'Sorry if I'm early,' James said. He had discarded his cords and wore green trousers with a pale lemon polo shirt. A brown leather belt was fixed around the trousers and matched the loafers on his bare feet. Very modern. He dangled a paper bottle carrier. 'I've got a decent sparkling to get everyone in the party mood,' he said and fished in the bag. 'And these.' He drew out a large box of matches.

Mona laughed. 'It's a good job I didn't go for the high-tech version where all you have to do is press a button.'

'That spoils the fun,' said James.

'Maybe. Sheila did say one of her neighbours is a fire fighter so we shouldn't have any disasters.' He looked quite crestfallen. 'I'm sure it will be exciting enough,' she said and motioned him out of the door. 'Let's get going.'

They walked through the early evening summer air. A warm breeze blew up the valley. The sounds of splashes and squeals were accompanied by the smell of barbeques. 'Someone's got the paddling pools out,' James said. 'Unlike your country, ordinary people don't have swimming pools. We'd all die of hypothermia.'

'Is it really cold in summer?' Mona said.

'This is very unusual. A decent temperature is 65 to 75 degrees Fahrenheit.

Mona stopped. 'That's more than us. We average 50 to 60 all year.'

'That's the trouble with getting all your information from films,' James said.

'Films are different. Everyone is clever, beautiful and rich, or kooky, beautiful and rich.'

'What is your role tonight?' James said. 'Apart from the fireworks?'

Mona spread her arms out. 'To float round and look the image of the charming American who is missing her home country.'

'Are you?'

'Sometimes and some things, yes. Other times and other things, a big fat no.'

'You often speak in riddles,' James said. 'Is that deliberate?'

'Do I?'

'With me. Yes.'

'I'm sorry. I don't want to burden people with my stuff,' she said and made the word sound as Yankee as she could.

'Perhaps some of us would like that,' James said.

'I'm sure you wouldn't. Oh, here we are. Follow me.' Mona led the way round the cottage to the garden. She must steer James away from such, intimate, yes that was the word she needed, intimate conversations. They were dangerous.

The garden was busy. Red, white, and blue bunting, interspersed with American flags hung between the fruit trees and the henhouse. Lights were twisted around the trunks and seats had been placed at small tables. They were all full and more people were seated on the lawn. A table had been set up with bowls of ice in which bottles of beer and white wine kept cool. In the corner of the patio a large barbecue was presided over by Brian and a younger lady. A fire extinguisher stood nearby.

'Sheila's in the kitchen,' Brian called out. He glared at James before flipping another burger.

'I'll pop in and say we're here,' Mona said. 'Get me a beer, will you?'

Sheila was unwrapping bowls of salad and coleslaw. Paper plates and napkins waited. Bottles of ketchup and proper American mustard for hot dogs were lined up like soldiers. 'Hi,' Sheila said and came over to give Mona a hug. 'Here's the guest of honour.'

'Please.' Mona shook her head. 'No fuss. I'm trying to be very British.'

'No chance. We're really going to make you feel at home today,' Sheila said and squeezed Mona's arm.

'You did that as soon as I saw the mustard. My mouth is watering already.'

'That means you can have the first hot dog and give us your verdict,' Sheila said and opened the fridge door. Inside were piles of burgers, ribs marinating in a sticky brown sauce and sausages, either flecked with herbs or chilli flakes. Sheila reached in and pulled out a plate of sausages. 'Can you give these to Brian,' she said.

'I've brought a friend, remember.'

'The more the merrier,' said Sheila. 'By the way Lydia won't be coming.'

'Oh?' Mona took the cold plate and balanced it on one arm.

'Her son, Tom, the one who is married is down here with his young family. They're taking her on a short holiday to the New Forest. It'll do her good to get away.'

'Is she better?'

'Yes,' Sheila said. 'She certainly seems on the ball whenever I call. Sausages,' she said and thrust a second plate at Mona. 'Or Brian will think his work's done and let the fire go down.'

'Sausages,' Mona repeated and went out to the barbecue. 'From Sheila,' she said and handed them to him.

'More?' Brian indicated the huge pile of meat keeping hot in a dish at the side of the fire. 'I'm melting here as it is.'

'What about a cool beer?' she said.

'I could hug you,' Brian said and wiped his forehead, leaving a small black mark. Mona picked up a paper towel and wiped it away.

'One beer,' she said. She selected a Budweiser, pulled off the top and handed it over.

Brian took it and drank deeply, his head thrown back and his Adam's apple bobbing up and down like a Halloween game. 'Aaaah, lovely.' He wiped his mouth with the back of his hand. 'That's what I like about you,' he said as he looked

184

at her. 'You know what I want. Like a sixth sense. It's a good feeling.'

Mona froze. Too intimate. Or is that what British men were like? All stiff and starchy on the outside. Open up a chink and out flows the crap. 'Must get back to my guest,' she said and searched around for James. He was seated on a blanket under the apple tree. She went across.

'Who is that giving me the evil eye?' he said.

'Who?' Mona looked around.

'The dude at the barbeque.'

'That is Brian Cartwright. Sheila's husband,' Mona said.

'Cartwright? As in Sheila Cartwright of Perkins Housing?' James said and handed her a beer.

'Sheila Cartwright is her name. I don't know anything about her work except it's something to do with housing. It's her party.'

'Oh,' James said. It wasn't followed by the usual pleasantries Mona was getting used to, things like, 'how interesting' or 'I must meet her' even 'have you known her long?' The list was endless. No. The tone of this oh was more like, oh shit. Except apart from the cow pat incident, she'd never heard James swear.

'Anything wrong?' Mona said. What was it the English did? Crossed their fingers? She wanted to cross her fingers, toes, and her eyes if possible.

At that moment Sheila came out of the kitchen. 'Everyone, please let me say one thing before the evening gets under way. I want to introduce you to Mona. Some of you know her already. She is from the other side of the pond and is the inspiration behind tonight's British version of Thanksgiving.' She searched for Mona. Her face crinkled into a smile which faded. Her eyes fixed on James, seated at Mona's side. The smile which returned would have frozen any hot meat instantly.

185

Chapter thirty-three Sheila

What the hell is he doing here? I haven't invited him. Shit, no. He must be Mona's guest. She isn't to know what a louse he is. I must warn her off. Not today. Later. I plaster on a smile. 'James, how nice to see you again.' I stretch out my hand.

James shakes it briefly. 'Yes. It was a very productive and shall we say, thought-provoking meeting?' He rolls his tongue round the words.

'Meeting?' Mona looks to me to James and back again.

I won't make a fuss. I'll simply state the bare facts. 'Yes. There was a meeting about the need for low cost housing in rural areas.'

'Isn't that a good idea?' Mona says.

I've spent most of my life keeping the peace. I can't any longer. 'It will be if we can guarantee no one gets shafted in the process. Villagers and tenants of course,' I say. Damn Mona. She should have said who she was bringing. I wouldn't have stopped him. It would have given me time to put on a more welcoming face. Something about the man irritates me. I don't trust him. I've heard all the stories about him. There's never smoke without fire.

'Perhaps we can meet for a coffee and discuss matters a little more, informally?' James says.

Is he soft talking me? Probably. I'm tougher than that. 'Yes. That would be very useful. You know where I work. My number's on the website. Give me a call.' Let him use the landline. It means I'm more in control of when he can get through. If he leaves a message, I can choose when to get back to him. Mobile phones might be great apart from one thing. You are always in danger of getting a call when you don't want it or are ill-prepared.

'Have a lovely time and look after Mona for me,' I say and escape back to the kitchen. Is there something between him and Mona? Surely not. It's too soon, isn't it? She'd hardly set foot in the country, and she was married. As if that mattered. I look through the window at the guests. This should be a great occasion. I should be proud. I don't feel that way. Somehow it has all gone horribly wrong. Not just the party. My dreams of the idyllic marriage, the beautiful home, the well brought up children, the loving husband were simply that. Dreams. Or had I allowed myself to be conned? Had I bought into the suburban dream only to find I'd created a nightmare? No. I'm being silly and emotional again. Damned hormones. The less there were, the more they wanted to make their presence felt. A giant kick up the backside to replace all the monthly PMT, the pregnancy and post-partum ups and downs in one final curtain call before a woman dries up like an old crone and no man ever looks at her again. Not that they did that now. Or if they did, I certainly hadn't noticed, and Brian wouldn't even if I ran around naked covered in glittery body paint.

I swallow hard. Get a grip. This is a party for Mona, and it will go well. For the next two hours, I swoop round the guests, tidying away plates and empty glasses, directing people to the kitchen where cheesecakes, apple pie, brownies and carrot cake can be doused in cream or dollops of ice-cream. At nine o'clock Brian shuts down the barbecue. I hand him a cold beer. 'You've done a good job,' I say. 'You deserve this.' My foot knocks against the table. There is a clatter of bottles falling over.

'People kept me well topped up,' he says.

'Not too well? Remember you're not a teenager anymore.'

'As if I needed reminding,' he says. 'Any food left in the kitchen?'

'Plenty. Help yourself.' I turn away. Is it me? Or is he being a miserable old git? I'd only wanted him to be careful.

After all the strain of the week, too many beers could make things worse. Sod it. He's old enough to look after himself, isn't he?

I check my watch. Nearly ten. Time for the fireworks. Mona had been over in the afternoon and she and Brian had set them up at the far end of the garden, away from the hen house. I clap my hands. 'At the end of any Thanksgiving party, I have been reliably informed there are fireworks. Thanks to Mona, we have our very own fourth of July display.'

There is a ripple of applause. Mona steps forward with James. 'It's my pleasure to start the display.' James hands her a lit taper. She walks towards the smallest array of Roman Candles. 'Do we have a countdown?'

'Of course,' I say. 'Come on everyone, ten, nine…'

On the sound of zero, Mona leans forward and holds the taper against the fuse. It fizzles. She steps back. I cross my fingers. With a bang, the sky is lit up with shoots of red, white, and blue stars. Thank goodness.

Brian, James, and Helen from the Old School House take turns to light the rest. Mona has retreated to the low stone wall around the garden and is gazing at the display as it unfolds. After each firework has burnt out, Helen douses them in water. It's good to have an off-duty firefighter in attendance. She should rent herself out for the evening.

The final star extinguished; the air of excitement subsides. People settle down again with a drink. It will be another couple of hours before anyone would leave. I never have a drink before everyone has been fed and after the fireworks, I pour myself a large glass of Merlot and try to find Helen to thank her for her help.

How is it at any party, it takes far longer to get around and say hallo to everyone? I've lost sight of Mona and James. Brian is somewhere. As long as he isn't intent on getting drunk. Usually, he'd end up with the guys from the pub quiz team as he plays golf with two of them. Well, he can't get lost in his own garden.

I am about to refill my glass when there is a yell, followed by shouting. 'Don't be stupid.' It's Mona's voice. There is a crash.

'What the hell?' I run towards the source of the noise. Brian is lying on the grass. He clutches his nose with one hand. Blood is seeping through his fingers. A few guests are cringing back against the wall in case anything else happens.

'The bloody pervert doesn't understand no means no,' James is saying as he rubs his right hand.

Mona pulls James away. 'It's just a silly misunderstanding,' she says. 'It's all cool. You see to Brian, and I'll take this guy home to get an ice pack on his bruises.' She shakes her head at me and mouths, sorry. 'It really isn't a big deal,' she says in a loud voice. 'These things happen.' She hurries James away.

'Not at my parties,' I mutter under my breath. I quickly change tack. 'Excitement over, everyone. A silly accident.' I help Brian to his feet and propel him to the utility room. 'In there.' I thrust him towards the stool next to the ironing board.

'I'm sorry,' Brian begins.

'Tell me tomorrow. I'm sure there's a rational explanation.' I open the freezer and pull out one of the cold compresses I'd kept in readiness for childish bumps and knocks when the grandchildren came to visit.

'I really am sorry,' Brian says. 'That man completely misunderstood.'

'Sit there while I try to keep the guests happy.' Yes. It's down to me again. All he had to do was cook some bloody sausages and burgers. I close the utility door behind me and venture outside. People are getting ready to go. No one kicks off round here. This isn't a Jeremy Kyle estate.

'There's plenty more drink,' I say. 'And there's food.'

189

It is no use. The party is definitely over. I am thanked profusely of course and told over and over how marvellous it has all been and what a pity Lydia wasn't here to enjoy it. I smile and do my best to act the gracious hostess. Trust Brian to screw it up again.

Within half an hour everyone has drifted away. A few helpful guests have collected up the plates, stacked the glasses on the draining board and tidied the tables and chairs. 'Don't leave the compress on for too long,' I call to Brian. There is silence. I open the utility door. The compress has fallen on the floor and Brian is asleep, his head back, mouth open and he is snoring gently.

I pick up the compress and put it back in the freezer. I close the door on the sleeping Brian. 'You can damn well stay there all night.'

I fill the dishwasher and switch it on. I collect a bin bag and throw every remaining scrap of food into it. I place the bag in the wheelie bin and go into the garden. An owl hoots from the trees in the valley and is answered by one in the wood. It is still light enough to see the outlines of the plants in the garden. I pack up the chairs and blankets. A fox leaps over the stone wall and sniffs at the grass where someone has dropped some food. I creep back inside and find a few raw sausages and burgers. I pile them onto my hands and return. The fox is still scrabbling in the lawn. 'Here,' I whisper and drop the food on the patio. The fox jumps back, stops and eyes me as if checking whether I am dangerous. I retreat to the shadows. The fox scuttles forward and picks up the food in his or her mouth before bounding away.

Gone to feed the cubs I suppose. I lean against the kitchen wall. I'm knackered.

Chapter thirty-four Mona

'Are you angry with me?' James said as he sat in Mona's kitchen, nursing his hand.

She threw him a tea towel and fetched a bag of peas. 'Wrap the peas in this and clamp it on the bruises,' she said. 'I need some coffee.'

'A drink would be nice. For shock, I mean?'

'Fat chance,' Mona said. 'You'll get coffee, same as me.' She took her time grinding the beans, heating the water, and letting the mixture stand before pouring. It gave her time to think. She should have screamed at Brian. It was sexual harassment after all. Except that would embarrass Sheila or hurt her and she liked Sheila. What had James seen?

As far as she could remember she had gone to get a second bucket of water for the spent fireworks when Brian had sidled up behind her. 'I need to talk to you,' he had said. His slurred words were a sure sign he'd had more than a couple of beers. More like a couple of crates.

'What about?' she'd said, expecting him to spill out a sob story about Sheila. Oh yes. He did want to talk about her.

'My wife. She doesn't understand me,' he'd said.

'Crap,' she'd said. 'I don't take notice of clichés.'

'No. It's true. We never talk. Not like us. Ever since that day when I mended your boiler, there's been a connection. A special bond. Don't you feel it?'

He'd lurched towards her, and one arm went against the wall. She was trapped. One punch to his solar plexus would have done the trick and created a disturbance. What would she say? 'I just punched Sheila's husband.' No. There had to be another way.

'Don't do anything silly, Brian,' she'd said.

'I'm not,' he'd said. 'I just want to know you feel the same. You must do. You're always so attentive to me.'

As if listening politely and showing compassionate

interest was a sign of sexual attraction? 'I am always interested in the lives of my friends,' she'd said 'Stand aside and let me go.'

'You understand. That means a lot to me. The fact we can talk. You don't judge.'

'I am Sheila's friend as well as yours. Let me go.'

'Just give me some hint that there's a chance of something more.' He'd leaned closer. His beery breath warmed her cheek.

'I said let me go.'

That's when James had pulled him away and punched him. Brian had gone down like a felled tree.

'Are you mad at me?' James' voice brought her back to reality.

She poured out two cups of coffee and pushed one towards him. 'Drink that,' she said.

'Are you mad at me?' James repeated. The bluff and bluster of their first encounter had evaporated like mist over the delta on a spring morning.

'Yes. Not for me. For Sheila's sake.' How did you tell your friend her husband had made a very clumsy pass at her and got caught?

'She'll think it's me being lary again.'

'Lary?'

'Yeah. Stroppy. Awkward. It's what she thinks anyway. It'll confirm her suspicions I'm a no-good capitalist out to rip off the poor and needy of the county while I rake in huge profits to be stored in an offshore tax haven.'

'Are you?' Mona couldn't help smiling.

'Sheila will be fine. She'll blame me and all will be well.'

'What do you think she saw or heard?'

'A squeal and her old man sprawled out in the petunia patch.'

'Nothing else?'

James shook his head. 'I don't reckon she was

eavesdropping. A woman like that wouldn't stand by hearing her old man chat up another woman. She'd be in there to land the first punch.'

'I hope you're right,' Mona said.

'I know I am,' he winced. 'He's got a hard jaw.'

'He might press charges?'

'Then he'd have to accept he was sexually harassing a woman and Sheila and the whole world would get to hear about it. I don't reckon he'd want that.'

'I hope you're right,' Mona said again.

'I know I am. He's like a big bag of wind—all bluff and bluster.'

'Hand,' Mona said.

James held it out. 'Will I live, Doctor?'

Mona removed the tea towel. His hand was red and a bit puffy. 'Wiggle your fingers.' James did as he was asked. 'You'll survive. I suggest you stay here tonight, in the spare room. You've probably had too much to drink anyway.'

James sat up. He looked happy. 'That's very kind.'

'No. It means you don't get stopped by the police or cause an accident in your state and waste this poor country's resources.'

'I do appreciate it though.'

'Good. Upstairs, second white door. First white door is the bathroom. I'm sorry I don't have any spare pyjamas but there's a new toothbrush in the bathroom cabinet.'

'I'll keep my pants and shirt on,' James said.

Mona pulled a face. 'Too much information.'

James stood up. 'See you tomorrow morning?'

'Sleep well,' Mona said.

As she waited until James was settled, she cropped and resized a photo she'd taken of the table with the pies and cheesecakes. It looked so much like home. She uploaded it onto FB.

Celebrating Thanksgiving with all these fabulous desserts. The cheesecake was delicious.

That was enough. She went upstairs and listened for a moment outside James's room. He was sound asleep, judging by the rhythmic breathing. She undressed and climbed into her own bed. Had a man punched another because he was jealous? Who would have thought it possible? It was like being a teenager again. Except that sort of thing never happened to her when she was younger. Other more worldly and sophisticated kids, yes. Not her. Did it mean James had feelings towards her too? No. It was too much. He was defending her. That's all. Even so, she'd be careful from now on to remain civilised so there could never be any more misunderstandings.

It was a long night. Mona kept waking up. She'd got used to sleeping in an empty house. It was strange to know there was someone else on the other side of the partition walls. Or were these proper brick and stone? She'd ignored the temptation to go downstairs and make a cup of tea. James might hear her. At least the dawn came early at this time of year. As soon as it was a decent light, she crept out of bed, dressed, and went into the kitchen.

She jumped at every creak and groan. Why did old places do that? She filled the kettle as quietly as she could and switched it on. The sound filled the kitchen. Was it always so loud? She made a pot of coffee and sat by the window. The sun was rising above the church and there was a light mist in the valley. The blackbirds were already singing, and sparrows squabbled and fought in the dust of what had once been a lawn. The few sparse patches of grass were brown and crisp. Should she have watered it? All the times she'd walked around the village, she'd not seen one sprinkler. She sipped the coffee. What was she going to say to Sheila? If anything? What excuse had Brian made? What if he said it was her fault? She liked Sheila. She didn't want to lose her friendship.

God, what if Brian had said she had been hitting on him? How many times had she seen him? Mona counted on her fingers. The first time was when he'd come to mend the boiler. The second time was when she arrived with the fireworks. They'd gone shopping together. What had she said to him? Had she encouraged him? No. It had been very businesslike.

All she had to do was get rid of James. If she was still planning an open day of paintings, she didn't have a lot of time left. Her lease ran out in September. That was six weeks away. Would she stay longer? It was tempting. Except it still felt like a holiday and not real life and that was what she had to deal with. Real life. Or her life.

She stood up and went for a shower. The sooner she woke James up, the quicker she could get rid of him and back to her painting. She'd set a date in her mind for the exhibition; Saturday 25th August. There would be plenty of time unless she was disturbed. She clattered up the stairs and sang loudly in the shower. Sod being a good hostess. This morning, James was an unwanted guest.

James must have had hearing problems. It was gone eight by the time he stirred. As soon as Mona heard his door open, she sprang into action. 'Breakfast in fifteen,' she called. 'There's clean towels for a shower in the cabinet.'

Fifteen minutes later James appeared. His hair was wet and plastered to his head. 'Good morning,' he said.

'Help yourself to juice and coffee. The eggs are nearly ready.' Mona flipped the eggs and pushed four slices of bread in the toaster. 'How are you this morning?'

'My hand's fine,' James said. 'More to the point, how are you?'

'I'm just dandy,' she said and leaned back against the counter. 'I suppose you are referring to the unfortunate incident with Brian?'

'Yes,' James said. 'If you want to go and see him, I'll back you up.'

The toaster pinged and the smell of warm bread filled the air. Mona lifted two slices out, placed them on a plate and arranged two eggs on top. She passed the plate towards James. 'Butter, pepper and salt are on the end,' she said.

'I mean it,' James said. 'He can't behave like that.'

'Like what? Mona said and took up her place at the other end of the counter.

'Like an old letch.'

'He's just a guy who had a bit too much to drink. Let's leave it at that, shall we?'

James looked down at his plate. 'So, there isn't anything between you and Brian?'

Mona smiled. The smile became a giggle. The giggle grew until it exploded. She threw back her head and laughed. 'Me and Brian?' she said between more outbursts. 'Not likely.' She dabbed at her eyes with a tissue. 'Me and Brian?' The giggles returned. She took several deep breaths. 'All gone,' she said.

'Good.' James looked up from his plate. 'I'm pleased.'

'Eat your eggs. They're getting cold.'

There were no further references to the incident. Mona made polite talk about the weather prospects and what she was planning to do today.

James looked disappointed. 'I hoped I might be able to take you to lunch. To make up for yesterday.'

'Sorry and there was no yesterday. It was a silly misunderstanding. That's all.'

James got the hint and left soon after. Mona avoided any discussion of when they might meet again. When she closed the door behind him, she let out a huge sigh. The last thing she wanted was to get involved with a man, any man. She had an exhibition to prepare.

Chapter thirty-five Sheila

I wake to the sun piercing through a chink in the curtain. The room is silent. There is no snuffling, sleeping form beside me. Where is he? I sit up in bed. It's not my room. Of course. Shit. I remember. I'd slept in Clare's old room. Anything was preferable to being with him. Not that we'd argued. I'd cleared up and left him asleep. A few hours later I'd heard footsteps going up the stairs to our bedroom. We need to talk. Today. I refuse to wait any longer.

I step into the shower and let the water flow over me. If only it was as easy to wash away people's problems. Or people? Was Mona involved? Had she encouraged him? I can't imagine she would. I fill my hands with lemon-scented gel and smooth it over my body. I work it to a lather and scrub at my skin. The sharp smell wakes me up. No. Mona isn't like that. It is probably Brian being a drunken prat. If so, does he have questions to answer?

There is no point in getting dressed up today. I pull on a faded pink T-shirt and a pair of denim shorts. It's already hot. No need for shoes. Barefoot will do. I skip down the stairs. No wonder children like going without shoes. It's empowering and light, as if I could skip away from my troubles and they couldn't catch me. The dishwasher has ended its cycle. I unpack and repack it with the last of the glasses from last night. Urgh. The floor is sticky under my feet. It will need a wash. Later. Usually, I'd worry about breakfast. Not today. Brian is more than capable of making himself a slice of toast. All I need is some fruit. I select an apple and a few strawberries, left over from yesterday and go out to the henhouse. The sound of clucking greets me as usual. I fill their food and water containers and open the door of the henhouse. One by one they strut down the ladder and peck at the grain. 'Good morning, girls,' I say and go to the back of the henhouse. I lift the second flap.

Snuggled down in the straw are three eggs. Omelettes for lunch. I throw the finished apple core into their run and Hettie rushes after it. Always partial to a bit of apple is Hettie.

I am washing the kitchen floor when Brian appears at the foot of the stairs. 'God, my head,' he says and rubs his brow with the back of one hand.

'And your jaw?'

'What about?' he stops. 'Oh. Yes. My jaw.' He wriggles his mouth and opens and closes it. 'Fine.' He goes to the cupboard above the dishwasher. 'Any paracetamol?'

'Second shelf next to the throat sweets.' I continue to mop. I hadn't expected him so early. Why couldn't he sleep till eleven today?

'The floor's wet,' he says as he pops two pills from the blister pack.

'That's because I'm washing it,' I say and slam the mop into the bucket. 'If you want some breakfast, there's bread, eggs and the kettle's just boiled for tea of coffee.'

'Have you?' he leaves the remains of his words unsaid.

'Yes. I have had breakfast. Ages ago. You can manage a simple meal for once, can't you?' I go into the utility room and pour the dirty water down the sink. Is that a waste? Should I have used it on the garden? Too late. I escape onto the patio with my tablet. I need a breathing space before I tackle Brian. It is not to be.

He sits down at the metal table and places two mugs of coffee on it. 'I thought you might like one,' he says and pushes a mug towards me. 'It's that new blend from the deli.'

He is trying. Perhaps I shouldn't be too hard on him. 'About last night?'

'I was an idiot,' Brian says.

'Yes, and an embarrassment.'

'I know. I was pissed.' He places his hands over his face.

'I'm a failure. At work. At home. As a father. As a husband.'

His shoulders are shaking.

I stay where I am. Every fibre in my body wants to be the nurturer, the carer, to take charge and say, "Let mummy kiss it better". It is too late for that. I take a deep breath. 'As far as I'm concerned, you've been a selfish, miserable git for the last few months. Before that you took me for granted and belittled any attempts I made to get a life for myself. You have one. You have plenty. All I had for years was the kids and the home.' That's more like it.

He looks up and wipes his eyes with the back of his hand. 'I thought that was what all women wanted?'

'Really? We've been married for thirty-three years. Life has changed. I've changed.'

'How?' Brian says.

'Jesus Christ, Brian. Isn't that for us to find out?' He looks confused. I relent and kneel down in front of him and place my hands on his knees. 'If we are going to make a go of this marriage after all this time, we need to understand each other. And that life is…well different. Expectations are different.'

'It was fine for my mum.'

'Your mum's life suited her. Your dad's life suited him. I'm not your mum.'

'What do you want?' Brian says. 'I can't reckon any divorce lawyer will grant you what you want on the basis of one small mistake.'

I stand up. 'One small mistake? Haven't you listened to a word I've been saying?'

'Yes. I have,' Brian says and winces. 'Bloody headache.'

'Self-inflicted. I have no sympathy.' I take a deep breath. 'If you have been listening to me, we need to talk about what is wrong between us and how it's happened, don't we?'

He holds up one hand. 'I understand. You're not happy. Well neither am I.'

199

He is back playing the little boy again. This time he isn't getting away with it. I sit back down on the chair opposite him. 'I don't think either of us can communicate with the other at the moment. We need a third party. Couples' counselling. If that doesn't work, we might have to do something different. Live more separate lives, perhaps?' Damn. I hadn't meant to say it. When it popped out, I realise it is a huge relief. Have I been holding everyone together for the sake of appearing the perfect married couple?

'What?' Brian's face turns pale.

'You heard.'

'If you think I'm going into some arty-farty room with a stranger who wants me to express my feelings or tell them I had a repressed childhood and I want to sleep with my mother, you can count me out.'

'That's crap. Counselling is more about being an adult and talking issues through. Like conciliation between management and unions.'

'Which of us goes on strike? I don't fancy a picket line in the lounge.'

I smile. For a moment there is a flash of the old Brain I'd fallen in love with years ago. 'It's a chance for us both to move onto the next stage. We're not mummy and daddy with little children anymore.'

'More's the pity.' Brian's voice is quiet.

'That was a good time, wasn't it? For us? I mean. You and me? We knew who we were. We didn't have a lot of cash. We didn't have much of anything. Somehow it didn't matter.'

'Do you remember making our own Christmas cards and crackers? We didn't have any snaps so had to shout BANG when they broke?'

'What happened?' I say the words as much to myself as to Brian. As soon as I say the words, I know. We'd put stuff before anything else and had bought into the dream that stuff makes us happy. Is that why we are at the beck and call of the children?

'Life happened,' Brian says. 'The big question is what do we want to do about it?'

'Our life has to change,' I say.

'That's easy enough for me. No job. No money once the redundancy payout has gone.'

'You can get another one, can't you? Or we can swap roles for a while. How do you fancy being a house husband?' I make it into a joke. I am deadly serious.

'It'll be one of a number of changes,' Brian says. 'To tell the truth, I don't want to go back to the world I was in. I'd like to do something for a charity.'

'Would anyone at the golf club have a lead? You've got some pretty good friends there, haven't you?'

'Not really,' Brian says. 'I called the treasurer and told them I might be late in paying the fees. He wasn't very helpful and to tell you the truth, I'm crap at the damn game. Can't see the point somehow.'

'Why do it then?'

'It's all part of the image, isn't it? Important job, flashy car, time at the nineteenth hole?'

I look out of the garden towards the hills covered in the deep green leaves of high summer. 'We were suckered in, weren't we? All this talk at university about being our own people, making our own lives, not following the crowd like our parents and what did we do?'

'We followed a different crowd. A very persuasive crowd too.'

'Will it work?' I say.

'We can give it a try, can't we?'

'Yes. We can give it a try.' I take the cups into the kitchen.

Brian follows. 'Let me get us some lunch. I can make a

sandwich,' he says.

I am about to tell him not to bother. I don't. 'That will be great,' I say. 'I'll have a glass of wine and catch up with the papers.'

There is a very long way to go but we have to start somewhere, don't we?

Chapter thirty-six Mona

Mona screwed up the piece of paper. She threw it on the floor. It joined a dozen others. She looked round the studio. Had she done enough? There were twenty paintings, three dozen small cards. The big watercolour of the valley was nearly completed. Did she need a few more? If she was honest, some of her efforts were tawdry. Most in fact. How on earth did she believe she had any talent? Why did she tell everyone about the exhibition? No one would come and anyone who did would see her daubings were no more than a poor amateur. Yet that Karen woman had wanted one. Mona pulled another piece of paper from her folder and picked up a soft pencil. She had to do a picture of the pub. The stonework was so typical.

Mona wiped a bed of sweat from her top lip. If anyone ever said England was cold and damp, she'd put them right. Day after scorching day was interspersed with sticky nights. Every window upstairs was thrown open in the hope of a breeze. There was none. She went to the sink and ran the water. It was so hot the water in the pipes was warm unless she let it flow for a few minutes. She filled a glass and drank deeply. Since the disastrous party at Sheila's, she'd spent every minute painting, distracting herself from the one question that haunted her waking moments. Sheila had texted of course. Mona had replied politely. That was it. The trouble was she missed her. Mona screwed up another piece of paper. She flopped down on the chair and looked at her phone again. She could call. Ask to pop round? No. She might see Brian.

What could she say? Perhaps if she left some space between them, Sheila might say something. Yes. That was it. She'd let Sheila speak first. If she didn't, it was all dead and gone. *Least said, soonest mended* as her old gran would say. What was her excuse? An idea pinged into her head. The

Wild Girls? What had happened to them?

She picked up her phone and called. It went to voice mail.

> *Hi Sheila*
> *How are you? How's work? Just calling in case I've missed some communication about the next meeting of the Wild Girls. I remember someone talking about wild swimming at a place near here. The weather is perfect.*
> *Let me know. If not, perhaps we can meet up for coffee or lunch?*
> *xxx Mona*

That would be the best way forward. She took a deep breath and returned to her painting. It would work out.

It was later that evening when the text came through.

> *Hi Mona*
> *Sorry not to be in touch. How are you fixed for breakfast tomorrow? We could meet at the shop at nine. They do a great bacon sandwich. If you can't wait that long for breakfast, the cappuccinos are tasty.*
> *Sheila.*

Mona smiled. It was going to be all right.

> *Nine tomorrow. Can't wait.*

She poured herself a glass of wine and sat outside as the sun dipped below the trees and the chorus of evening birdsong faded to be replaced by the faint call of an owl. It was the first decent night's sleep she'd had for weeks.

'Say nothing. Act cool,' she repeated as she dodged the children hurtling along Lower Street to the school. So much nicer than being bussed. A whistle sounded. The shouts subsided. That's why they were in a rush. Daren't risk the wrath of a teacher or a late mark. Kids are the same the world over.

She sidestepped a mother with a buggy and walked down the narrow path to the shop. The windows and doors were already wide open. 'I'm looking for Sheila,' she said.

'We're looking for Lydia,' Jen said. 'Have you seen her?'

'No. Not for ages,' Mona said. 'I thought she was on holiday.'

'She was. She's been coming in to help most mornings. This is the first one she's missed.'

'Give her a call,' Mona suggested.

'I've done that. There's no reply.'

'Do you want me to check on her after I've been to the studio?'

At that moment Sheila burst through the open door. She was wearing a pale lemon T-shirt and cream stretch cropped trousers. Had she gotten a face lift? She looked younger. 'Hi, Mona, how are you?'

'Good,' said Mona and returned the kiss on both cheeks. 'Jen here was saying she was expecting Lydia today. I said I could pop in on my way home and check on her?'

'No need. Her son's back in England for a short stay. She told me they were planning on a few bits of DIY on the house.'

Jen frowned. 'It's not like her to miss a session at the shop. She's been regular since...'

'I'll give Chris a call if you want and find out what's up.'

'Please,' said Jen. 'I'd pop over myself except we're short of cover today.'

'Consider it done,' Sheila said. 'Only if you can provide two cappuccinos and two bacon rolls?'

'Coming up' Jen said and bustled into the kitchen.

'Do you want to eat inside or out?'

'Outside will be lovely,' Mona said. 'No one will believe me when I tell them how hot it's been.'

'Let me take a photo of you,' Sheila said.

Mona handed over her phone. They went outside and Mona sat at the small table in front of the shop. She put on her sunglasses. 'I reckon this will suit,' she said.

'Great. Smile.' Sheila clicked and handed the phone back.

'I'll upload this now,' Mona said.

'Can you see with your sunglasses on? I end up sending the wrong thing to the wrong person.'

'Technically challenged I am not,' Mona said. 'There. When the West Coast wakes up, they'll see me sunning myself.'

'That's what I can't get over. I thought it was always hot on the West Coast.'

They were skirting round the subject. Mona changed tack. 'I want to say a very big thank you for the party. I'm not going to apologise for James. He was an asshole.'

'I won't apologise for Brian. He was an even bigger…er asshole.'

Mona lifted her hand in a high five. 'Heh, girl, it says it all. Asshole is the only way to describe some men.'

'And their behaviour. At least I knew James could be an …'

'Asshole,' Mona suggested.

'I expected better from my husband.'

'Was it the job?' Sheila raised one eyebrow. 'He told me about the promotion he wanted. Did he lose out?'

Sheila nodded. 'Big time. He resigned and we have a lot to talk about.'

Mona's heart froze. 'Uh huh?' What had he said? Was it about her?

'I told him a few home truths and how I want some changes. I've been the good wife and devoted mummy for far too long. I want some time for me.'

"So, you guys are cool?'

Sheila shook her head. 'No. We've got a long way to go. We are talking and there's plenty to talk about. What happens after the talking depends.'

'On what?'

'On whether we still want the same things.'

'If not?'

Sheila turned her face half away from Mona. 'I suspect he wants changes too. We'll try to work it out.' She turned back to Mona. 'Thanks for reminding me of the Wild Girls. It was Mary who was going to arrange the swimming session. I called her this morning and if you're on, we plan to go this Saturday.'

'Tell me more,' Mona said. The other subject was closed. Obviously, Brian had said nothing, and Sheila hadn't heard Brian's attempts at a chat up line. He'd get over it. He had more important things to think about with Sheila. The relief was huge.

'Here's Jen with our breakfast. How do you fancy some wild swimming on Saturday?'

Jen placed two large granary rolls, encrusted with poppy seeds and grains on the table. Out of each one hung rashers of grilled bacon. 'What's wild about it? Not wild animals I hope?' she said and unloaded two frothy cappuccinos, doused in chocolate, and a bottle of ketchup and one of brown sauce from a wooden tray.

'No. We head out to Chester Park. There's a specially designated swimming area in the lake,' Sheila said.

'Ooh, will it be muddy and slimy?' Jen said. 'What about changing?'

'There's little booths to change and we get into the water from a jetty. There's no need to put your feet down. We swim around. The water is cool and silky.' Sheila hugged her arms round her body. 'I went with the children years

207

ago. It was so beautiful, surrounded by trees and meadows.'

'Better get me cossie out of moth balls,' Jen said. 'Text me the time and place and if you need a lift, I'll get Martin to drive us. We could have a picnic?'

Sheila clapped her hands. 'Great idea. Let's get the men to drive us and we can have Prosecco and smoked salmon sandwiches with strawberries and cream. I'll contact Moira and she can send out lists for donations of food. There's plenty of paper cups and plates left from the barbecue and most people have at least one cool box.'

'Count me in,' Jen said. 'We must remember to pack rugs to sit on.'

'It'll be like Ratty' s picnic from *The Wind in the Willows* ' Sheila said. 'Although perhaps not. Mole did sink the boat, didn't he?'

Jen laughed as she went back into the shop. 'I'm swimming, not boating,' she said.

Mona lifted her cappuccino. 'To the next Wild Girls event.'

Sheila lifted her cup in reply. 'The Wild Girls swimming party, with picnic.'

Mona tapped her cup against Sheila's. How strange so many events ended with food. It was like being a child again when cookouts happened every weekend. 'To swimming and picnics,' she said.

Chapter thirty-seven Sheila

I knock on the door of Lydia's cottage. 'Hi, Chris, I didn't realise you were back,' I say to the young man who answers the door.

'Yes. I'm back for a good while. Mum's sorting through some old photos. Do you want to come in and see her?'

'Can I? It's just she was expected at the shop today and everyone was a bit worried when she didn't turn up.'

Chris slaps his hand to his forehead. 'Sorry. That's my fault. I'm trying to get both of us organised. I'm not quite up to speed with her extensive social life,' he says and grins. He steps back from the doorway.

I follow him into the cottage. Lydia is seated at the table in the lounge. In front of her is a pile of photos. She picks up each in turn and stares before placing it in one of two groups. She looks up. 'Oh, Sheila, nice to see you.'

'And you. What's all this?' I indicate the table.

'That's Chris's idea,' Lydia says. 'He's getting all the advice he can on my condition. Reckons a memory book with photos and the names of people in my life will help later on.'

'Really?' My voice squeaks in shock.

'Don't sound so outraged,' Lydia says. 'I'm used to the idea. I plan to get all my affairs in order before…I suppose I should say before it's too late.'

'It's just a precaution, Mum. That won't happen for years.' Chris pokes his head round the kitchen door.

'It will happen sooner than you realise,' Lydia says and is quiet.

'Enough talk like that,' I say briskly. 'Jen was expecting you today at the shop. I'll say it was an oversight.'

Lydia frowns and looks at Chris. 'Was I supposed to be there?'

Chris puts his hands together as if he was praying. 'My

fault again',' he says. 'I need a bigger board for all your activities.'

'It was the same when the children were young,' I say and feel a pang of regret. Would I want to go back to those days with playdates, as they're called now, sleepovers not to mention after school clubs, homework, and music lessons.

'Mum was an expert at organising us too,' Chris says. 'Do you want a cup of tea? I was about to make one.'

'No. I can't stay. This is a flying visit. Brian and I are in the middle of, let's say some restructuring.'

'Building work?' Lydia says. 'Chris wants to put a shower room where the larder used to be. I'm not sure.'

'It's for your future, Mum,' he says and leans over to kiss the top of her head.

'Stop fussing,' she says and shoos him away. 'Well?' she looks at me.

'Nothing as grand, more restructuring our life,' I say and hope she'll leave it at that.

'Good luck,' Lydia says. 'Pop in again, will you?'

'Yes. I'll do that as soon as I can. Will you see me out, Chris?'

'Of course.'

I stop on the front step. 'She seems very lucid. What's the prognosis?'

'No change and no chance of any miracle cures. Today it's as if Mum is back in control. Yesterday she couldn't put on her shoes. Tomorrow? Who knows?'

'Not much point of me asking her to the Wild Girls event?'

'Unless it is very familiar and close to home, no. On bad days I don't let her out of my sight.'

'Thank goodness she's got you. If it gets too much, let me know,' I say.

'I will. Tom and I are putting aside some cash for extra support when we need it.'

210

'She's lucky to have you,' I say.

'Your children would do the same,' Chris says.

I say nothing. I doubt they'd lift a hand. 'I'll pop round later this week.'

'Yes. Take care.' He closes the door behind him, and I make my way home, walking in the shade of the hedges and trees to avoid the heat of the sun.

Brian is at the kitchen table. The contents of what we call *The Croak File*, all the documents about the mortgage, insurances and savings are spread out in front of him. A pile of what looks like the utility bills, broadband, telephone, and heaven knows what else teeters on the edge. He has a calculator and is scribbling figures on a piece of paper.

'Anything wrong?'

'Might as well get started,' he says and looks up. 'You do realise I don't want to go back to the work I did, even if I could get a job.'

My heart constricts. 'Was it that bad?'

He snorts 'Pah. I knew as soon as the new CEO took over, I was a dead man walking.'

'Why was that?'

'New brooms like their own people in key positions.'

'Why did you apply?' It is the first time I'd heard any of this. Poor Brian. He'd lived for his work, or so I'd thought. Had I been wrong? Or had he used this as an excuse while I'd been wrapped up in my own life?

'I couldn't go without a fight,' he says 'I took a chance and lost.'

'Surely that means you're entitled to redundancy pay. Severance? You have rights, don't you?'

Brian takes a deep breath. 'I resigned. I refused their offer of an alternative.' He makes the signs of speech marks with his fingers.

'Would it have been so bad?'

He tilts his head on one side. 'Imagine having to work for the James bloke you've been moaning about for weeks? More work, less staff, same money, and same expectations. That's about it. I was being sidelined and I'd have to take orders from some of the people I'd trained up. Oh, she knew what she wanted. It wasn't a blast from the past, like me.'

'I understand.' One encounter with James has been enough for me to realise I need to feel respected and valued to work with a person. That's why I like Karen. A boss or co-worker like James would be a nightmare.

'Do you? I've worked for that bloody firm, helped build them up, brown nosed the movers and shakers on the board, and this is the result. I wasn't taking charity.'

'Yes,' I speak firmly. 'I do understand. The thing we have to work out is what we do now.'

Brian indicates the papers spread before him. 'That's exactly what I'm doing or attempting.'

'Can I help?' I sit down. 'I can input all the outgoings and income into a spread sheet.'

'Taking us into the twenty-first century and dragging the old man kicking with you?'

Here it was again. The old Brian. The cheekiness. The ability to make fun of himself. 'I'm surprised you're not sitting here with a quill pen and a double entry ledger. You'd be like Scrooge in the film.'

'Well Bob Cratchit, make us a cup of tea and we'll get started.'

I fill the kettle. While I wait for it to boil, I go outside. All my precious plants in the vegetable garden are spindly, despite attempts at watering. The peas and beans are late, and the potatoes stunted. The grass crackles under my feet. It is like walking on toast. I refill the bird bath with clean water. A starling flies down and flutters above the surface before landing and splashing itself. Water falls onto the withered lawn. I'll have to refill it later. The poor birds mustn't suffer.

'Here you are,' I say and place a mug at Brian's elbow. 'Where do I start?'

He holds out a list. 'As far as I can work out, these are the outgoings we can't avoid; Council Tax, utilities, insurances that sort of thing.'

'Great. I'll start with expenditure.' I pause. 'Do you remember how we had to budget when we first bought this place? I reckon we counted every penny.'

'We had to. We still might.'

'That sounds ominous.'

'We'll find out sooner or later,' Brian says and picks up a sheaf of papers about the mortgage.

I open the laptop and create a new file. *Budget 2018*

After half an hour Brian hands me another sheet. 'This is our income if you work three days a week and I get a job that brings in twenty thousand and I'm being very optimistic.'

I don't need any formula to calculate the difference. It is obvious before I type in our income in the required field and hit *enter*. A red figure appears in the small box I'd labelled *EXTRAS*. It is meant to cover holidays, unexpected bills, repairs, clothes, and the odd meal out or trip to the theatre. Is this what we'd worked for? I scan the figures and check again. I show Brian the screen.

'I thought as much. We'll have to cut back,' he says.

'What if you can't get a decent job?'

'We cut back some more. Let's check where we can make any savings.'

'Don't forget my additional pay,' I say.

'What?'

'I told you ages ago about my promotion. It'll mean more money and I will be working full time.'

Brian claps a hand to his forehead. 'Sorry. I've been so

caught up, I'd forgotten.'

Another hour passes, Satellite TV is ditched first. A new deal on the electricity and gas nets a saving. The household bills can be reduced. It will be tight. We can do it, just. With my extra money, we'll still have a bit for extras. Not as much as we want.

'Of course, I need a car,' Brian says. 'The company one has gone back. That'll have to come from our savings.'

'I know we didn't want the children to have a debt, so we paid for their university course. I thought we'd have had a bit more of a buffer than that,' I say. I'm angry. How had we let this happen? Why hadn't I taken more interest?

'It was the extension, the new garage and the kitchen,' Brian says. 'It took up a chunk of our savings and we extended the mortgage, remember?'

'We'll be OK, won't we?' I never dreamed we'd end up in debt or worse, impoverished like my father.

'If I get a decent job. Yes. If not...' Brian looks at me. 'We could downsize. That would help a lot.'

'Downsize? There's not a lot of smaller cottages in the village. When they do come up for sale, they're snapped up.'

'Who says we have to stay?'

'Are you serious? I thought you loved it here?' Is that the answer? Leave the village where I've got so many friends. Where I know every path and walkway? It was something I'd thought about when we were older. Not yet. 'Perhaps you can find another way of earning a bit of cash. What about your woodwork?'

Chapter thirty-eight Mona

What did a fifty something wear to a swimming party? Mona held up the black one-piece before shoving it aside. So, she was plump. Who cares? There were plenty of worse things than carrying a few extra pounds. She had to finalise the list of paintings for the exhibition. It was less than a month away. Did she have enough? She closed the front door of Lavender Cottage and headed down the narrow alleyway to her studio. She waved to Jim with the immaculate garden. How did he do it? He had produced a succession of fruit and vegetables and his glass houses were stuffed with tomatoes, peppers, cucumbers, and chillies. She'd met him as she'd leaned over the hedge to admire his efforts. He'd spoken to her and that was it. Funny how eager people were to talk when you lived in the countryside.

She walked on, past the playgroup. The children were all wearing sun hats and their skins shone with the slick of sun cream. At least a dozen were kicking a ball around until someone who as yet had not grasped the rules of soccer picked it up and ran off to screams and shouts and the odd tear. A few were seated on a mat under the tree, engrossed in their own games of make believe with toy cars, planes, dolls and teddies. Had she missed out by not having children? Probably. She wasn't convinced. Some women are natural mothers. She was not. Her mother had felt the same. Her life revolved around bridge, golf, and personal grooming. A lumpy daughter with no sense of style and little interest in the latest fashions must have been such a disappointment.

Mona unlocked the door of the studio. Cool air wafted out. She stepped inside and pulled back the curtains. Time to start work. For the next two hours she checked each item against the description for the brochure. The plain white frames Sheila had volunteered Brian to make suited the images and made it uniform. She'd take another batch to him this afternoon. Sheila had said he'd had no luck with finding a job. Mona made a note to give him a bonus when the task was over. Not that she had much to spare. She hadn't budgeted for canvas, paint, and paper as it was.

'Anyone home?' A familiar voice called through the open door.

'Come in, James,' she said as he came towards her holding out two soft and melty ice-cream cones.

'Better than coffee. Best eat it while it resembles ice-cream.'

'Thanks.' Mona took the cone and licked the dribbles of white and pink liquid before they reached her fingers.

James plonked himself in a chair and swirled his tongue round the top. 'Nothing is better on a hot day than an ice-cream.'

'Or any day.'

'I won't disagree,' James said. 'How's it all going?'

'Perfect. I've got another ten for Brian to frame and I'm done. I wish the Open Day was closer.'

'I don't,' James said and bit the end of the cone. He chewed before answering. 'It means you've got no more reasons to stay. Perhaps I should steal them in the middle of the night.'

Mona frowned. 'What for?'

'Like Penelope who kept unravelling her weaving each night, so she'd never finish the shroud she'd promised.'

'A bit grisly, isn't it?'

James crunched the last of his cone. 'Not when you realise, she was using the trick to keep away unwanted suitors,' he said.

'Well, I'm not fighting off any would-be suitors. Am I?'

James looked at her and folded his arms over his pale green polo shirt. 'Aren't you?'

'No. If you're still thinking about Brian, that was all a

silly thing on his part. He didn't mean anything by it. I can tell you, hand on heart, there is no one remotely interested in a middle-aged Yank like me.'

'Are you sure?'

'Yes.' Even as she said the words, she knew it wasn't completely true. Brian had used her as a dream, an escape from the stress of the job and his home life. She'd done the same, although not with a man, with a dream, her dream of escaping here. It had kept hope alive for months if not years. That was what most people needed, hope for the future. She stalled. 'Are you telling me you know someone in this village who has feelings for me?' She raised a hand to her face and fluttered it like a caricature of a Southern Belle.

'I do.' James said. 'Me.'

That was all she needed. 'Jesus you British aren't backward in coming forward. So much for the stiff upper lip. Or does that help?' A few jokes would lighten the situation.

James ignored the jokes. 'I'm serious,' he said. 'I want to know if you have any feelings for me. Or if you might have in the future?'

How could she let him down? It was the last thing she'd wanted. Brian? That was simply a depressed man in desperate need of a boost to his morale. James was different. Yes, he was pleasant enough to be with and good looking, once he'd abandoned the hunting, shooting, fishing image of the hillbillies. She simply wasn't ready. She might never be ready for another relationship again. Did it matter? She'd come over here for space and to heal. That's what she still needed. 'I'm very flattered you think of me in that way.' Jeez, was that a line from Jane Austen?

'I know. Don't tell me, you're happy being single.'

'For the moment. Yes.'

James' eyes flashed. 'Does that mean things might

change?'

'Things might be different once I'm divorced, everything is settled and I'm back home. For the moment, there's been too much upset for me recently to consider another relationship.'

'You don't sound too sure,' James said.

'I'm damaged goods.'

'I don't believe that,' James said. He changed tack. 'We've all got baggage of some sort.'

'Some baggage is harder to shift than others,' Mona said. She held out her hand. '*Friendship is certainly the finest balm*, as Jane Austen once wrote.'

'Yes. Didn't she continue with the words *for the pangs of disappointed love*?'

'Oops. Someone knows his Jane Austen. I would have thought you were more Stephen King. Or Ludlum? Dan Browne, even?'

'The beauty of a 1970s English education was that English Literature O level blasted Shakespeare and the classics at you for two years. The quotes you had to learn are learnt for life,' he said. He shook her hand. 'I'll be content with friendship for the moment,' he said.

'Thank you,' Mona said and squeezed his hand. 'That means a lot to me.'

'If you change your mind?' James said.

'I won't,' Mona said. 'If you don't mind, I've got more work to do.'

'Of course.' James stood up. 'Give me some flyers when you've got them printed and I'll spread them round. You might be discovered and get so many commissions you'll have to stay.'

Mona shook her head. 'You wish.'

'Yes,' James said. 'I do wish.' He tipped an imaginary hat. 'Here's looking at you, kid.'

'I'll be in touch,' Mona said. 'You must come to the open

218

event.'

'I'll be there.' James tipped the imaginary hat again and closed the door behind him.

'Well, girl, did you ever expect two declarations of love when you set foot in the place?' She shook her head. 'Crazy, just crazy.' Except what James had said about getting people to come to the open day wasn't crazy. She collected ten of her favourite paintings and lodged them along the wall outside her studio. She propped the door open. She'd take a photo and put it on Facebook. Some of her friends might ask to buy one of the paintings of the countryside.

She arranged the paintings and got out her phone. The sun was too bright. She moved them closer to the stone wall. That was better. If she took the image at an angle, she'd get a nice view of the steep pathway to the side. The piercing blue of the sky accentuated the greyish stone of the wall and the crisp white frames of her paintings. It matched the white of the street sign with its black letters. The pale pastel shades of her artwork fitted perfectly. It all looked very English, very rural, and old worldly. There was a romantic dreamlike quality about the photo. It fitted. For the last few months she'd been in a dream-like world; a world so far removed from her previous existence she shuddered at the contrast. Yet there was something to be said about the urban bustle. She loved both. If there was any way she could combine them, she'd be in heaven.

That evening she posted the photo on Facebook. Within a few minutes she'd got a dozen likes and two comments. One from someone who wanted her painting of the church. She'd been vague about questions as to where it was. She'd message the person once she was back home with details. No one could tell from a picture, could they?

Chapter thirty-nine Sheila

I leave Brian sleeping. Since the bombshell of his suggestion about downsizing, I'd scoured online house sale websites for possibilities. There are none. No. That is wrong. There are plenty if we're prepared to move away. I'm not. Not yet. We can keep up the mortgage repayments for a year. After that we'll have used up most of our savings. If Brian doesn't find a decent job, we'll face that later. I reverse the car and set off down the hill towards the town and the by-pass. The sun has already scorched the blue from the sky. Windows of the houses I pass are flung wide open. Anything for a breath of air. The forecast promises no respite. The trees are already dull green, dusty and parched. It will be an early autumn and a long winter. I flick on the radio. It's about the fires on the hillsides. Poor people in the north. Who would have guessed a place renowned for its damp weather would succumb so easily? Could it happen here? No. The hilltops are grass, not bracken and the woodlands are full of sappy beech and ash.

I switch to a classical music channel. That's better. I pull into the car park. Should I sell the car and use the bus regularly, not when I feel like it? That's a tough ask. I'll need it for work, for meetings and appointments with people in their homes. Perhaps Brain will be the one who has to use the bus? Upstairs in the office Karen is leaning back in her chair fanning herself. 'Phew. Did you know you can't buy an electric fan in the whole of England? Remind me to order half a dozen for next year,' she says as I sit down at my desk.

'You'll never use them,' I tease. 'I reckon next year we'll be in a mini ice age. That's how predictable our weather is, global warming or no global warming.'

'James Frobisher has been on the phone already. He says he would like some tenants lined up for October. Reckons he can get the units finished by the second week.' She pulls a face. 'Units? Why can't he call them flats? Bedsits? Maisonettes?'

'Isn't that what everything is today? Units of some sort?'

'Anyway, I said I'd pass the matter onto you.'

'You do realise I'm not his greatest advocate?' I don't mention the incident at the party between him and Brian.

Karen stops fanning herself. 'There's one thing I know about you and that is you will carry out all your duties with absolute professionalism.' She smiles. 'Let me know what you come up with by the end of the week.'

I sit down. A warm glow spreads from head to toe. Karen trusts me. She regards me as a professional. After all the years of being Mum, Sheila on the PTA and *my wife*, I am a professional. All the hundreds of years of imprinting that a woman should be a good mother and a dutiful wife dissolve like salt in hot stew. It had been important at the time. Now though I am forging a life as Sheila the professional and it feels great. 'I'm onto it.'

It is nearly four o'clock and I have identified six families and four individuals who would benefit from rehousing. Half are known to social services. I leave messages with the social workers to get in contact. The office phone rings. 'I'll take it,' I call to Karen who is fixing everyone a cold drink. 'Perkins Alternative Housing Association.'

'Afternoon, Sheila. Is Karen around?'

It's James. 'She's busy right now. Can I take a message?'

'Yes. We spoke this morning about the possibility of selling off the smaller three-bedroom cottage to provide a bit of funding for the conversion of the two maisonettes. 'I've got another proposition that I'd like to run by her.'

'I'll see if she's free.'

Karen must have heard me. She takes the phone and mouths *thanks*.

'James, what can I do for you?'

I go into the kitchen area and finish the drinks which I take round the office. By the time I get to Karen's she is typing frantically.

She takes the drink. 'Our Mr Frobisher is never short of new ideas,' she says.

'Good ones?'

'What do you think of using one of the two-bedroomed maisonettes as a tied house for a general handy man, supporter, friendly face to the more vulnerable tenants?'

'It could be perfect if the right person exists,' I say. 'Is this what the money from the sale of the three-bedroomed will be used for?'

Karen nods. 'If we could do any sale privately it would save a lot on estate agent's fees, and it might be quicker. Do you know of anyone?'

'No. I don't,' I say.

'No matter. I'm letting the Trustees know about the proposed change of plans. James is certain he can get the builders to readjust the specs. The only issue is it will mean two less units, but it might make it easier to place vulnerable tenants.'

'It's something we've talked about before.'

'Yes. James reckons it was you who gave him the idea.'

'Me?'

'Reckons he took notice of your arguments about people in villages being isolated. This could be the answer and provide a small job for someone.'

I go back to my work. This would make it easier for me to find suitable tenants and with support, there would be no feeling they had been dumped on the local community. Have I misjudged James?

It's six-thirty in the evening. Brian is cooking. I am doing nothing. It is weird. I feel guilty. My phone rings. It is Mark. 'Heh how's the job going?'

'Brilliant,' he says. 'We're getting full houses for the

shows and the comedy open mic is going down well too. The poets don't drink enough though.'

'I thought that was part of the deal. Get drunk and write poetry.'

'Not now,' Mark says. 'It's all very serious.'

'I see.' I wait. What does he want? Mark never phones for a polite or interested enquiry about us.

'This new flat I'm renting with a bunch of friends; we need a deposit.'

'That's not unusual.'

'The thing is the others are a bit short, so I offered to pay up front.'

'Very generous of you.'

'Can you lend me some money?'

There it is. The usual bleat. 'How much?'

'Great, Mum, you're a diamond.'

'I haven't agreed. How much?'

'Twelve hundred?'

'Pounds?' I squeak.

'Not Euros, with Brexit and all that,' Mark says and laughs.

'Don't try to be funny. Are you telling me that between the four of you, you can't find three hundred quid each?'

'That's the trouble. We don't have any savings. Not like people of your generation. Life's far more expensive for us.'

I switch to speaker phone and walk up the stairs. I fling open Mark's bedroom door. 'From what I can see, you have two games consoles, a number of old phones, a CD player, a DAB radio and downstairs in the garage are two decent off-road bikes. Why not sell them?'

'That might cover my share. What about the others? I said I'd get the cash.' His voice is quavering.

'Grow up, Mark. Your friends have probably got as much useless crap lying round as you. Get them to sell and you'll be fine.'

'I promised.'

'Sorry. You promised something you can't deliver. However hard it is, that's the fact of the matter. With your father's redundancy, we're short of cash too.' I walk back down the stairs. Brian pokes his head round the kitchen door. He mouths 'OK?' I nod and mouth back, 'Tell you later.'

Mark's voice sounds through the room. 'That's not very fair. I bet if Claire needed cash, you'd help out. What if the twins needed to go on a school trip?'

'I'd say the same. We've supported both of you for too long. We need to conserve funds and that means no handouts.' As I say the words, I hear the familiar accusatory voices in my head. *Call yourself a decent mother? Anyone else would make the effort.* This time I ignore them.

'I didn't realise.'

'Well, you do now,' I say.

'Sorry, Mum. I suppose I'd better collect my stuff at the weekend.'

'There's a few toys that would fetch a tidy sum on eBay. All your Beyblades and Doctor Who stuff must be worth a bit.'

'That's my childhood,' Mark lets out a wail.

'It's long past,' I say. 'Use everything to create a better future.' God, I sound like an advertising campaign for some New Age fad. 'Clear the clutter today for a brighter tomorrow.'

'I suppose I'll have to,' Mark says.

'Yes.' My voice softens. 'I suppose you will.' I change tack. 'If you plan to be here at the weekend, let me know in advance. Your father and I might be going out.' I end the call. I stand for a moment and blink hard. I've done it. I finally stood up for myself, like Mona would. She'd never take any nonsense from anyone. There is the sound of someone clapping their hands.

Brian is leaning against the door frame. 'Well done. Tough love is always tough. It's what's often needed.'

'I feel so awful,' I say.

He holds out his arms. 'Come here, old girl.'

I run towards him and let him hold me tightly. It is the closest we have been in months.

Chapter forty Mona

At least the weather was still warm. Mona drew back the curtains to let in the sunlight. No one would ever believe her when she told them back home that England could be hot. She checked herself. That was the first time she'd admitted she planned to go home. Yes, she'd told everyone she'd be staying till September. It had all seemed so distant in April. Here she was in late July. September was only a few weeks away. It was beautiful here and she'd made some fabulous friends. She'd have stories to tell till Thanksgiving about the quirky village, quaint town, and breath-taking countryside. And yet she couldn't stay. She had to go back. She had to face Ethan and demand a divorce and her share of the settlement. She flexed her knuckles. Just let him try to weasel his way out of this one. She'd already checked out real estate prices and could afford a small apartment in East Santa Cruz. That would suit her. She could rent gallery space and her savings would cover her till her pension was released, providing she wasn't too extravagant. It would be fine.

She put on the one-piece swimsuit, added a yellow T-shirt and shorts. She must remember to take her bra and panties, or she'd be going commando on the way home. At least she was driving to allow Sheila and two others to have a drink. Wine. That was another thing to remember, and it needed to be properly chilled.

The swimming area was in the grounds of an old derelict mansion. Someone had created a platform to enter the water which was greenish brown, even on such a bright sunny day. It looked cool and inviting. Sheila had spread a tartan rug on the grassy bank, away from the families and teens who had commandeered the flattened beach-like space. How the hell did anyone get all that sand and gravel here? Not that it mattered. Mona preferred soft grass to scratchy gravel. It was another of the things Ethan had insisted upon; holidays had to be by the sea. She'd lost count of the times they'd been to the same island in the Caribbean, to the same hotel and spent the same two weeks in the same way—a day on the hotel beach, followed by a day on another beach which Ethan had driven to in the hired car and the pattern was repeated.

'Not anymore,' she murmured.

'Sorry?' Jen said as she unpacked a canvas chair and placed it between two cool boxes.

'Nothing. Murmuring to myself again. It's so pretty here,' Mona said. 'Is this what they call wild swimming?'

'Not as wild as some would like it,' Sheila said, indicating Helen who was already dragging a rubber ring down to the water's edge. 'She reckons this is pretty tame.'

'Tame suits me,' Mona said. 'Do you need a hand?'

'Can you fetch the picnic hamper from the car?' Sheila said.

'You mean the one that sat on my lap all the way here,' said Jen.

'Sorry,' Mona said. 'I supposed we could have done with a bigger car. I didn't expect so much luggage.'

'The English know that on any day out we need enough food to feed three times as many people as in the group, clothes for all four seasons and a choice of seats in case we get sore bums from sitting on the grass or stung by hidden nettles. Oh, and don't forget insect repellents, hay fever, sun lotions, tissues and God knows what else.' Jen wagged a finger at everyone.

Mona stretched out a toe and touched some poles attached to striped material. 'Is this God knows what else?'

'Oooh no,' Jen said. 'They're essentials. Wind breaks.'

'Wind breaks?' Mona said.

'You put them up if its windy and shelter behind them, so you don't get cold.'

227

'Why don't you stay at home on cold days?' Mona said.

'Because we'd never go anywhere if we did that,' Jen said and burst out laughing.

Mona walked back to the car and collected a brown wicker basket. It was the type you'd see in old films or cartoons. It rattled as she carried it and placed it on the tartan rug.

'Jeez that's a weight.'

'There's smoked salmon and cream cheese sandwiches as well as the usual ham and mustard, onion quiche, slices of Margherita pizza, mushroom vol au vents, green salad, mixed salad and a big, iced fruit cake. That'll keep us going,' Jen said.

'It'll keep us going for a week.' Sheila took one end of the basket and helped Mona place it in the shade of a tree.

'Like that bit in *The Wind in the Willows* when Ratty packs a picnic and reels off a whole list of stuff?' Mona said. '*Cold tongue, cold ham, cold beef, pickle gherkin salad, French rolls, cress sandwiches, potted meat, ginger beer, lemonade and soda water.*' I learnt that as a kid.'

'All very English, especially the bit about ginger beer.'

'You can leave me to unpack and keep the jaspers off.' Jen flapped at a small insect with her hat.

'Jaspers?'

'Wasps.' Sheila pointed out a small black and yellow insect.

'We call them yellow jackets,' Mona said.

'Pesky little things can smell a picnic a mile off. That's why I've got a pot of jam,' Jen said.

'Jam?'

'Yes. Whenever you go on a picnic, place an open jar of jam away from the food and the wasps will congregate there. I like good old-fashioned strawberry, myself.'

'Jeez, you Brits are something else. You feed the critters you don't like.' Mona shook her head.

'We do have our strange country ways,' Sheila said and pulled off her T-shirt and shorts. 'Ready for a dip?'

Mona looked at the rest of the Wild Girls. Some were splashing round in the shallow water. Others were lounging on huge rubber rings.

'I suggest we follow their example and go for a swim before we have lunch or we'll have to wait,' Sheila said and slipped on a pair of rubber beach shoes.

'Yes. Mustn't swim for an hour after eating,' Jen said. She looked around. 'Lydia would have liked this.'

'Has anyone seen her recently?' Mona asked as she peeled off her shorts and folded them up.

'Her son says she's able to go out for a little walk. He's placed a tracker on her phone in case she gets lost and anyone who sees her keeps a check. She has a set route. Down past the lake, up by the farm and along the road to her cottage. She does it every day.'

'Is she safe?' Mona said.

'Yes.' Sheila crossed her fingers. 'The medication is working for the moment. It won't last but Chris is grateful for the return to something like normality. I wouldn't call it that,' she added and sniffed.

'No. Anything is a delay, not a cure.' Jen shook her head.

'What would you do if it happened to you?' Mona said.

'I've never thought about it.' Sheila frowned. 'I suppose I hope I wouldn't realise. Just sink into oblivion.'

'Martin and I have signed powers of attorney to each other, in case of illness and incapacity,' Jen said. 'I must say I found it very upsetting to do. Made me admit to my mortality. Scary stuff.'

'It's harder for the families than the person, isn't that what everyone says?'

'I suppose it takes everyone and every family in a different way,' Sheila said.

'I suppose all we can do is enjoy the moments we've got

because that's all we've got,' Mona said.

'Exactly,' Jen said. 'You two get off for a swim. I'm going to sit here in the sunshine and guard the goodies.' She placed a straw hat on her head and opened a dog-eared book.

'Race you to the water?' Mona said.

'No,' Sheila said. 'My racing days are over. A sedate stroll to the water.' She paused. 'Then I'll race you.' She ran down the grassy bank towards the jetty.

'Heh. I kinda call that cheating,' Mona said and trotted after her. 'Watch out when I'm in the water though.'

Sheila had already plunged into the lake and was floating on her back. 'Come on in, the water's lovely,' she called.

Mona dipped a toe in the greeny brown surface. 'Jeez' she gasped. 'Lovely and cold more like.' She stepped gingerly down the mossy ladder until her butt was inches above the water. Any moment a splash or a slight wave would freeze her. What the hell. She plunged her body below the surface so only her head and neck were showing. The shock was over in a few seconds. Her skin soon accustomed to the temperature and with the sun hot on her hair, perhaps it wasn't so bad after all. She struck out in a splashy crawl and caught up with Sheila.

'What do you think?'

'It won't replace the Caribbean,' Mona said and wiped a stray piece of weed from her face.

'Try not to swallow any water,' Sheila said. 'It's not just kids who pee in lakes. There are plenty of farm animals further upstream.'

'God, get me out of here,' Mona said and strained to keep her mouth away from the water.

"Only kidding. It's probably cleaner than a lot of swimming pools at the height of the holiday season.'

'Give me a Santa Monica pool with inflatable chairs and a palm tree any day,' Mona said.

'It's an experience,' Sheila said.

'It certainly is. Race you to that tree.' She set off, leaving Sheila far behind.

Chapter forty-one Sheila

Mona might have set off first, but she's no match for me. I overtake her within ten strokes and power ahead. A twisted branch from an alder hangs low over the water. It is secure enough to hold my weight and had been a favourite jumping place when the children were small. I'd watched, ready to dive in and rescue the skinny bodies as five, six or more children scrambled on and pushed each other off, in the old game of *Who's the King of the Castle?* Do kids play that anymore? Probably not. I'll have to ask the twins when I see them next although since Claire had heard the news of her father's redundancy, she'd kept her calls to a minimum and any conversations were on the subject of the twins or my work. Had I cosseted her too much so she wasn't happy talking about family problems? Too late to do anything about it.

'Where the hell did you learn to swim like that?' Mona says as she grasps the branch, panting.

I reach down my hand and help her scramble alongside. 'I was school champion for three years until the inevitable happened.'

'What was that?'

'I discovered chlorine made my hair go frizzy and green when the sun shone. I hated it.'

'Were boys involved?' Mona says.

'Inevitably. I wanted to look cool, elegant, and sophisticated. Not like the Jolly Green Giant.'

'Heh, did you have him here too?'

'Yes. I can even remember the jingle "Ho ho ho, Green Giant",' I sing. 'I don't even like sweet corn.'

'That's because you don't eat it fresh,' Mona says. 'There's nothing like fresh corn with butter. It's the first thing I'm going to eat when I get back home. That and a stir fry from Panda Express, with beef, broccoli and noodles.'

It is the first time I'd heard Mona talk seriously about going home. 'You miss it. Don't you?'

Mona swings one leg over the branch and sits on it like a horse. 'Yes and no. I've met some amazing people, made some huge changes in my life and I need to get back to continue those changes.'

'Do you think you'll ever come over back? To stay? Not for a holiday?' For some reason, I'm willing her to say yes.

'Of course. I've got friends over here who mean the world. But it isn't my world if you see what I mean. I'm an American. Always have been, always will be.'

'It's funny. I've got used to you being here. It feels as if you've been in the village for ever.'

Mona reaches out her hand and pats mine. 'Heh, it's not the end of the earth. You can visit me next time. I'll be over here again if the paintings sell well. I might need a stock of them.'

'Good. I'd hate to think this was it,' I say. For the first time in years, I'd felt a bond with a woman that wasn't linked to our children. I'm sure too that at least a few grains of Mona's grit have rubbed deep into my own skin. Self-determination doesn't come by pandering to others all the time and putting yourself last.

'You kidding? This is the start. Is that Jen over there?' Mona nods towards the bank where a woman in a blue swimsuit is waving a hat. Mona waves back. The figure beckons us.

'Oh oh, seems we're needed. Must be time for lunch,' I say. 'No racing this time?'

'Great, my stomach needs some food.' Mona slips off the branch and into the water. She bobs up and down while she waits for me. Together we swim from the cool shadows of the trees, into the full glare of the sun. No motorboats or jet skis pollute the air. Splashes, the cries and shouts of excited children and the occasional adult voice carry across the water to mingle with the twitters of a late brood of swallows, the squawk of a duck and the drone of an aircraft high overhead. We reach the jetty. Jen is pacing up and down. She has her phone in her hand.

'Is something wrong?' I know there is. I climb out and Jen hands me a towel.

'I've had a phone call from Lydia's son, Chris. He wanted to know if we'd seen her. I said we were at the lake. He wants you to call him.'

'Did he sound worried?' I squeeze the water from my hair.

'A bit. He said Lydia had set off for her usual walk, but she hasn't got back by her normal time. He checked her phone tracker and she's either dropped her phone by the front gate or deliberately left it there.'

'We didn't see her on our way here, did we?' Mona says.

'That's what I told him.'

'I'll give him a call after I've got changed.' I'm not worried. It's a small, safe village. 'She can't be far. Everyone knows to look out for her, and it isn't as if she lives in the city. Where can you get lost in our village?'

An hour later I'm more concerned. I listen as Chris talks. I put down the phone. The others look up, waiting for my words. 'What's going on?' Mona says.

'Lydia hasn't been seen since eleven o'clock. She's usually like clockwork with her walks. I said we hadn't seen her. Chris has called the police but it's still too early even though she could be classed as vulnerable. He's walking around the village asking people if they've seen her and wanted to know if there were any special places Lydia liked to visit. I said the churchyard where her husband is buried was a great source of comfort for her. He could try there.'

'Do you think we ought to go back and offer to help search? She might have fallen?' Helen says.

234

'I don't want to break up the party,' I say. 'Yet somehow I feel I need to do something.'

Jen stands up. 'That's settled. We're going back,' she says. 'We can all help in our own way, even if it's checking our garages and sheds. When Mr Lancaster from the top of the hill had dementia, he could be found in people's sheds. He didn't do anything. He reckoned he was back as a nipper and was with his granddad.' Jen speaks as she packs away the food. No more words were needed. It was a tacit agreement. The Wild Girls had to help out.

Mona lets me out of the car on the main road. I walk the remaining few hundred yards. A helicopter is circling overhead. It isn't uncommon round here. Off road cyclists, unfamiliar with the steep terrain are prone to spectacular accidents and the air ambulance is often called out. The road through the woods is the site of dumped, stolen cars and the police use infra-red heat seeking cameras to detect bodies. Bodies? I shudder. Is this connected to Lydia's disappearance? Surely not. It would only be a matter of time before she is spotted. She might have walked into town. It is an easy downhill stroll with no major roads. She could be in Tesco's at this moment.

'Right, dump stuff, change into walking boots and trousers and head off,' I mutter under my breath as I open the door of the cottage. A note is propped on the table. Brian would never think of texting her. He isn't that generation.

> *Gone to search the upper warren with Graham and his dogs. Seems Lydia used to go up there regularly when the children were small. Will call you later. xxx*

I dump my damp things in the utility and go upstairs. Should I call Chris? Or will he be out searching too? Surely someone has stayed at her home in case she wanders back?

235

No. I'll change and walk across to Lydia's house. Someone will know how best I can help, even if it is only making tea and sandwiches.

As I walk towards the chapel, a police car swoops past. I watch as it stops, and the officers climb out and follow the path down towards the lake. Something is going on. Has Lydia been found? I take my phone out. 'Brian? What's going on? Where are you?'

'With Graham. A fellow dog walker found Lydia's hat and a letter by the lake, hidden under the bracken. I'm heading down there.'

'I'll meet you.' I hang up. My hands are shaking, and I shiver in the warm air.

A letter? Why would Lydia write a letter? She'll soon be found in the gorse and bramble-covered gulleys around the valley edge. She must have fallen or twisted her ankle. Knowing Lydia, she'd be too proud to call for help. I try to remain positive. Something tells me it's not going to be like that.

Chapter forty-two Mona

Mona stared out of her bedroom window at the scene around the lake. A police cordon had been set up and a diver was preparing to get in the water. What had that letter contained? Sheila had texted her over an hour ago. It was terse.

> *Lydia's hat and a letter have been found by the lake. Fingers crossed it's all a hideous misunderstanding.*

Somehow her gut reaction told her to prepare for the worst. Should she go down there? She hardly knew the lady. Yes. She'd met her once or twice. It was in the early days when Mona's mind was buzzing with new experiences and not a little culture shock. Obviously, those who'd lived here a long time had a history that went back many years; gossiping at the school gate, play dates, parties, shared moments in a long life. Things Mona had put behind her when she moved over here. She'd wanted a new start. She'd got it. What was the old saying? The grass is always greener? Or be careful what you wish for? She'd had her break. It was time to get back to the people who shared her history. Ethan could go to hell. She wanted to see her old friends again, to go back to the places she loved, to pick up the pieces and resume the life she'd abandoned. Except this time, it would be different. Very different.

She peered through the window. Still no signs of any action below at the lake. A couple more people in the white suits of the SOCOs prowled round the edge of the water and a few uniformed police were poking through the undergrowth. At least there'd be several hours of decent daylight left. Would they rig up arc lights? No. Surely it would all be over by then?

Mona moved away from the window. It was Sheila she

237

was concerned about. Her face had gone a strange grey shade when Jen had told her the news. Funny how shock does different things to different people. Would Brian understand? Should she go down and check if there was anything she could do? She hated waiting here. Far better to be active. That was it, she'd pop down in case there were any familiar faces. If Sheila wasn't there, she'd call in on her way back.

Mona closed the front door and sniffed. The air smelt fresh, salty, clean, unlike the sweaty, diesel-tainted fug of the past few weeks. She shivered. It was cooler than it had been. A slight breeze rippled the treetops. She went back inside and pulled a cream sweater from the coat stand in the hall. That would do.

Mona walked along Lower Street to the steep slope that led to the lake. Everywhere was quiet. A few people were sitting in their gardens. All faces were turned towards the lake. 'Heard any more?' she said to an old man. He was leaning on the dry-stone wall that divided his neat rows of flowers and vegetables from the scrub of the valley fields.

He shook his head and drew in a breath between his teeth. 'Nothing so far. Her son's down there. Reckons she knew what she was doing.'

'You think she deliberately left the note where it could be found?'

'That's what people do, isn't it?'

Mona frowned. 'Like a cry for help?'

The old man ran a calloused hand through what remained of his sparse grey hair and hitched his brown cord trousers higher around his waist. 'He reckons she'll turn up and wonder what all the fuss is about.'

'I hope you're right,' Mona said.

'It'll mean she gets the help she needs,' he said. 'You'll see.'

The conversation was at an end. Mona moved on. A

small crowd had gathered on the bridge overlooking the lake. Mona spotted Sheila. 'Heh, you. How is it going?'

Sheila turned and faced Mona. Her eyes were full of tears. 'The police divers are ready to search. The surveillance helicopters have spotted a shadow in the water.'

'Could be a log? Or a boat?' Mona said. 'The old boy up the top reckons she'll turn up and wonder what all the fuss is about.'

Sheila began to cry. Mona pulled her closer. 'She's dead,' she said between sobs.

'We don't know that,' Mona said.

Sheila broke away. 'Chris told me about the letter. There were two. One by her hat and another had been posted in their own letter box on the cottage wall. He found it this evening.'

'What did it say?'

Sheila motioned for Mona and her to move away from the silent watchers. 'She knew what she was doing. She wanted to die, to kill herself.'

'That's not easy,' Mona said. Yes, guns and knives dispatched people pretty quickly. This wasn't the same. If you wanted to kill yourself, drowning was one hell of a hard way to go about it, wasn't it?

'The letter said she was tired and wanted people to remember how she was and not how she would become.'

'Was it a definite suicide note or a ramble?'

Sheila lowered her voice. 'Lydia knew what was happening to her and she hated it. Chris said she had some very lucid moments. This must have been one of them. If that shape is…' her voice faltered.

'You can't walk into water and drown, can you?'

'Remember how the cold sapped our breath away when we got into the lake? This is what water is like here. It rarely warms up. The surface, yes. A metre below and it's cold as hell...I don't mean hell...'

'I know what you mean,' Mona said.

'Within a few minutes the body starts to shut down. That's it.'

There was a movement in the crowd. A murmur of sound rippled round. A police diver had bobbed up and signalled to the crew onshore. A small rubber dinghy with an outboard motor sped to the spot. The motor was cut, and the machine lifted when they got closer. Mona strained to hear what was being said.

'Something's up,' a man in the crowd said.

Sheila clutched Mona's arm. Mona placed her hand on it and squeezed. 'It'll be fine,' she said.

They watched as the diver descended again. The two small craft bobbed on the spot. A buoy was cast on the water. The crowd was silent. A police officer walked towards them. 'Ladies and gentlemen, we have to clear this area. We need space for a vehicle. I would recommend you all go home. This area will need to be searched. Please make your way home or at least to a place on the road.' He signalled to another uniformed officer with a roll of blue and white tape in his hand.

'We'd better do as he says,' Mona said. 'Come back to mine unless you want me to wait with you until Brian gets back?'

'I need to be at home.'

'That's all decided. This way.' Mona placed one hand under Sheila's elbow and steered her up the slope.

Neither of them looked back. They didn't say anything until they reached Sheila's cottage. Brian was still out. 'At times like this, don't you all recommend a cup of tea?'

'I'd prefer a glass of wine,' Sheila said. 'Bottles in the cooler, glasses in the cupboard next to the freezer. If you need a corkscrew, there's one in the top drawer under the sink.'

'Coming up,' Mona said.

Mona watched as Sheila sat in the conservatory. She placed her phone on the table. Her face was etched with lines. Is that what we all really look like? Somehow Mona had never thought of Sheila as the same age as her. She'd appeared younger. Not today. Is this what worry did to you?

She placed a glass of white wine on the metal table. 'It could be anything, couldn't it?'

'What? The diver and the ambulance and the need for a space?' The same thought hung between them, unsaid, unacknowledged but there, like a dark cloud on a summer's day.

They sipped the wine and waited. Mona was about to refill their glasses when Sheila's phone rang. She picked it and switched it to speakerphone.

'Brace yourself, old girl. Graham and I are with Chris. He's been told the police have found the body of an older woman in the lake.'

'Is it?' Sheila said.

'Chris is going down there. Prepare for the worst,' he said. 'I'm staying with him. He might need some support.'

'Did you hear that?' Sheila said.

'Yes,' Mona said.

'It's her, isn't it?' Sheila said.

'We can't be sure,' Mona said. 'Not until there's been a positive identification.' The words sounded false in her mouth. The coincidence of another woman of Lydia's age in the lake when all efforts to find her somewhere else had failed was unbelievable. Yet as they sat there, it was all they had left. Belief in the impossible, the improbable. It was comforting for them both.

Chapter forty-three Sheila

I pull out the purple and pink flowered dress I'd worn to Brian's sister's second marriage three years ago. At least it still fits. Just. It doesn't matter. No one is interested in what anyone wears to a funeral. I dress slowly and carefully. For once I'm using lipstick and have painted my nails a vivid shade of purple. I'd found a chunky pink necklace from a charity shop and three bangles in glittery pink. The instructions said to wear bright colours. I'm not going to let Lydia down.

'All right, old girl?' Brian calls up the stairs. 'We need to make a move to collect Mona and Jen.'

'Coming,' I call down and place a white straw hat festooned with pink and purple flowers on my head. It doesn't match and I always look a fright in hats, more like a scarecrow than a sophisticated woman about town. This is for Lydia. I plonk an oversized pair of sunglasses on the end of my nose—easy to disguise the tears I'm sure will fall.

Downstairs Brian is dressed in navy trousers and a blue golfing shirt. He holds out his arms. 'Chin up, old thing. We'll get through this somehow.'

I smile and let him hold me for a few moments. Since the argument, we'd had many long discussions over a glass or two of wine and Lydia's death has changed everything. There is a sense of urgency and a need to sort this damn mess out before it's too late for us. I'd forgotten how caring he can be. Or had I been so caught up with other people I'd forgotten I am a wife too? At least we seem to understand each other and are making an effort, tiptoeing round more sensitive conversations. They can wait. For a while.

I take a deep breath. 'Ready.'

Mona and Jen are waiting outside the school. The crematorium is a few miles away in a stunning parkland. It was Lydia's choice. She was to be cremated and her ashes buried with her husband's in the churchyard at a private committal later that month. She and Doug must have talked it all through before he died. That took courage. To recognise and accept your own mortality. Chris had told them the will had been written while Doug was alive and had everything detailed down to small items of jewellery and porcelain to be distributed to her friends and more distant family. Brian and I ought to have the same conversation. Later. Everything is too raw at the moment.

Brian stops the car. Mona is dressed in a bright orange shirt and yellow trousers. Jen wears a red dress with a pinched waist and white wedge-heeled shoes. 'Vintage,' she says as she climbs in. 'A genuine copy of a 1950s dress to honour Lydia's birth decade. eBay,' she adds.

'Nice thought,' Brian says.

I move the glasses to cover my eyes. If they fill up so easily, what the hell is it going to be like in the service?

Usually, a car containing us lot would have resembled a cage of parakeets, all chattering and giggling. Today conversation starts, stutters and stalls. Silence is preferable.

The car turns off the main road and follows a side road through trees, past weeping willows overlooking a lake where ducks and their ducklings squawk madly. Several wooden buildings like barns with large windows and stained glass stand at the edge of the car parks. 'Lakeside is the place.' I point to a sign.

The road winds round past more trees to a building with a curved roof, like a ship's sail. 'This is it,' Brian says. People of all ages spill over the car park and onto the grass between the rose bushes. Everyone is dressed in bright colours. It is more like a wedding than a funeral. Brian parks the car and our party join the group. Amongst what must have been distant friends and family, a fair number of familiar faces from the village are present, including the vicar who is dressed in a green jacket and jeans. Her dog collar fights for space with a jewelled chain and heavy cross.

'I thought the vicar would be leading the event,' Brian says as a celebrant in a pale pink suit calls everyone to file into the hall.

'She's sharing the service. Lydia had it all worked out. Like Doug's,' I explain.

'I wasn't there.' Brian looks away.

'No. You weren't.'

'It was beautiful,' Jen says. 'Very spiritual with just the right element of religion without being bogged down in Old Testament readings and ancient psalms. 'Very Christ-ian,' she emphasises the word *Christ*.

'Wow. This is some fabulous place,' Mona whispers as we follow a lavender-edged path and enter the hall. Pale beams, pale wooden seats and cream walls set off the stained-glass windows in which plants and trees, mountains and rivers have been depicted. Sunlight shines through and the floor and walls are speckled with colours. We sit down. I pick up a booklet that has been placed on each seat. On the front is a photo of Lydia on her wedding day and her name. Nothing else. She looks so young. I sniff. Mona hands me a tissue. 'Let it out, girl,' she says. 'Let it out.'

Except I want to be strong for Lydia and for myself. It is no use. The vicar stands up. 'Welcome everyone. Please stand as we say our farewells to our dear friend Lydia.' There is a rustle as everyone obeys and a creak as Lydia's wicker casket is wheeled into the hall. From an unknown source the sound of *Jesu Joy of Man's Desiring* fills the space. I watch as the green wicker casket, so alive, so fresh bears Lydia to the front where it is placed on a dais next to a photo of her surrounded by a bouquet of meadowsweet and pink roses.

The music fades away. 'Please be seated,' the celebrant says and takes her place at a small stand. 'We are here today to say farewell to Lydia, mum, sister, aunty and friend.'

There follows a poem, a reading, more music, and everyone joins in the hymn *All Things Bright and Beautiful* before Tom, Lydia's eldest son, stands up to do the Eulogy. Who had known Lydia was a former champion netball player? Or that she turned down a chance to go to university to marry Doug? Their struggles to have children. How little we know of each other's lives? I glance at Mona. What did I really understand of her need to move here? What had she left behind? I turn my head to look at Brian. Even we had lost what really went on in each other's lives. When did we stop talking, really talking, not about the children and their problems, or whether we should get a new television? That was trivial. What really matters is the stuff left unsaid. The dreams we each still have and the need to continue to dream and have dreams. I realise I'm never going to be a ballerina, climb Everest or make a billion pounds. Does that matter? What really matters is whether we still have some dreams together. I squeeze Brian's arm. He smiles down at me. Will it work? I'd give it a damn good try.

Tom clears his voice. 'I want to read the letter Mum left. It explains why she took the decision she did. And I accept that.

> *'Dear family and friends,*
> *I don't know who will find this letter. I've slipped one in the letter box so if the cows chew this up, another might get to someone who can show it to the people I love most, my two sons, my grandchildren and all the fabulous people I have in my life. I know Reverend Sally will probably disagree, but I don't think people who take their own lives are condemned to eternal misery. My God has too much compassion and common sense for that.'*

Tom pauses as heads turn to the vicar. She smiles and

shakes her head. He continues.

> *'I know this illness is one from which I'll never recover. Any improvements are temporary. It is a long, slow decline and I don't want that. I want people to remember me as I am and was. Not as I know I will become. My life has been in order since Doug fell ill which is why you are here; I will be cremated, and my sons will go with the vicar to inter my ashes alongside Doug. We will be together again. I firmly believe that and will wait to see you all when you too leave this earth for a better life.'*

He stops as a young girl from Lydia's last class joins him and reads aloud.

> *'Weep not for me though I am gone;*
> *into that gentle night.*
> *Grieve if you will but not for long,*
> *upon my soul's sweet flight.*
>
> *'I am at peace,*
> *my soul's at rest.*
> *There is no need for tears.*
> *For with your love I was blessed;*
> *for all those many years.*
>
> *'There is no pain,*
> *I suffer not,*
> *The fear now all is gone.*
> *Put now these things out of your thoughts.*
> *In your memory I live on.*
>
> *'Remember not my fight for breath;*
> *remember not the strife.*
> *Please do not dwell upon my death,*
> *but celebrate my life.'*

As she sits down Tom joins hands with his brother, the vicar, and the celebrant. 'We have to leave Mum here. Please come and join us in the pub for a drink and a bite to eat. The landlord's ordered an extra barrel or two and the wine is Mum and Dad's favourite. Finally join with us in singing *Lord of the Dance*.'

Lydia's casket remains on the stand as we all file out. It doesn't seem right to leave her there. I want to go up to it and place my hand on it to say a proper goodbye. Except people will think I'm silly. Instead, I bow my head as I pass and whisper 'Goodbye, Lydia. I'll miss you.'

Chapter forty-four Mona

Mona threw herself into painting, often working into the night. She'd walk home along the moonlit streets, stopping as a fox or badger crossed her path or stayed motionless, hoping she wouldn't see them. The owls called across the valley in an endless sing song of To whittt....whoo. She made friends with a few cats out on the prowl and crawled into bed, grasping a few hours of sleep.

When the alarm sounded the following morning, she cursed her idea as she dragged her tired body out of bed. Why had she let herself be talked into this? She resented the bare canvases that demanded her attention. Yet as soon as she opened the studio door and saw the results of her work, it was worth it. If only people came along. She'd already put something on the village Facebook page, stuck posters round the telephone poles and on every notice board. What was the least number of people she'd need to feel it had all been worthwhile? Ten. That was enough. If she sold two paintings, she'd be happy. James would buy one and Sheila had already chosen a view of bluebells in a woodland glade. All the Wild Girls had promised to attend. That was at least ten. Perhaps she'd reach her modest target after all.

Mona was ready early and was about to leave when there was a knock at the door. It was James. 'Thought you might like a bit of Dutch Courage,' he said and waved a half bottle of champagne. 'Here or at the studio?'

'The studio, please,' Mona said. Why was she so nervous? 'In case anyone is as early as me.'

They cut across the small track by the shop. The door was open. 'See you later,' a voice called out as Jen stuck her head through the door. 'I finish at eleven. Make sure the coffee is on.'

'Is that a sale?' James said and winked.

'Who knows? I reckon if two people turn up and I sell one painting I'm a winner.'

'Oh, ye of little faith,' James said and did a mock bow. 'You'll be swamped.'

'Optimist,' Mona said and crossed her fingers he was correct.

By the end of the afternoon Mona had sold ten paintings, seven small prints, three of her acrylic experiments in a more abstract style to represent flowers, and the cakes, wine and coffee had been depleted. She checked her wallet and had made a profit of several hundred pounds. It was a start. Everyone had admired the large canvas of the valley. James was clearing away the debris. Sheila nudged Mona's arm. 'What are you going to do with the large picture? I spotted several interested parties.'

'It's a present,' Mona said. 'Certainly not for sale.'

'Lucky beggar. If there was another, I'd buy it,' she said. 'To hell with the budget.'

Mona smiled to herself. She planned to present it to Sheila on her last day. Not at the airport as Sheila had already offered to drive her there. That would be too tacky. As the month had passed and after Lydia's funeral, she'd become more convinced she had to return as planned.

A voice called from outside. 'Is Mona around?'

Mona froze. She recognized that voice.

'Another punter,' Sheila said. 'Better find out what he wants.'

'You go. I don't want to see him.'

'Why? Who is it?' Sheila said.

The voice called again. 'Heh, anyone at home? I've come a long way to see my wife.'

'Wife?' Sheila held onto Mona's arm. 'Is that?'

'My ex or rather my soon to be ex? I think so.'

'Do you want me to stall him?' Sheila said. 'I can get

249

Brian and James to help out.'

Mona shook her head. 'I can't. That would be cowardly. The one thing I've learnt over the last few months is nothing good comes from running away. Leave him to me.'

'Yell if you need me,' Sheila said as Mona crossed the studio floor and went out into the bright sunshine.

'How are you, darlin'?' Ethan was leaning on the dry-stone wall. A small rucksack perched next to him. A cigarette dangled from one lip. Since when had he started smoking again? He dropped the butt end. It smouldered on the dry path.

'How did you know where I was?' Mona said, her voice as flat as the sands on Pacific Beach.

Ethan smiled. 'There ain't many Bell Pitches in England.' He held out his phone. There was the photo she'd posted of her artwork, all lined up against a stone wall. In the corner was a small sign that said *Bell Pitch.* 'All I had to do was stick in the image and check them all out. Easy.'

'Why are you here?' Mona said.

Ethan's eyes narrowed and his voice became harsh. 'You walk out on me, no address, no fucking nothing and wonder why I'm here? You're my legal wife. I need to know what's going on.'

'No, you don't.' Sheila was standing in the entrance to the studio. Behind her Brian and James were silhouetted against the interior of the room.

'Introduce me to the welcoming committee,' Ethan said.

'We're friends,' Brian said.

'Strange, I reckoned I knew all of Mona's friends. She must have been very busy while she's been on her little holiday.' There was no mistaking the venom in Ethan's voice.

Usually, Mona would have shrunk away. Not today. 'They are my friends and part of the new life I'm going to create when I get back to the States. We're history.'

'You? Make a new life? You won't last five minutes. You'll be running back to me within days.'

'That was the old me. I've survived the past few months. I can do anything.'

'Come on, let's get out of here and talk,' Ethan's voice took on a wheedling tone.

Mona had heard it all before. Threats were followed by persuasion, flattery and if that didn't work, he'd pretend he couldn't live without her. It was all crap. 'No. You go. I'll make arrangements to see you when I get back in the middle of next month. By that time, I'll have contacted my lawyers. I want out.'

'You don't mean it,' Ethan said. 'Unless you've lined up one of these dorks to fall back on. Wasn't that your modus operandi? Find a sucker, bleed him dry, ditch him and on to the next one?'

'Firstly, one of these dorks is married to me,' Sheila said. 'Secondly we know that is all untrue.'

'It's more like your method, isn't it, Ethan?' said Mona. 'Find a lonely woman, make her think she's of value before little by little stripping away her self-worth until she relies on you for everything?'

'That's a bit harsh, isn't it?' Ethan said. His tongue flickered over his lips and his face flushed.

'I mean it. Go back home.'

Ethan held up his hands. 'Heh I've just arrived. Can't I stay for a few days to recover from jet lag?' He tried to make it sound like a joke.

'I'll take you to the station. You can be in London in an hour and a half. There's plenty of sightseeing to do.' Mona folded her arms and waited.

'We can make sure you do get on that train,' James said.

'Are you threatening me?' Ethan stepped forward and thrust his face at James.

James side stepped. 'No. Simply making sure a friend of

251

a friend gets away safely. There are some nasty villains in the countryside. We get a lot of thefts, not to mention the poachers and badger baiters. You don't want to risk getting caught up with them.'

'You are making a big mistake, all of you,' Ethan said.

'No. You are. I'll take you to the station. We can go back to my cottage to collect my car,' Mona said.

Ethan looked at each one in turn before he spoke to Mona. 'Seems like I'm beaten.' He held out his hands. 'I'll take you up on that lift.'

Had she talked him round already? It all seemed too good to be true.

Chapter forty-five Sheila

'If you want to get away,' I step forward, 'we can clear up here and I'll stick the keys through the letterbox.'

Mona glances round.

'After all, the sooner you despatch your friend to the station, the sooner you get your life back on track and we can celebrate the success of the day. You do remember I invited you to supper tonight?' I say.

Mona looks confused. I wink. 'Oh yes. Must have slipped my mind.'

'So that's it, is it?' Ethan takes a step toward Mona.

James jumps in the way. 'Not so fast, tiger. The lady has been very generous. I'd leave you here to stew. Take our advice and go home. It'll be easy to sort everything out when you're both in the same place.'

Ethan runs one hand through his hair. 'I suppose you're right,' he says. He holds out his right hand. 'No hard feelings?'

No one moves. 'Come on, let me take you to the station,' Mona says. She turns to James. 'If you can bring the smaller canvases back with you and the cash box. I'll leave the big ones for another day. Oh, and the bin bag of trash. It's got all the rags I used to clean off the darn stickers. I don't want the place to stink of white spirit.'

'Consider it done,' James says. 'I'll leave it by the front door.'

I stand by the wall and tap Mona's arm as she walks past. 'Come around to us straight away. You shouldn't be on your own tonight.'

'I'll think about it,' Mona says as she leads Ethan back to her cottage.

I watch until they are out of sight before I return to Brian and James who are clearing away the remains of what shops like to call nibbles. 'I don't trust him.'

Both men stop what they are doing. 'Do you think he might hurt her?' Brian says.

'No. He's not that stupid. He is devious though. I'd have taken him to Heathrow and waited till he got the hell out of here,' I say.

'Mona's got our numbers. I'll call later to check on her. I suspect she'd rather be alone. It's been quite a day.' James keeps glancing towards the open door.

'He's got a damn nerve,' I say.

'And bucket loads of intelligence. I would never have spotted the name on that Facebook page. Not that I spend any time on it,' Brian says.

'Correction. You don't spend any time.' I punch his arm in a teasing way and he smiles. I feel closer to him and it's good.

'Too busy trying to find a job.' Brian clears a table of paper plates and stacks the borrowed glasses into boxes. 'I'm either overqualified, too old or under qualified.'

'How can you be all of those?' James says.

Brian ties up the top of a bin bag. 'Take IT. I can work the company's systems but that's about it. Under qualified. For any bog-standard admin post I'm overqualified. I'm too old for most places that offer training. They want youngsters. I'll end up on a supermarket checkout although with my luck, I'll be too young. The retired teachers have got there before me.' He is smiling. His voice though is grim.

I go up to him and put my arms round him. 'Something will turn up.'

'What sort of skills do you have?' James says.

Brian ticks off on his fingers. 'Project management, procurement, dealing with angry customers, investigating loopholes in systems, preparing reports, liaising with specialist companies…'

'With a bit of basic DIY if the quality of these frames is

anything to go by. Am I correct?'

James nods towards my favourite painting of the valley.

'Yes. Brian designed and masterminded the extension and did all the finishing touches.' If there is a hint of pride in my voice, I don't care.

'I might know of a vacancy,' James says.

'No.' Brian shakes his head. 'Not after what I did to you.'

James shrugs. 'That was all a misunderstanding. I hoped we'd moved on.'

'We have,' I say and kick Brian's foot.

'Ouch.' He rubs his shin.

'Touch of cramp,' I explain to James. 'He gets it from time to time. What's this possible vacancy?'

James leans against the table. The pile of pictures wobbles. I steady it with my hand. 'By the end of the year I'll have twenty properties. Some flats, some houses, some sheltered accommodation and some small workshop units like this one.'

'The sheltered accommodation will be under our care,' I say.

'Yes. Even those units need some overseeing unless you plan to do it?'

'We outsource.'

'At a very high per unit cost, am I right?'

'Yes of course. Good people are hard to find.' Where is this conversation going?

'My business partner has an idea to take on an administrator who will check the premises on a regular basis, notify us of any repairs and generally act as a sort of trouble shooter. We also want someone to oversee the new projects as they come on stream in Bristol and Swindon.'

'Yes?' Brian says. His eyes are shining. He is interested.

'There will be a certain amount of time spent with our more vulnerable tenants. As a one stop shop.'

I clap my hand over my mouth. 'That's what you were

talking about? A friendly face?'

'My business partner liked the idea so much, we reckoned it could be extended to a more specific post with a wider remit.'

'What about the salary?' I say.

'Negotiable, depending on hours,' James says. 'We want someone who can act as the tenants' champion and the developers' champion when we take on contractors. Make everyone feel they really are being listened to.' He pauses. 'It might suit you.'

'Yes. It might,' Brian says.

'Why don't you come to my office on Monday and meet my business partner. He can tell you more.'

'I will.' Brian's face is glowing. 'This might be the break I need.'

James holds out his hand. 'Let's get this place cleared and we can have a pint in the pub—if he's got any decent beer left after a hot day.'

'Good idea,' Brian says. 'Thank you,' he adds. 'You must have thought I was a bit of a fool?'

'No. I like people who are passionate.' James turns to me. 'Do you still think I'm the capitalist spawn of the devil?' he says.

'I might allow myself to be convinced otherwise. It could take a while. What did granny say, 'The proof of the pudding is in the eating?' '

'My gran said that too. And another one, 'Don't look a gift horse in the mouth.' '

'Let's get that beer,' says Brian. 'The pub might even run to a burger and chips.'

'Great,' says James. 'I really can't stand all these little bits of what do they call it… party food?'

'I'll text Mona and tell her where we are,' I say. 'She might want to pop along later.'

The air is cool, and a fresh breeze is blowing the clouds

across the sky, obscuring the moon as we cross to the pub. 'I hate the end of summer,' I say. 'I feel cheated I haven't done any of the things I dream of each year.'

'Such as?' Brian says.

'Oh, a festival. I've never been to one.'

'Sleeping on a bumpy field, in a tent surrounded by thousands, no hundreds of thousands of stoned and pissed yoof is not my idea of fun,' James says.

'It doesn't have to be a big one. One day at smaller, more family orientated would suit me.'

'We could give it a go,' Brian says. 'As you're talking about summer, I'd like to go to an outdoor theatre performance. We haven't done that in years.'

James pushes open the door of the pub. 'I feel a summer bucket list is overdue,' he says. 'Except you'll have to wait till next summer. A couple of weeks and it'll be the equinox and after that—'

'It's all downhill to Christmas,' I say and laugh.

'How did you guess. What's everyone having? My shout.' James leans over the bar to check which beers are on tap. 'What I can't understand is why Mona didn't kick her ex's backside out as soon as he turned up.'

'Get me a drink and I'll tell you what I know. They have a history, and it goes back a long way,' I say.

'Tell me more,' James says.

'Get the beers in and I will.' I find a table and sit down. I'd give James as much detail as I can without breaking any confidences. It's something I've learnt to do well.

The summer evening light has turned to dusk by the time we have finished the burgers and a second pint. 'I needed that,' James says as he pushes his plate away. 'Pity Mona didn't feel up to coming out. Should we check on her?'

'No. Her message said she wanted a long bath and an early night. I'll go and see her tomorrow.'

'I reckon it's time for another pint.' Brian collects our glasses.

I'm staring out at the valley. 'Someone's got a big bonfire,' I say. 'Or their barbecue is alight.'

Brian comes over and joins us. I point to the flicker of flames. A plume of smoke drifts over the nearby gardens. 'Reckon someone's shed is on fire,' Brian says.

'That won't please the neighbours,' James says.

'There's no shed. It looks more like a conservatory.'

'Should always have a barbecue a long way from the house,' Brian says.

'It's close to Mona's cottage,' I say. 'Really close.'

'Bugger. I hope it doesn't spread,' James says. 'I'd better get over there.'

'Do it quickly.' I jump up. 'I'm certain it's coming from Mona's garden. Her house is next door to Laburnum Cottage, and I can see the tree.'

'You're right,' James says. 'It is Lavender Cottage. I think the damn thing's on fire. Call the Fire Brigade!' he yells as he runs out.

I get out my phone. If it is Mona's cottage, is she inside? Or is she still at the railway station with Ethan?

Chapter forty-six Mona

Mona pulled the plug and let the bathwater drain away. The steamy room was filled with the scent of lavender and rosemary. She wrapped a towel round her body and padded back to her bedroom. She'd already poured herself a glass of wine. A plate with some cheese and biscuits waited with a new crime thriller from a young Asian writer set in the North of England. Next time she was over here she'd like to explore more. Scotland? Hadrian's Wall? York? Liverpool was a must. Next year perhaps, if she could afford it.

She smoothed body lotion onto her legs and arms. Bliss. Thank God Ethan had gotten onto the train. He'd been remarkably docile on the journey down. Had he finally realised it was all over? He'd offered her a hug. She'd let him, briefly, and he'd arranged to get in touch with her once she was back home. It was funny hearing the word *home*. For a while she'd come to think of this place as her home. It wasn't. At least it meant she could settle in a new place. Once the divorce was through, where could she go? Where would she want to live? She'd always fancied somewhere more hilly and cooler. She wanted winter. A proper winter. With snow and ice and log fires. She replaced the cap on the bottle and slipped on an old T-shirt. Ethan would be in London by now. The train only stopped at Kemble, Swindon, and Reading. Yes. He'd be miles away.

She curled up in bed and reached out for her glass of wine. 'To the future,' she said and took a sip. Yes. This was better She couldn't face talking to Sheila, James, and Brian. That would happen tomorrow.

She opened the book and settled back on the pillows. Something floated past the window. Smoke? No, she was imagining it. Someone was having a barbecue probably. There it was again. It seemed very close. She sniffed. That wasn't the smell of woodsmoke. It was more like gas. She'd check the windows downstairs were closed or the place would stink tomorrow.

She stepped out of bed and padded to the window. She opened it and looked out. Shit. The smoke was coming from her garden. No. Not her garden. From her porch. She ran downstairs. The porch was ablaze, and smoke was curling into the lounge. Water? No. If she opened the door into the porch the flames would quickly spread. She couldn't leave the place. What if it all went up in smoke? What was the number for the emergency services? She'd get out. She had to. The kitchen door? That was the best way. Nine nine nine? That was it She entered the number. 'Fire!' she called as she ran towards the kitchen and closed the lounge door behind her. 'Fire!'

'Mona, are you all right?' It was James. He burst into the kitchen. 'Get out. Sheila's called the fire brigade. They'll be here. Come with me.' He grabbed her by the hand and dragged her outside.

'The cottage? My paintings?'

'Your life,' he said and thrust her towards Sheila. 'Hose pipe?' he called to the neighbours who had gathered.

'All done.' A man in wellies was heading towards the flames with a hose. He'd draped it over the stone wall. Other neighbours were using buckets. The flames licked at the outside of the cottage. Thank heavens Mona had shut the doors.

Too late. A flame flicked from the porch to the old outhouse. There was a bang and the outhouse crumpled. Flames shot towards the sky. 'Shit what's that?'

'There was an oil tank inside. Must still have had some oil in it,' James said.

They watched as flames touched the dead branches of fir trees that should have been felled years ago and the sad skeletons of ash trees, ravaged by ash dieback. There was a crackle and bracken on the edge of the woodland glowed, flickered, and caught alight. Sparks drifted into the air and floated over the treetops.

'If those sparks reach the gorse on the hilltop, the whole bloody place will go up,' a man shouted.

Mona watched as a chain gang of men and women poured water onto the walls and the surrounding gardens. A flashing blue light made them jump back as the fire engine arrived and the fire fighters got into a well-rehearsed routine. James took charge. 'No one inside,' he said.

'Good. Stand back folks. Soon get this out.'

'What about the woodland?'

'We'll send another tender up there. Don't worry.' A fire officer in breathing apparatus headed towards the flames with a hose.

Within minutes the fire in the gardens was contained and brought to a smouldering mess. Hoses doused the trees as another fire tender negotiated the steep path along the hillside. More hoses were unfurled, and water cascaded through the branches.

'That was close,' murmured Brian. 'Those trees could have gone up. The place is tinder dry.'

'About time someone did something about all those dead ones. Woodland needs managing,' the man who alerted them about the gorse spoke loudly and shook his head. 'Accident waiting to happen that is.'

Mona stepped away from the crowd of onlookers, and those who had been helping put down their buckets and watched as the fire crew got the blaze under control. She walked slowly towards the entrance hall of her cottage. It was a mess and what was left of the garden that hadn't been trampled by boots or deluged by water was scorched.

The crew manager walked towards James and Mona. 'Anyone any idea how it started?' he said.

'No,' Mona said.

'I spotted a bloke fiddling around about an hour ago,' the neighbour with the hose said.

Another fire fighter stepped forward. 'Reckon this might be for the police.' He held up a charred cloth. 'Smells like a spirit of some sort.' He bent down and peered at the remains. 'Looks like a bottle of spirit was in the bag.'

'Yours?' The crew manager said and looked at James.

'No. Mine,' Mona spoke before James could answer, 'I use it for painting. I'm sure there wasn't a bottle in the bag. I kept some in the outhouse though.'

'Is that the outhouse?' The crew manager nodded towards the small building by the wall.

James took control. 'Let me check with you.'

A few minutes passed. James returned. 'There are no bottles of any spirit or petrol, not even a Gerry can for the lawn mower.'

The crew manager spoke into his radio. 'Possible arson attack.'

He turned to James. 'Your property is it, sir?'

'Yes. I rent it though.' Mona stepped forward.

'If I were you, I'd think very carefully of anyone who might hold a grudge.'

'Ethan,' Mona said. 'My ex. He was here a few hours ago. I thought he'd got on a train back to London.'

'I think we'd better leave any further speculation for the experts,' James said.

Three hours later Mona collapsed into an armchair in Sheila's front room. 'I won't need to stay here long,' she said. 'James and I are going to check the place tomorrow. There's little damage except to the porch. Even the smoke didn't really get inside.'

'You can stay here as long as you like,' Sheila said and poured a cup of hot chocolate. 'Drink this. It'll help you sleep.'

Mona took a sip. 'Reminds me of winter holidays at my

grandma's place. Thick snow, roaring log fires and chocolate with marshmallows.'

'A bit like here, on occasions,' Sheila said.

'We won't pry but if you want to talk, we're ready to listen,' Brian said and perched on the end of the sofa.

'Nothing to tell. I told them about Ethan. The neighbour Mr?—Clements, that's it, gave a good description which fitted with mine and they picked Ethan up at Stroud station. I reckon he wanted to get caught,' Mona said.

'Why?' Sheila sat next to her. 'Wouldn't he want to get the hell out of here?'

'He likes the dramatic,' Mona said. 'If this was his big gesture to scare the shit out of me. It didn't work.'

'He could have killed you,' Brian said.

'Not to mention endangering the rest of the village, criminal damage to the woodland and beyond. We've been lucky,' Sheila said.

'I don't think he ever intended that,' Mona's words tumbled out, 'it was another attempt at control. That's what he's been doing all his life. With me, anyway.'

'Will they prosecute?' Sheila's face was grim. 'I bloody well would.'

'I'd throw the fucking book at him.' Brian slammed his fists into an open palm. The slap echoed through the quiet.

'It's James' property. He will have a say,' Mona said. 'Any potential damage and threat to the woodland is up to the owner.'

'Do we know who that is? I was told it still belonged to the old couple who had the small holding where we used to take Claire and Mark to feed the horses.'

'They sold it years ago to a company,' Brian said. 'One of those that promise you can buy a bit of your own woodland and sit in it.'

'I think Ethan's scared. He never expected it to take light. He doesn't know how dry it's been lately.'

'Scared or not he could have killed someone and the whole village could have gone up,' Sheila said.

Brian smiled. 'Not with people like Mr Clements around and the rest of the neighbours. I reckon they'd give the fire brigade a run for their money.'

'There's plenty of evidence. It's amazing how many people saw Ethan walking up the main road and going into the garden' Sheila said.

Brian's smile faded. 'No one thought to say anything, did they? So much for Neighbourhood Watch.'

'They probably thought he must be a friend as he went around the back rather than knocking on the front door.'

'Funny how no one saw him start the blaze,' Brian said and shook his head.

'The fire officer reckons he found a couple of pieces of rag. I've been using white spirit to clean my brushes and the bin bag by the door was full of them.' Mona shook her head. 'It's all my fault.'

'Bin bags don't suddenly combust,' Brian said.

'What exactly happened?' Sheila said. 'Or are they still speculating?'

'Ethan claims he got off the train at Kemble. He took a taxi back here and knocked on the door. There was no answer, so he threw away his cigarette and walked off.'

'That's not enough to start a fire, is it?' Sheila said.

'You'd be surprised,' Brian said.

Mona yawned. 'Sorry.'

'No. I'm sorry,' Sheila said. 'You're worn out. Get to bed.'

'I'm a bit smelly and smoky,' Mona said.

'It'll wash off tomorrow. What you need is sleep.'

Sheila led her to the spare bedroom. The quilt was already turned back, and crisp yellow sheets waited. Sheila had left an old T-shirt as a night dress. Mona stripped off and pulled it on. She collapsed into the bed, dragged the quilt over her and curled up, like a hamster in its nest.

Tomorrow she'd decide what to say to James. She didn't really want to prosecute Ethan. He needed help. Serious help. There were no longer any twinges of affection. That had died long ago. It might not be up to James, though. What about the owner of the woodland? Arson was serious, wasn't it? Except Ethan wasn't that spiteful, was he? This was an accident, a stupid accident.

Chapter forty-seven Sheila

The phone rings. 'How are you?' I motion Brian to be quiet.

'Mona?' he mouths. 'Any decision about Ethan yet?'

Brian squeezes closer to hear what is being said. I do not switch to speaker phone. It is too revealing. 'Keep me informed. You know we'll do all we can.'

I switch off and put the phone away. 'I hope she and James will insist on prosecution. That man's a danger to her and everyone else.' Brian's face is grim.

I collect my bag. 'She says she's meeting James later today. Ethan's claiming it was all a mistake. Reckons he dropped his cigarette and that must have started the blaze.'

'I don't believe him' Brian says and helps himself to a slice of toast. He smothers it with marmalade and drops the knife in the sink. A few stray crumbs scatter on the counter and the floor.

For once I do not reach for a cloth. Who cares about a few crumbs? There are more important things in life.

'If the evidence isn't there, all he'll get is a reprimand.' I change the subject. 'Are you going to call James today about the job?' I hate to think we're accepting charity. There's also an issue with my role. Could it be construed as a bit of a bribe or a softener? I hope not. The money would help us over a sticky patch and give Brian more chance to search for something more—what? More senior? Except does Brian want that? More lucrative? We could cope financially. Just. It would give us more time together and that was certainly needed.

'He sent an email first thing today. I'm meeting him at the new development in Queensway at ten.'

'If he offered you a proper job, with a contract and all that, would you take it?'

Brian pauses. 'Yes,' he says. There is no doubting the certainty in his voice.

'Good for you.' I mean it. This might be the chance we need. 'I'll be back at six. Get the supper on, there's plenty of food in the freezer.'

'I thought I might have a go at a pasta bake. I've seen you do it plenty of times,' Brian says. 'Unless there are secret ingredients you've hidden from me?'

'No such luck.' I lean across and put my arms around him. 'Have fun.'

'You too.' Brian kisses the tip of my nose. He hasn't done that for decades.

My cheeks flush hot. 'Better be off.'

Outside the rowan trees rustle in the breeze and I shiver. Is this the end of the hot spell? It is nearly September. The starlings have stripped the berries from the rowans and pigeons are gobbling the first elderberries. Blackberries hang in the hedgerows and the old apple tree is weighted down with fruit. My bare legs are cold. Is it time for tights? Not yet. I must wait till September.

It is mid-morning when my personal phone rings. I hate taking calls, unlike so many of the younger members of staff who are constantly checking for messages and cute videos of puppies and kittens. I'm old school. Work means work. This time I answer. It is Claire.

'Hi, Claire. How are the twins enjoying the holidays?'

'They love it. They've got football club this week.'

'Good. Work going OK?' I wait for the request to help out. Since Brian has been at home, I've half expected Claire would ask him to take over day care.

'Work's fine. I was wondering if you and Dad would like to come over for supper tonight. Nothing special. Shepherd's pie, salad, and ice-cream suit you?'

Have I heard correctly? 'Tonight? A meal?'

'Yes. About six? The twins will love to see you.'

I waste no time in accepting. 'Of course. It'll save your dad from cooking. He was planning on pasta bake.'

'I know. He's been pestering me for a recipe for a week. I sent him a link on YouTube.'

'Oh, you did, did you?' What else has been going on behind my back?

'Yes. He said as he wasn't working, he wanted to take on more of the chores. I told him he's welcome to do my ironing any time.' Claire laughs. She sounds more like my little girl.

'I'm beginning to think I've underestimated your father,' I say. 'I'll tell him.'

'See you at six,' Claire says and rings off.

I text Brian.

Pasta bake is cancelled. Claire has invited us to supper. We need to be there at six. And what's all this about secret cookery lessons?

Brian replies.

Oh dear. Rumbled. I need all the help I can get. This cookery stuff is trickier than it looks. Spared for tonight. Saves me slaving over a hot tin opener. Off to see James. Love you.

Love you? He hasn't said anything like that in years let alone written it as part of a bog-standard message. I am about to put my phone away. I stop and send an emoji of a smiley face and a heart.

'Everything all right?' Karen appears at the end of my desk.

'There's something I need to talk to you about.'

'In my office in ten?' Karen says.

'Yes. Fine.' It will give me time to work out what to say. Brian hasn't been offered the job yet, has he? What if it is a clash of interests? What if I could be accused of letting my own feelings get in the way of making a decision? Not that

268

I'd ever allow it to happen. People gossip and where there's gossip, there's often a nasty smell of scandal. What did her gran say? There's no smoke without fire? That was it. How awful if Brian accepted the job and I had to tell him to turn it down. It would destroy the confidence he is getting back.

Karen is waiting when I knock on the door. 'What's the problem?'

'Why do you think there's a problem?' I sit in the chair opposite Karen.

Karen moves the paper files and folds her hands in the space. 'Because if it was a mundane run of the mill issue, you'd have dealt with it. If it's slightly problematic, you'd have taken action and told me about it afterwards. You're a real professional.'

I know I'm blushing. 'It's a little trickier than most.'

'Start at the beginning and I want all the gory details.' Karen rubs her hands together.

This is the best chance I'd have, and it had to be done. I take a deep breath. 'It's Brian…and James Frobisher.'

'If you're going to tell me they've decamped to the Cayman Islands with all the loot, I won't believe it,' Karen says.

'James has offered Brian a job.'

'Management, I hope. I can't see your Brian as a bricklayer or a builder's mate.'

'Something like that,' I say.

'Go on.' Karen leans back in the chair.

'James has offered Brian a post as project manager and trouble shooter for his property portfolio.'

'What does that entail?'

'He will be overseeing the redevelopment of any new properties James buys and…' I hesitate. 'He wants him to be a sort of first line of support with the tenants if there is a problem.'

'I see.'

I cross my fingers and edge towards the front of the chair.

'You thought it might interfere in some way with your role as the housing officer who assigns tenants to some of these properties?'

Relief sweeps over me. 'How did you know?'

'James mentioned it to me last week. We've often thought a friendly face popping in once a week was better for our more vulnerable tenants than speaking to us, however kind and understanding we claim to be. A disembodied voice on the phone is not the same as flesh and blood. Besides, it might save us a mint of cash. We waste a lot of energy on petty niggles, like a timer needing readjustment, testing the alarms or a blocked sink. Brian can check if it needs real work or simply a thump. If you get my meaning?'

'You don't mind?'

Karen folds her arms across her ample chest. 'Let's be honest. What can you or Brian do that is against the law?' She doesn't wait for an answer. 'Nothing. All repairs must be carried out by our insured traders. You have no say in who does the work. Brian has no say in who we take on. Job done.'

For a moment I don't know what to say. 'I'm so pleased,' I stammer out.

'No worries,' Karen says and passes her mug over. 'Get us a coffee, can you? I'm due to call Miss Ellis with the news that her request for another transfer is unlikely. It will be a long conversation.'

I skip out of the office. Hopefully Brian will be offered the post properly and our lives might start looking up.

Chapter forty-eight Mona

Mona parked her car opposite the police station and paid for two hours. It wouldn't last longer than that, would it? She had no gripe about Ethan as long as he left her alone and they could deal with the divorce through solicitors. James might be angry about the damage. She'd cleaned up, washed all the inside curtains, and hired a carpet shampoo to get rid of any smoky smell. The front porch would need a bit of repair and the floor was scorched. Ethan could pay for that and have cash left over from his weekly expenses.

Even if the porch needed rebuilding, she knew his bank balance. That had been one of the problems. How can someone insist on saving every penny and making their joint and single lives a misery. Or perhaps that was part of his obsessive nature?

She pushed open the door of the police station. James was already waiting. 'I didn't see your car,' she said.

'By the church,' James said. 'Hopefully it won't take long. The duty officer knows we're here.'

Mona sat down in one of the grey plastic chairs. It was quiet. Shouldn't police stations be full of criminals dragged in by uniformed officers, pale-faced men and women in civvy clothes speaking out of the corner of their mouths and a dear old lady explaining she'd lost her cat? Or had she been watching too many reruns of old cop shows? Where were the cells? Her dreams were interrupted. A small woman in uniform with short, blonde hair walked towards them. 'I'm your Liaison Officer, Sergeant Jenkins. Call me Lauren,' she said and stretched out her hand.

'Pleased to meet you,' Mona said.

'This way.' Lauren tapped in a code on a keypad and a wooden door to the left of the desk opened. 'We're using the family suite,' she said.

Mona and James followed. It sounded more like a hotel

than a police station. The suite was set up like a lounge with assorted armchairs, a sofa and low coffee tables. There was even a small kitchen, and a closed door had a sign for a toilet.

'Sit down, please.' She pulled up a grey armchair to join two blue ones by the smallest table, opened her file and brought out a sheaf of papers and a small tablet. She placed both on the table. 'Can I get you a tea or a coffee?' she said.

'No thank you,' Mona and James spoke at the same time.

'Let's get started.' She flicked through the sheaf of papers and pulled out a typed sheet. There was a signature at the end. 'This is your statement,' she said and handed the paper to Mona. 'This is yours,' she said to James. 'Please read through them and tell me if there is anything else you would like to add.'

Mona skimmed the words. She knew what she'd written. There was no mention of the difficulties between her and Ethan or the friendship between her and James and the embarrassing incident with Brian. That was history. This was a simple case of a separation that had gone wrong.

> *I admit I should have contacted Ethan and told him where I was and what I planned to do. I was so caught up in my new life, the old one was left behind.*

Did that make sense? Yes. To her. What about the police? Surely, they'd let Ethan off with a caution. She'd made it plain she didn't believe he wanted to hurt her. If he'd wanted to, he'd have made sure it happened. He didn't know the property was owned by James. There was no deliberate act against James, was there? Were prosecutors more lenient in the UK? Besides she'd clearly indicated that the white spirit was hers and the bottle could have been in the bag of trash along with the rags.

She glanced across at James. What had he said? The

damage was easily repaired. And Ethan? Would he understand and finally let her go? Mona looked up at the sergeant 'This is fine.' She picked up the pen and signed her name and added the date. 30th August. It would be Labour Day soon back home and the end of the summer. She needed to be there. She'd start clearing up the studio today. Her lease expired on the 5th September.

'Yes. That seems accurate,' James said and scrawled his signature. He pushed the paper back to the sergeant. She collected both statements and placed them back in the file. 'Are we free to go?'

'Yes, unless there are any questions you want to ask me?' The sergeant smiled.

'What happens next?' Mona said. 'I know how we do it in the States and I suppose your system is like ours. I'm not sure though.'

The sergeant nodded her head, folded her hands on the table. 'The perpetrator is on bail until any decision has been made. As there appears no deliberate threat to life or property and the damage is under five thousand pounds, it could be a caution. Especially as the defendant has personally offered to pay for the restitution of any property that has been damaged.' There was a pause. 'We believe the evidence all points to an unfortunate accident.'

'What about the woodland? Isn't that like a national park?'

'The owner has taken full responsibility for not keeping the trees properly maintained.'

'I see,' Mona said. 'When will we know?'

'All the paperwork will go to our officer in charge. She will decide.'

'And then?'

'If there was evidence to show any deliberate act, the case could go to court except the circumstances all suggest it was a one-off and will not happen again and no harm was meant.'

James stood up. 'We'll wait to hear from you,' he said and held out his hand.

'Thank you,' Mona said and followed James' lead.

'I'll show you out,' the sergeant said.

Mona dragged the fresh air into her lungs. Despite the peace and quiet of the station, the smell of disinfectant and sweat intermingled with the unmistakeable sense of poverty and despair. It was something she hadn't encountered in years, not since she'd worked as a volunteer student counsellor in a Los Angeles suburb. Or should that be ghetto?

'Coffee? Or something stronger?' James said.

'Coffee would be wonderful,' Mona said. 'It's feeling colder today.'

'Summer's over,' James said and indicated the clouds barrelling in from the west. 'We'll be in for a real wetting later today. Come on.'

They sat in the small coffee shop tucked at the end of an alleyway off the main street. 'You seem distant. Is anything wrong?' James asked.

'Why do you think the sergeant thought Ethan might be let off with a caution?'

'No real evidence Ethan wanted to hurt you or damage the house. He just comes across as a sad old git who can't get the idea he's going to be a divorcee very soon,' James said.

'What about the owner of the woodland? If that was me, I'd want him strung up. Think of the damage he could have caused.'

'He didn't though, and I know the owner is very embarrassed that he's let it get into such a state.'

'You know the owner?'

'Very well,' James said and shifted in his seat.

'The owner isn't linked to Frobisher and Kingswood

Estate and Lettings?'

James held up his hands. 'Oops. Rumbled. Mr Kingswood is my brother-in-law.'

'I see,' Mona said. 'That still doesn't explain why you should carry the cost.'

'If the damage had been a lot, it would have been worse. I said it'd cost me a couple of hundred and it's a kick up the backside to make sure the woodland is properly maintained in future. Job done.'

'Is that all?' Mona replaced the cup before she'd taken a sip.

'I've got a chippy and a plasterer and decorator lined up. I can reuse a door from the refurbishment I've been doing. It's a nice old one and not up to the latest HMO requirements,' James said. 'That's houses with more than one tenant.'

'I know.' She looked at James. 'Did you deliberately underplay the damage?'

James shrugged. 'What good would it do to keep Ethan here, possible fine him or bang him up? The sooner he gets back home and you sort out your differences, the better for everyone.' His voice took on a grim sound. 'You both need to be free to move on, once and for all.'

'How did you know about Ethan and me? About us being together as kids, I mean?'

'Sheila told me the details when I quizzed her after you left with Ethan.'

'What exactly did she say?' Had Sheila told him of the abuse? She felt her legs tense before twisting them round the chair, as she'd done so often when she was younger.

'You were high school sweethearts. The relationship broke up and you moved on. You met up again years later older and wiser and decided to give it another try.' He held out his hands like a priest in supplication. 'Very understandable.'

Mona relaxed. Her legs untwined and she stretched them out. 'More gullible and easily taken in, I'd say.'

'No. There are plenty of others who fancy another crack at their first love. The old emotion runs deep.'

'I would have wanted to teach him a lesson.'

'Would you? Really?'

Mona thought for a moment. 'I suppose not. I'd rather let it all get sorted and everyone can move on.'

'My point entirely,' James said. 'Does that mean you're moving on too?'

'Yes,' Mona said. 'It's time to go home and start over.'

'Pity,' James said. 'Not about starting over, about going home. We've got used to having you around.'

'Part of starting over is facing up to what I'd run away from,' Mona said. 'It's time to stop running.'

Chapter forty-nine Sheila

Brian stops the car outside Claire's house. 'You've been very quiet since you got home. Anything wrong?'

Should I ask him about the interview with James? He hasn't said anything. 'How did it go today?' There it's done. 'The meeting with James, I mean?'

'Oh, he was in a bit of a rush. Had to meet Mona at the police station to go over their statements. He reckoned Ethan could be let off with a caution.'

'Surely he deserves more than that? He practically tried to kill the woman, didn't he?' I can hear my voice getting louder and squeakier. I can't stop it.

'Mona says he's learnt his lesson. I believe it. We all make silly mistakes and the older we get the sillier they become.'

'Mistake my backside.'

'Now, now. Where's all your forgiveness of us lesser mortals?' He punches me lightly on the arm.

'He should be locked up.' I pause. 'You still haven't answered my question.'

'The job is mine if I want it. I sign a contract at the end of the week and start properly on Monday. If I want it that is.'

'Do you?'

'I thought you said there might be a conflict of interest in your role as housing officer and James's interest in social housing?'

'Karen assures me there is nothing to worry about.'

'Just as well. I signed the contract anyway,' Brian says and laughs.

This time I punch his arm. 'You bugger.'

'Your face has been a picture all evening.' He turns to face me. 'Why didn't you come straight out and ask me?'

'I wasn't certain how you'd take bad news. It's been difficult in the past.'

'You mean I've been difficult?' Brian says. There is no time for me to reply. 'I have been difficult. Bloody difficult. That's certainly in the past. This is a new start for both of us.'

I reach out and squeeze his hand. 'As long as you really want the job. I don't want you to take something that's…well…'

'Below me you mean?' Brian puffs out his chest. 'As if a captain of industry like me will miss the rough and tumble of the board room, daggers drawn at every meeting, a thousand emails all cc'd so everyone knows what everyone else is doing, even down to the collection for the cleaner's leaving present?' He pretends to bang his head on the steering wheel. 'Sucking up to shareholders, endless minutes of pointless meetings that end up with more meetings and always looking over your shoulder to spot who's crawling up the ladder behind you to muscle in on your job? No chance.'

'I didn't realise it was that bad?'

Brian stares ahead. 'Neither did I until I stopped. I was so caught up in the crap, I couldn't see a different life. This will suit me for a few years.'

'You make it sound as if it's temporary.'

He turns to face me. 'Listen, Sheila, none of us know how long we've got left. The kids are off our hands. In a few years we might want to sell up, move somewhere else, travel for a year. I don't know.'

'We need to be open to options. Is that right?'

'God, you sound like the CEO when he was considering takeovers. Yes, that is exactly it. Let's be open to as many different options we find attractive or intriguing.' He holds out his hand. 'Shake on it, Mrs.'

'I can do better than that.' I bend closer and give him a kiss on the cheek.

'Really?' Brian puts his arms round me. 'Like the old days

in the Golf GTI?'

'Granny, Grandpa, what are you doing? Mummy told us to hurry you up.' Two small faces appear at the side window.

'Laters, baby,' Brian says in a fake American accent.

'Promises, promises,' I say and climb out of the car. 'We were talking about Grandpa's new job.'

'Are you going to be an astronaut?' Nick says.

'Don't be silly,' Emily interrupts him. 'He's too old and fat.'

'Old and fat, am I?' Brian jumps out of the car and picks Emily up. He twists her upside down.

'More,' she yelps as he puts her over his shoulder in a fireman's lift.

'Me next.' Nick pummels Brian's back.

'Oh, I think an old, fat grandad like me can manage two pipsqueaks.' He transfers Emily to his hip and holds her round the waist with one hand. With the other, he scoops Nick upwards. 'Hold on tight,' he says. 'The galloping horses have arrived,' and he charges across the lawn towards the back gate.

I lock the car and follow. It is the game he'd played with Claire and Mark when they were the same age. He hasn't done anything like that in years. I'm pleased about the job except there was no mention of money. Does it really matter? We're not destitute. We'd manage. We had before and what's the point of new stuff all the time if we're too knackered or miserable to enjoy it? The same goes for fancy holidays. We might not be so flash with cash, but Brian will have more time and I'll make sure we spend plenty of it together and take the grandchildren for picnics, treasure hunts, beach barbecues. All the cheap, easy stuff I'd enjoyed as a child and with Mark and Claire when they were small. I push open the gate. It is time to tell Claire what has happened.

'Heh, good to see you.' Claire comes forward and kisses me. 'We decided on a barbecue. To celebrate the end of summer.'

I nod in the direction of the two men both poking at chicken drumsticks and steaks as if they were gourmet cooks. 'Which one is in charge?'

'As long as we get a decent meal, I don't care,' Claire says. 'Come on, let me get you a drink.'

By the time the children are in bed, I could have climbed in with them. I fight back a yawn. 'Sorry. It's been a long day.'

'Stay for coffee, please,' Claire says. 'We've got something to tell you.'

I follow her into the kitchen. Please not another baby. 'You're not pregnant, are you?' Should I sound excited? I can't.

'No,' Claire says and laughs. 'He's had the snip.' She jerks her head in the direction of the lounge. 'No more kids for us. It is about the children though.' She pours coffee and hands me a mug.

'What about them?' My hands shake. Same old worries bounce up. Illness? Are they moving away?

Claire must have noticed. 'Don't get all stressed. Can you remember me telling you Nick was going through a clingy phase?'

'I thought that was over and done with?'

'It got better over the half-term holiday when the children were doing nothing except playing. As soon as they got back into the routine, it started again.'

'Any idea why?'

'Yes,' Claire says. 'Too much activity and not enough play. We stopped the after-school clubs, except for swimming and piano for Emily and swimming and guitar for Nick. Heh presto. Two happy kids who sleep well and we can have their friends round to play. I've cut my hours, so I finish at four. The money we save on those dammed clubs, not to mention all the equipment makes up for any lost income. At weekends it's football and ballet on Saturday morning and nothing else.'

I was not expecting this. 'Don't you feel they're missing out?' I repeat Claire's excuse since they'd been little.

'They're missing out all right,' she says. 'Missing out on being kids.'

I look at my daughter with admiration. 'We've mistaken busy-ness for happiness '*What is this life, if full of care, we have no time to stand and stare?*'

'What's that?'

'A poem I had to learn by heart at school. It's true. We spend too much time charging around, we have no time to do nothing. As if it's some sin or we're guilty of bad parenting.'

'That's exactly how we feel,' Claire says.

'I suppose I'd better tell you our news,' I say. 'It's been the summer for changes.'

'Must be the weather. The heat makes you stop and stand still.'

'Let's go and find out what your husband and your father are doing, and he can tell you all about his new job.'

'New job?' Claire's mouth drops open in a perfect circle.

'It's not what you'd expect. It's demotion.'

'As long as he's happy and you too,' Claire says.

We take the mugs into the lounge. Will it work out? Who knows? That's the trouble; life doesn't come with an insurance policy. We all have to take our chances. I'll accept happy for now, rather than happy ever after. Like that bit at the end of the film, *Shirley Valentine*. She could see the images and hear the waves lapping on the shore.

Shirley watched as her husband sat on the shoreline, his feet in the water and his suitcase by his side, dressed in a suit like his Sunday best. She hadn't known if it would work out. Sometimes you have to walk forward into the unknown and hope for the best.

Chapter fifty Mona

How had she managed to acquire so much stuff? Clothes? Books? Paints? Brushes? Pastels? Pencils? Not to mention sketch books and the small pile of as yet unsold canvases. Not that she minded the artist's materials. They'd come in handy. *Walks in the Cotswolds*? She placed the book on the thrift pile. She corrected herself. Charity shop. What about the clothes? She'd get a box and post them to herself. Not that she'd need them for a while. The summer was over and with any luck, she'd be in Vermont within a few months.

The phone rang. Funny? Who knew her landline? If it was another call about the slowness of the internet she'd whistle down the mouthpiece. That should put the scammers off.

'Hi?'

'Mona?'

Her hand shook. Her knees quavered in sympathy and the pit of her stomach opened up, like a sinkhole. 'Hi, Ethan. What can I do for you?' How the hell had he got her number.

'I'd like to thank you and your landlord for your hospitality. Not,' he said.

What was it about the way he said the word *landlord* that was creepy? Suggestive? Sexual?

'Where are you?' Mona said.

'At Heathrow. Let's say I'm no longer welcome in this suckhole country. I have in fact been told to leave.'

'Damned right you ain't welcome.'

'That's as maybe. I'd like to finish if you don't mind.'

'Enlighten me.' Mona's hands clenched. Fear had been replaced by anger.

'When I get home, I'm packing up. You're right. We aren't working as a couple. I agree a divorce is the best option.'

Why did he sound so formal? 'I appreciate that.'

'However, I think you have behaved badly. We could have talked. You've made it clear you want nothing more to do with our marriage.'

God, he was so damned pompous. It was his refusal to admit anything was wrong, after all. Not hers. She bit back the temptation to tell him what to do with his suggestion. 'Marriage needs two people to make it work and to let it fail.'

'Are you saying your idea of running away, without telling anyone was because of me?'

Mona sat down on the seat by the blackened wood of the porch. The smell of burning lingered. 'It wasn't my idea to set fire to someone's house, was it?'

'You're changing the subject. As I was saying, I will not contest any divorce. I will divide everything evenly and until it is settled, you may stay at the apartment. As soon as I get back, I'll collect clothes and some essentials.'

'Have you got a place to stay?' Despite all the abuse, there was still concern for his wellbeing. She wasn't that spiteful.

'I'm taking a transfer to a different state. The post comes with a serviced apartment. I won't even need towels.' There was a note of triumph in his voice unless she was imagining it.

'Which state?'

'Not that it really concerns you. Since you ask. Alaska. It'll be a new start.'

'Alaska? Wow. Bit of a difference,'

'As I said, I will be in touch via a lawyer about selling the apartment. You can have your pick of the furniture and fittings. The only thing I ask is that you pack up my personal stuff and send it to me when you move out. I'm thinking my books, paintings, my parent's photos. Stuff like that.'

284

'Yes. I understand,' Mona said.

'Good. My flight's being called. Got to go. Thank you for your cooperation. It's a pity you didn't think about that earlier and we might not be in this position. Goodbye.'

The phone went dead. That was it. The end. Full stop on their marriage. Why wasn't she running around the room, jumping up and down and cheering? She felt guilty, that's why. He'd always managed to make her believe any problems in their relationship were all her fault. It was the same the first time round. Except she'd been younger and more gullible. When they met again, she'd sunk back into the same patterns of behaviour. Could they have made it work? A familiar sensation crawled over her skin. Damn him. The scheming SOB had done it again. Made her feel she was the one at fault. She shook herself. She'd left because she hated the person she'd become; fearful of upsetting him, making her think he was doing her a favour, and this was the worst bit, inferior, unworthy of success, admiration, respect—only worthy of the crumbs of approval he occasionally scattered her way.

At least she wouldn't have to see him again. She had the apartment, not that she intended to stay there; long enough to engage a realtor and a specialist divorce lawyer to make sure Ethan didn't shaft her. She'd need to clear the crap to the thrift shop before packing up Ethan's stuff and shipping it to him. The cost would come out of the proceeds of the sale. She counted on her fingers. October. She'd be in Vermont for the Fall. It would be a great place to paint.

The doorbell rang. She turned. It was James. 'Come in,' she called.

'Anything wrong? You look a bit peaky.' He was at her side in a second.

It would be easy to let a man like James take care of her. Except she'd never wanted that. 'A call from Ethan has…'

'Knocked you off your perch? Made you go all of a doodah?' James said.

'That's what I like about the Brits. We might share a common language. Somehow, I reckon you've got the best sayings. Yes. I'm feeling I've been knocked off my perch.'

'Fancy a pub lunch?' James said and took hold of her hand. He looked round the room. 'You'll tackle this a lot quicker with a decent meal and a glass or two of wine.'

'For once I agree with you. Except you must let me pay. As a way of saying thank you for letting me this place and sorry for causing you so much upset.'

'What upset?'

Mona pointed to the damaged building. 'Ethan,' she said.

'That? He paid over the odds. Gave me five grand for a couple of days work and a new door. Reckon I should be treating you.'

Another familiar feeling crept over her. Pity. Why did Ethan still have that effect on her? 'Isn't that a bit over the top?'

'What?'

'Oh, I don't know. forget it. I'm being a sentimental old fool again.'

'Should I have refused payment? Said it was all fine and let him off without any come back? Or charged him a pittance?' James' eyes bored into her, like they did the first time they met.

'No. You did the right thing.'

'I know I did,' James said. 'I've met plenty of people like him. Controlling. They make you think everything is your fault and they're the ones to be pitied. You end up feeling guilty. I bet that's why you went back to him.' James tilted his head on one side. 'And might do again?'

'No,' Mona said. 'That's all in the past. We're divorcing and he's moving a very long way away.'

286

'If he tries to wheedle his way back in, it's all part of the plan, remember that.'

'What plan?'

'Did you ever go fishing as a child? Or have a friend or a relative who did?'

'No,' Mona said. 'What's that got to do with Ethan?'

'Same behaviour. He baits the line, casts it and waits, throwing out a few maggots from time to time to entice you closer.'

'Urrggh,' Mona said. Yet he was right. Ethan had always known when to turn from spiteful to kind, from ignoring her to taking an interest and every time she'd fallen for it and thought he'd finally changed.

'You took the bait, he played you, drawing you closer until you were trapped.'

'You make it sound so deliberate.'

'It is in a way. Except I wouldn't be certain Ethan does this all consciously. It's part of who he is, and it'll take a hell of a lot of therapy to change. If he ever believed he needed to change.'

James was telling her what she already suspected. Ethan would find another victim. Men like him always did. If that person ever discovered what he was really like, he'd move on to someone else. 'Well, this time it won't be me,' Mona said under her breath.

'Enough of him. What do you fancy for lunch?'

'Somewhere very English. A pub with beams and a view,' she said.

'The food?'

'Shepherd's pie or fish and chips.'

'Pity I didn't come around earlier. We could have headed off to Weston for a proper fish supper on the pier.'

'Next time,' Mona said.

James grasped one hand. 'Is that a promise?'

Mona extricated her hand. 'In a few years, perhaps. Not

before.'

'Pity. I thought you couldn't get enough of my magnetic charm.'

The words were said lightly enough. Mona wagged her finger at him. 'Was that a cue for a compliment?'

'I can only hope,' James said. 'Come on or the best tables will be taken and over lunch we can plan how you can enjoy your last few days over here. Any ideas?'

'There is one thing I need you to do,' Mona said.

'What's that?'

Mona fetched a tube from behind the pile of paintings. She unrolled a large canvas.

'It's our valley. Here's Lydia's old cottage. There's the school, the chapel and the row of houses where Sheila lives.'

'Can you keep this until after I've gone? I want Sheila to have it and I want it to be a surprise.'

'It'll be a lovely surprise. I'll makes sure she gets it.'

'I've done one for the shop too.'

'Nice one,' James said. 'If I was a sentimental man, I'd give you a hug.'

'Hug away,' Mona said.

As James hugged her, Mona let herself imagine a time when she might be tempted to find another partner. That was for the future. For the moment, she was content to explore what it meant to be the new Mona.

Chapter fifty-one Sheila

'I didn't think we'd get everything in the car,' I say and stow Mona's suitcases on the back seat.

'That's only half of it,' Mona says. 'I sent two parcels by Fed Ex. It's costing me a fortune and I thought I could travel lightly.'

'You couldn't leave all the art materials behind, could you?'

'Not to mention all the presents. I never expected people to be so generous. I've enough mementos of the area to set up my own shop.'

'Sorry the books aren't in electronic format.' The search for original copies of all of Laurie Lee's work had been worth it, not to mention the books of old photos of the area.

'I love them. They'll be on my coffee table so everyone can see them.'

'That's what I'd hoped.'

Mona climbs into the car and fastens her seat belt. 'Heathrow, here we come.'

Before we set off, I'm going to do what I used to do when we went on holiday. Except that was ensuring Brian had packed the tent poles and I'd packed the stove. This time, it's a bit different. 'Passport?'

'Yep.' Mona taps her bag.

'Show me, please, or I won't start the car.'

Mona unzips her bag and draws out her passport, the eTicket and her phone. 'Credit cards, cash and keys?' she says and draws them out one at a time.

'Hand luggage?'

Mona leans over the seat and picks up a small rucksack. 'In here is my laptop, tablet and all the leads.'

'We're ready.' I'm satisfied and put the car into gear.

The journey passes in that strange limbo land of talk.

Neither of us wants to mention the departure or the inevitable change to a friendship that has built up over the past six months. Instead, we both choose safe topics like the weather, the traffic and mutual acquaintances. Only when Mona has checked in, paid for her extra luggage and is ready to go through immigration into the no-man's-land of international departures do I suggest a last coffee.

'I know where,' Mona says. 'This was the place I stopped on my first morning.'

'What do you want?'

'No, let me. I must use up this English money.' Mona pulls out her wallet.

'Just a black coffee. I'll get us a table.' I squeeze my way between trolleys of luggage and buggies. The table looks out over the incoming runway. It's better than watching the planes go out. Somehow it makes the departure less imminent.

'One black coffee and one cappuccino, English style for me,' Mona says. 'I do like the huge patches of chocolate on top.' She scrapes at the foam with a spoon and licks it.

My eyes prickle and fill with tears. 'Sorry. I'm such an emotional idiot.'

'Sorry for what?' Mona pats my hand.

'I wanted to appear calm and in control. Not a mess.'

'Saying goodbye is never easy,' Monas says with a sniff. 'I don't hold with all that crap about it being easy. Parting means that.'

'I know you were only here temporarily. I suppose over the course of the summer it slipped my mind. Or I chose to forget.'

'It's been a wonderful summer,' Mona says. 'In spite of Lydia. I wish I'd gotten to know her better.'

'We don't get many years like this. Yes, you and Lydia would have been good friends. She had spirit, like you.'

'I don't just mean the weather.'

290

'No?' I wish we'd had more conversations like this.

'No. The whole place is special, like a dream scape. Hell, Shakespeare could have written *A Midsummer Night's Dream* and set it in the Cotswolds.'

'Yes,' I say. 'Whenever stuff happens, I look out at the landscape. There's something reassuringly permanent about the hills and valleys.' In contrast to our fleeting worries and short span of time on this planet I want to add. I don't. It sounds sentimental and yet it's true. In a hundred years from today, our worries will be forgotten, the landscape will still be there.

'There's something else.' Mona studies her hands. I give her space. 'When I got here, I was running away. I'm going back and I'm ready to take charge of my life.'

'Like the Lady Ragnell,' I say, remembering a favourite story from my childhood.

'Who? Not another Royal? No one will ever believe me when I tell them I lived close to Charles and Camilla.'

'No. This is a story from King Arthur.' I haven't thought about it for years. Why has it come back today of all days?

'Go on.' Mona takes a sip of her coffee. 'I love a neat story.'

'It's a good one,' I say and hope I can remember it. 'King Arthur will be killed unless he can find out what it is that women most desire. Sir Gawain finds the answer from a hideous creature called Ragnell who demands he marry her in return. On their wedding night, he pretends to find her desirable, and she changes into a beautiful princess.'

'What is it that women desire, except a million dollars, to be able to eat and not put on weight and World Peace?'

'Ragnell tells Gawain that women desire sovereignty, the right to exercise their own free will.'

Mona slaps a hand on the table. 'Too darn right. That's what I'm going to do. Any chance you can find me a gorgeous knight?' She laughs. 'Or one with a pulse?'

'You had a good chance with a certain gentleman in the village.'

Mona smiles more to herself than at me. 'Yes. James was a great guy. First though I have to do what I want to do. I have to be me.'

'After that?'

Mona sighs and spreads out her hands. 'Who knows?'

We sit for a while in silence. 'I'm sorry the *Wild Girls* didn't get the chance of more outings. We should have done some exciting stuff.'

Mona frowns. 'I don't think being a *Wild Girl* is about doing stuff. Isn't it more about *being?*'

'What do you mean?'

'It's about how we live our lives, being independent, not accepting how society wants us to be. You want a career and no kids? Great. You want to be a stay-at-home mum? Great. You want both? Great. Marry? Live together? Live alone? Eat ice-cream at midnight?' Mona's voice drops a tone. 'It's Ragnell all over again. Let us exercise our own free will to be the people we need and want to be. End of story.'

'I wish I had your strength of mind.'

'You have.' Mona slaps her hand on the table again. No one takes any notice.

'Have I?'

'Yes. You sorted out your work, your kids know where they stand, and you and Brian are communicating. That's pretty good in my book.'

I gaze out at the runway. A jet thunders down. 'You inspired me,' I say.

'Me?'

I turn back to look at my friend. 'Yes. I met this strong woman who comes over here, doesn't know anyone, sets herself up and makes a life. What isn't there to admire?' I blink hard. Damn, tears are close again.

'Funny, you inspired me too,' Mona says.

'I don't believe that.'

'You did. You have a sense of belonging. I haven't had that since I was a kid. It's something I want and I'm going to get.'

I reach forward and take Mona's hands. 'That's the nicest thing anyone's said about me in years. Thank you.'

We hold hands. 'That's the thing about being a Wild Girl,' Mona says. 'We recognise strength in each other, and we're not frightened of taking risks to be our own people.'

'That deserves a toast.' I'm feeling more cheerful. A bit of Mona's positivity has again rubbed off on me.

'Not in coffee.'

'There's a champagne bar further along. How about one drink to celebrate the successful start of a new movement; the Wild Girls who demand the right to be who and what they want to be?'

'I'll drink to that,' Mona said. 'Let's go, Wild Girls.'

Thanks

With thanks to my husband Peter and the family and friends who have always believed in me. Thanks also to the members of Catchwords Writers group in Cirencester, the Wild Women Writers of Cheltenham and the original Wild Women group who enjoyed a brief flurry of activity in 2018. Although it was a few years ago, the staff and students of the MA in Creative and Critical Writing at the University of Gloucestershire from 2014-16 are also still appreciated. Thanks to my fellow attendees and the tutors at Swanwick Summer School whose support and inspiration is a pleasure to experience.

Finally, none of this would have been possible without the expertise of the team at Black Pear Press to whom I will always be grateful.

About the Author

After a career in education and leadership training and development, Dr Pam Keevil completed an MA in Creative and Critical Writing at the University of Gloucestershire. Her first book, *Virgin at Fifty* was published in 2018. With her husband, she has co-authored two self-development books, *Finding Happiness after Covid 19,* published in 2020 and *How to be Happy* which was an Amazon number one in the summer of 2021. She lives near Stroud and when not writing, enjoys ballroom dancing, playing the piano and observing the changing seasons in the countryside.